TAINTED HEARTS

ANGELIC ACADEMY
BOOK THREE

ALISHA WILLIAMS

For more information, please address: alishawilliamsauthor@gmail.com

Book Cover Design: Haelah Rice Covers
Formatting: Sweet Chaos Publishing

CONTENT WARNING

This is a paranormal reverse harem. If you're looking for heavy world building and lots of magic and adventure, this series isn't for you. It has a contemporary vibe. This is a bully, academy, enemies to lovers, best friends to loves, fated mates, rejected mates and step-brother romance. It will contain MMM content heavily throughout the series. Starting with book three, there will be a female in the harem and this series will now have FF. This female is only with the main girl. This book doesn't contain a trigger list, how every to be safe, I will mention that there is death and mention of past abuse of both an adult and a child.

If you are good with everything mentioned above, then happy reading.

To all my readers who have been so understanding and patient with my pace of this series. Paranormal isn't my main genre, so it takes me a little bit of time in between books. Thank you for sticking with me and coming along for Abby's journey as she collects her mates.

CHAPTER ONE

ABBY

Gripping the door handle of the closet, I slowly turn it. When I get enough room, I peek my head out of the gap, looking up and down the hallway.

The coast is clear, has been for at least ten minutes, if the silence outside was any indication.

Stepping out, I close the door and lean back against it. Shutting my eyes, I take a deep breath and think of how I'm going to approach this. How do I tell my mates that their dads *are* the bad guys?

Michael is, that much we already knew, but Raphael and Gabriel too? How fucked up is it that God's three most trustworthy men are slimier than some of the people who work for my father?

"Little Bird?" Zed's low, husky voice has my eyes popping open. "Are you okay?"

For a moment, I wonder if he's asking about what I just

heard the dads talking about, but then I remember everything that just happened outside with Isaac.

My heart shatters all over again for him. Tears prick the back of my eyes as I stare up into Zed's troubled ones. "Shhh," he soothes, pulling me into his arms. I go willingly, wrapping my arms around him tightly. I inhale deeply, his scent settling me a little bit, while his touch makes my body hum in a comforting way.

"Why does life have to be so fucked up?" I murmur against his chest.

His hand rubs up and down my back as he places a kiss on the top of my head. "I don't know, baby." He lets out a deep sigh like he has the weight of the world resting on his shoulders. "But you have me. You have Leo. And you even have Luke and Noah. Hopefully, someday, you will have Isaac too. We will be by your side no matter what. Whatever is thrown at us, we will fight it together."

"I hope you're right on that one," I say, my gut turning as I peer up at him. "Because I just overheard something that's going to make life a hell of a lot more complicated."

His eyes darken, jaw ticking. "What did you overhear?"

Biting my lower lip, I tell him. "When I came up here, I heard yelling. Wanting to find out what was going on, I eavesdropped outside of my mom's room. Their dads were in there, fighting about something. I only caught the tail-end of things, but it sounds like the dads had a plan of some sort. They're afraid that what they're doing will piss God off, and Gabriel and Raphael no longer want to do it anymore. Michael did not seem happy about it."

I try to remember word for word what they said, relaying what I can to Zed.

"I knew Michael was an asshole, but fuck, he really is a

monster," he scoffs, shaking his head. "Whatever he's up to, we need to find out and fucking expose him."

"I agree, but first we need to tell the others. I don't want to sit on this information, but I don't know if the guys are mentally able to hear this after everything with Isaac."

Isaac, that poor broken boy. I might not be ready to welcome him with open arms, but it doesn't change the fact that he's my mate. And the whole reason why he's been such a horrible person was because he's so fucked up by the shit his father did to him.

I can't think about working on us being mates right now, I need to put Luke and Noah first. They've earned it. They've shown me that they're not as bad as they made themselves seem; they've made it up to me and want to be good mates.

Keeping this from them wouldn't be being a good mate on *my* end.

"How about we sleep on it? Give them a night to process everything they found out about their mate. In the morning, I'll make everyone a big breakfast, and we can talk then, okay?"

"Yeah." I nod. "That sounds good."

With an arm wrapped around my shoulders, Zed leads me downstairs.

"Starbright." Leo's waiting for us by the front door. "Are you alright?"

His worried eyes search my face. I give him a half-hearted smile. "Not really. But I know I will be. I have you guys." I look around and see he's by himself. "Where is everyone?"

"Noah and Luke took Isaac down to the basement. Libby, Penny, and Bennett left. They said to call them if you need anything. Also, the dads all left. Didn't even know they were here," Leo says, scratching the back of his neck.

"About that..." I cringe.

3

When I'm done telling Leo everything I told Zed, he's staring back at me with bewildered eyes and slack jawed.

"Fuck." He lets out a breath as he runs a hand through his blond waves. "That's... that's messed up."

"I'm starting to think anything involving these guys is fucked up," I retort, rubbing my eyes. I'm tired, this whole night has taken a toll on me, both physically and emotionally.

"Come on, Little Bird." Zed bends down and scoops me up into his arms. "Let's get you to bed. We can decide our next step tomorrow. Right now, you need sleep. I don't like seeing my mate upset."

Giving in, I close my eyes and snuggle into his embrace. We don't even make it up the first set of stairs before I'm passed out.

The next time I'm coherent, I hear Zed and Leo talking.

"What do we do? There's so much going on all at once, I don't even know what the first thing to deal with would be."

"Not much we can do about the dads right now. I think it's best to help Abby connect with her mates and get as much of that settled as we can. Go about our lives as normal while trying to dig up whatever information we can on what she overheard. At least we only really have to worry about one of the dads right now. It's, unfortunately, the worst one of them all, but it's two less people to worry about. Not that we would let them get away with their involvement in whatever it is they're doing."

"How are you doing?" Leo asks Zed, and Zed goes quiet.

"What do you mean?" Zed asks a few long moments later.

"You just found out your father has been treating your little brother horribly for who knows how long. I know you well enough by now, Zed. You've never had a reason to like Isaac, but I saw the way you reacted to what's been happening to him. At the end of the day, you and him aren't that different. You've both been treated like shit by the same man."

"He's not a fucking man," Zed growls, his voice low but powerful. "He's a coward. A stupid, childish person who gets pleasure by making others feel small and worthless to make himself feel big and powerful."

They keep talking, but sleep overtakes me again, sending me into a dream. I feel a familiar tug, and I know right away it's my bond. But it's not my bond with Zed or Leo that's pulling at me.

Next thing I know, I'm standing inside the room in the basement. The same room where I first saw the guys being intimate together. A sight that very much had my pussy pulsing to say the least.

But it's not raw, wild sex I find myself astral projected into.

They're all on the bed and under the blankets together, but Isaac is fast asleep between Luke and Noah. The two of them are having a hushed conversation over his head.

"What the fuck do we do now?" Luke whispers as he looks down at his mate's sleeping face. "I want to kill his dad. I fucking hate him."

"I do too." Noah cups the side of Luke's face. "But we can't let rage take over right now. He needs us." Noah's face crumbles as he looks down at Isaac next. "All this time, he's been enduring so much hurt and pain, all because he thought he was saving us." Noah kisses Isaac's forehead. "You stupid, stupid man. I love you so much. I wish you would have just come to us. Why did you think you needed to save everyone but yourself?"

"We need to do better," Luke says next. "We need to be open and honest because I'm getting real sick of all these lies and secrets. This isn't what it should be like with your mates.

We would die for him, just as much as he would for us. He needs to stop trying to save us when we don't need saving."

"Tomorrow, we'll talk about everything. Get it all out on the table. Then we move forward. It's all we can do because Isaac isn't the only mate we have to worry about now."

"Abby," Luke sighs wistfully. "It's taking everything in me not to go upstairs and beg her to join us. It's like the bond is pulling me toward her. I crave her, every moment of the day. Just like I do you two."

"I know." Noah flops back onto his side of the bed. "I do too."

"Life could be amazing, you know? Once Isaac shows Abby that he can be a good guy. Once he's won her over, once we build something with her, we could be happy. I've been thinking about it a lot lately. And fuck, Noah, it really makes me happy."

"One day at a time," Noah whispers up to the ceiling. "It's not going to be easy. It's only the beginning really. We practically have to start all over again. All of us in this new bond. And that includes Leo and Zed. Because whether we like it or not, they're a package deal."

"I'm not mad about it," Luke responds, making me smile. "Leo is cool, and Zed... well, he's not too bad, when he's not scaring the shit out of me."

That has me snorting a laugh. They both look over my way, and I slap a hand over my mouth, heart pounding erratically. *No, they couldn't have heard me, right?*

Even that night, Isaac didn't see me, he only sensed me.

"Abby?" Luke asks, eyes searching the room.

"You don't think?" Noah looks to Luke.

My feet move me forward, the bond pulling me toward them. I stop next to the bed, next to Luke, but their gazes are locked on where I was standing before.

Reaching both hands out, I brush my thumbs over their cheek bones.

They both suck in a shocked breath, eyes fluttering shut. Even in this state, I can feel our bond hum to life. And in this moment, none of the past matters, only they do.

"My mates," I whisper. "What are we going to do?"

Removing my hands, I let them fall to my side. They don't open their eyes, seeming to just enjoy the lingering feel of my touch.

My eyes fall to the broken boy between them. "You are haunted, so damaged that it turned you into this muddied version of yourself. I really hope everything changes from here on out. Because if not, I don't know if I'll ever truly be able to forgive you."

Leaning forward, I brush my lips across his forehead in the softest touch. But the bond... it's like a kick to the gut, roaring to life.

Tears fall, one landing on his cheek. In his sleep, he lets out this haunted sound that I feel deep in my soul.

Seconds later, I'm sucked out of the room and tossed into darkness. There I stay in a dreamless sleep until I awake in the morning.

I thank the silent void of my mind for the rest. Because I know it's not something I'm going to have very much of.

What has my life come to?

CHAPTER TWO

NOAH

I've been up for an hour now, just watching my mates sleep. Luke's head rests on Isaac's chest, while I'm on Isaac's other side, playing with his silky black strands.

"Mhhm," Isaac hums sleepily. "That feels nice."

His eyes blink open slowly. "Morning."

He gives me a soft smile, but I watch it fade as his mind catches up. "Hey."

"How did you sleep?" He looks like he aged ten years overnight.

"I wanna say like shit, but it's hard to not have a good night's sleep when it's spent between the two of you."

My lips curve up into a soft smile. My heart hurts for him. Last night was gut-wrenching to watch. Finding out what he did for us makes me love him more, but at the same time I want to kick his ass for making decisions for us.

After a long talk last night with Luke, we've decided to make things work with Isaac, but there are some conditions.

8

"We need to talk."

He sighs, but nods. "Yeah, we do."

"What are we talking about?" Luke asks, his voice rough from sleep.

"What Isaac needs to do for us to forgive him," I answer Luke, but my eyes stay on Isaac.

"I'll do whatever it is." I can see the sincerity shining in his eyes.

I cast Luke a look, and he nods, giving me the go ahead to be the lead in this conversation. "No more lies. We are open and honest about our feelings to each other and our mate." His eyes flash with... something at the mention of Abby.

"Done."

"You are to work hard to win her over because, Isaac, I don't think you deserve her forgiveness any time soon. You were the worst of us all. And I don't think we will have any type of happiness unless we're all together. The hurt from a bond mate is a hell of a lot to handle."

"Trust me, I know." He rolls onto his back, his head tilted up to the ceiling as he closes his eyes. "Being away from her, hating her, being mean. Fuck, it almost killed me."

"Then why did you do it? Why keep going after her when Luke and I told you how wrong it was?"

"I don't know," he groans. "I was just so angry... with my dad and the fucked up shit he does. With myself for being a coward and letting him treat me that way. I needed someone to take the blame, and she seemed like the easiest target. I used my hatred toward her dad and projected it onto her."

"You need to get over that. Whatever her dad did, it has nothing to do with her. God doesn't punish children for their parents' sins, and neither should you. We need to stop blaming her for other people's wrongdoings."

"I know, I know," he sighs harshly. "I already feel like

shit. It might have seemed like I enjoyed hating her, but fuck... I *hated* hating her." He grabs a handful of hair and pulls. "Gah, my head's all fucked up. I don't know what to do."

"Start by apologizing. I know it won't count for much, but it's a solid first step. Then work on building a friendship."

"You know how hard it is to be around her, wanting to drag her into the nearest empty room and fuck her?" he asks me, raising a brow.

Luke snorts. "Ahh, yeah. Trust me, we do."

"The bond is a powerful thing, but you can't let it fuck things up. You're going to want to touch her, to hold her, kiss her, fuck her, but you can't do any of that. Not until you've earned it. If that's even something you want."

"It is," he confirms, sounding defeated. "But you're right. I don't deserve any of that. I don't deserve her. Hell, I don't even deserve you guys."

"Enough of that," I growl, grabbing the back of his head and pulling him in for a kiss. He moans against my mouth, his tongue eagerly pressing between my lips. I open for him, and I'm the next to groan as I taste him on my tongue.

"Fuck," Luke grunts. "You're gonna make me blow my load."

Our eyes open at the same time before we laugh into the kiss.

"I've missed this. I've missed you. Both of you." For the first time in, maybe ever, Isaac looks at ease. Maybe getting everything off his chest helped relieve the burden he's been carrying. Or maybe he's just so defeated that he doesn't have it in him to fight anymore.

He doesn't get to give up. We won't let him. We will be by his side to hold him up when he can no longer do it himself.

I feel guilty for pushing him away these past few weeks,

10

but I couldn't keep sitting by and watching him treat Abby like that.

She's not at all what we made her out to be. She's sweet, funny, extremely sexy, and a real badass.

Both Luke and I were shocked to find out she was our mate, but we weren't pissed. We've felt something toward her from the start. Now, it all makes sense.

We enjoyed getting to know her before we found out, and now that we know, hopefully, it will get better.

I plan on being with Abby whether or not Isaac is. But I'd much rather we all work things out. We've been through so much that I think we all need some happiness. And that's going to start today.

"Can we just lay in bed and cuddle?" Isaac asks, laying back onto the bed, his eyes passing between us.

"Alright, who are you and what have you done with our domineering, control freak of a boyfriend?" Luke asks, raising a brow.

"Haha," Isaac deadpans. "Please?"

Luke's eyes dart up to mine. He needs us. *Shit.*

"Yeah." I lean over and kiss Isaac on the forehead. "We can do that."

We all cuddle together and lay there; no more words pass between us, but the bond hums to life. It's almost complete. We just need Abby here with us. *Soon.* Because I need her just as much as I need them.

When we get to the top of the basement stairs, we all stop at the sound of Abby's laughter. A warm tingly feeling rushes over me like a blanket, and my feet are moving before I even realize it, with the need to be close to her.

"Stop!" She's laughing so hard her face is red as Leo and Zed tickle her. She's dressed in one of their shirts and a pair of panties. Licking my lips, my cock grows hard. I want that. I want to be able to be carefree when I was with her. She looks so happy right now... so in love.

"You will," Isaac says, as if he could read my mind. "Just give it time. You will have that too. I'm sorry." His brows crush together as he looks toward our mate. "I'm sorry I took away the time you could have had with her."

I don't say anything, because he's right. In a way, his need for us to hate her stopped us from getting to know her, from finding out we were mates sooner. If only we welcomed her with open arms in the beginning, we would have known her earlier and avoided so much pain. But sadly, that's not how it turned out.

"Hey," Luke says as we step into the kitchen.

The three of them stop, but as soon as Abby is free, she ducks out of their arms and darts over to Luke. "Save me!" She giggles as she hides behind him. "They're gonna keep going until I piss my pants."

"You're not wearing any pants," Luke points out, a smirk gracing his lips.

She rolls her eyes. "Whatever."

The moment she touches him, I can see the way they both pause, sucking in a breath. It's going to take some getting used to. The guys and I, we're used to it by now. It's not that our bond has dulled, but our bodies have come to recognize the spark. Each bond is like its own wavelength. Similar, but different.

She bites her lower lip, leaning into Luke as he wraps his

arm around her. When he kisses the top of her head, her eyes flutter closed.

I need that. So, I walk over to her next. "Morning, Hellcat," I murmur, dipping down to press a kiss to the top of her head. I don't want to push her or rush anything, but damn, I need to feel her.

She lets out a little pleasure-filled whimper and pride fills me that I did something right.

"Pancakes, anyone?" Zed asks, holding up a plate with a stack piled so high it looks like it's about to topple over.

"Fuck, yes," Luke groans, tucking Abby under his arm and bringing her over to the table. Pulling out a seat for her, she sits and lets Luke get her a plate. She watches him with a smile. Leo and Zed watch him too with observant eyes, protective of their mate, and rightfully so. But I'm happy to see they are okay with one of us doing something for her.

After Abby has her plate, Luke, Leo, and Zed plate their own, taking a seat at the table with her.

"Are you coming?" I ask Isaac, stepping toward the table. His eyes dart over to mine, like I snapped him out of a daydream.

"I'll let you guys eat. I'm not that hungry." He's lying. He just doesn't want to be in the way, thinking he's unwanted.

"Sit," Abby's request surprises us all.

He looks at her with shock. "It's okay, really. You guys eat, I'll—"

"I said, sit," she says more firmly, raising a brow as if she's daring him to argue with her. Leo snorts a laugh, trying to hide it by shoving pancakes into his mouth.

"Better listen, little brother. I've seen her pissed off. It's sexy as fuck, but she could totally kick your ass if she wanted to," Zed throws out.

Isaac isn't normally speechless, but he looks at the two of

them like he's wondering if he's even awake right now or if this is all a dream. Zed called him *little brother*, not in a condescending way either, and Abby is insistent he eats with us. Poor guy looks like his head is going to explode.

"Come on." I grab his hand and pull him over to the table. I take the free seat on the other side of Abby, making Isaac take the one on the other side of me.

We sit and eat. Leo and Zed joke around, and I find myself a little jealous that two of her mates are so close, like best friends. *Will Luke and I have that with them too? What about Isaac? What does it mean for him and his older brother now that Zed knows the real truth about their father? Will he keep hating him, or will they build a brotherly bond?*

"I need to tell you three something," Abby says after she's done eating, placing her fork onto her plate. She pushes her chair back and stands, moving around the table to stand between Zed and Leo. Placing a hand on each of their shoulders, they place their hands on top of hers, as if giving her support for whatever she's about to say next.

"Okay," Luke says. "What's up?"

"After what happened last night." Her eyes find Isaac's, a flash of sympathy on her face before continuing to look between the three of us. "I came inside to get away. I ended up hearing a fight, and well... I wanted to know what was going on." She shrugs. "So I eavesdropped. It was your dads; and they were fighting, mostly Raphael and Gabriel were fighting with Michael. I'm not sure what about exactly, but from what I heard, Michael has them doing things they no longer want to do. Michael was pissed, like raging pissed, but your dads." She pauses, looking at Luke and then me. "Said they just wanted you to be happy and they were done. I'm not sure what they're done with, but by the sound of it, God won't be too happy with whatever they were up to." She looks at Isaac. "Your dad, however, I don't think he's done."

Her words don't seem to surprise me. I love my dad, he's not a horrible guy, but I've always had a feeling he was into something he shouldn't have been. I've seen the way his demeanor changes when he's around Michael. I always just assumed it was because, out of the three of them, Michael was the leader.

Isaac laughs, but it's not out of humor. "Of course he's up to something. When is he not?" He shakes his head.

"You're not mad at me?" Abby's brows furrow together.

"Why would we be?" Luke asks, genuinely confused.

"Because I just accused your dads of being up to something, most likely nothing good."

"Look," I sigh, standing and walking over to her. "We love our dads."

"Not all of us," Isaac snarls.

I try again. "My dad and Luke's dad aren't as bad as Isaac's, but they aren't exactly fathers of the year. We understand that being the sons of archangels comes with a lot more pressure than any other pure blood, but the way they pushed some things on us while we were growing up, we've started to question things."

"So, what do we do?" she asks.

"You leave that part to us." I look at the guys, and they nod. "We'll find out what's going on. I think, by now, they know we're done being their little puppets."

"You don't have to do it alone, you know. I'd like to help in whatever way I can."

I give her a warm smile. "We won't leave you out. Anything we find out, we'll let you know."

"Come on, Little Bird." Zed pulls her down onto his lap and gives her a searing kiss that has her moaning. My cock twitches at the sound. When they break apart, her face is flushed, but the love she has for him makes my heart yearn for her to look at me like that someday. "We gotta get going to my place. Mom wants to hang out with us for my birthday." Zed stands, taking her with him. Leo gets up and follows them out.

"See you guys later!" Abby calls out as they leave the room.

"Well, fuck," Isaac sighs heavily, running a hand through his dark locks before scrubbing his face. "What the hell do we do now?"

"Is it kinda sad that I'm not surprised at all about what Abby said she overheard?"

"I'm not. I knew from the moment my dad first hit me that everything he's been spewing to the pure bloods is bullshit. I'll bet you anything that's what she overheard our dads talking about. No doubt it's my dad leading this fucked up bullshit."

"So, what? We do some digging, see what they've been up to. How the hell do we do that?" Luke asks.

"I don't know!" Isaac snaps. "Fuck. Sorry. It's just a lot to deal with, everything that's happened in the last twenty-four hours."

"I know." I pull him to his feet and into my arms. He goes willingly, burying his face into my chest.

"I'm sorry," he says again, but he's not talking about getting upset.

"I know," I repeat. "We love you, Isaac, so damn much. It's us against the world. And now we have another mate to think about. So, tomorrow, you're going to start your groveling with your first big gesture toward winning her forgiveness."

"And what is that?" he asks, pulling back to look me in my eyes.

"You're going to dump Heather. Publicly. You tell the whole school who Abby is to you. No more secrets, no more lies, and no more hiding."

"My dad isn't going to be happy about that," he mutters, looking a little pale.

"And he's never going to get you alone again to be able to hurt you. We won't let him. He seems set on keeping up his perfect reputation, so he won't cause a big fuss if we intervene. We just have to make sure we don't show that we know something is going on."

"Alright." Isaac nods. "I hate Heather anyways. I'm more than happy to be rid of her."

"We never should have been forced to be engaged to those horrible girls," Luke growls.

"Starting tomorrow, we're taking our lives back. Beginning with claiming our mate the way we should have and treating her with the respect she deserves. Nothing less. Do you understand?" I direct that toward Isaac. Normally, I'm the quiet one, I only speak up when I feel the need to. And right now, is one of those times.

"She's never going to forgive me," he mopes in defeat. "But I'm going to try to do what I can to make up for what I've done."

"It's a start."

CHAPTER THREE

FRANKIE

"Francesca!" my father calls, banging on my bedroom door. Groaning at the use of my full name, I roll out of bed and get up to answer it.

"Yes?" I say with a sigh. Today is my first day off in weeks, and I just want to spend it relaxing, maybe take a nap.

"Lucifer has requested to see you." His face stays blank, always in soldier mode.

That has my back straightening. "Why?" I ask, hating that there's a bit of panic in my voice. But it's the Devil, how can I not be a little worried? The man is scary as fuck. And I live in hell with a lot of demons, so I should be used to it.

"When the King of Hell asks for your presence, you don't ask questions. You do as you're told."

"Okay." I nod. "Just give me a moment." He nods back and steps away from the door.

I close it and rush to put on something more appropriate to see my king than a pair of sleep shorts and loose tank top.

Feeling like my uniform is a safe bet, I get changed, throwing my bright red locks up into as neat of a bun as I can.

Taking a look to make sure I'm presentable, I head out of my room. The whole way to Lucifer's office I try to figure out what he could want. Does he want me to move positions? To fire me? No, I'm a good soldier, there's nothing I did that would cause him to get rid of me. *Right?*

I give the door three hard knocks and wait for him to answer. "Come in!" His voice is loud and booming, making an unsettling shiver run through my body.

Letting myself in, I close the door and wait for him to direct me further. He looks up at me from his desk. "Francesca, take a seat." He waves his hand toward the chair in front of his desk.

Taking the seat, I try to ignore the way my heart is pounding in my chest. I'm normally not one who gets rattled very easily, but like I said before, this is the King of Hell. If you're not afraid of him, to some degree, then you're stupid.

"So, I'm sure you're wondering why I've asked you here today." He folds his hands together on his desk, raising a brow at me in question.

"Yes, sir." I nod.

"You see, my daughter, Abigail, is on earth." At the mention of her name, my whole body becomes alert.

"Is she alright?" I ask, a little too eagerly.

His brow raises higher. "Yes."

Letting out a sigh of relief, I relax back into my chair.

"Why are you so concerned with my daughter, Francesca? Because that is not a reaction one might have to a stranger. Do you know my daughter well?"

"No, sir." I shake my head. "I've only met her once. The last time she was in Hell."

Okay, so I only talked to her once, but I've been watching her behind the scenes for years now.

"Very well," he continues. "As I was saying before, Abigail is on earth. She is staying with her mother and her sorry excuse of a husband." The way he curls his lip, I can tell he despises both of them. "I'm not one to give personal information away, but seeing what I'm about to ask of you, I feel like you should know as much as you can."

"Okay..." My brows furrow in question. What is he about to ask of me that would require me to know about Abby's life?

"My daughter was supposed to go to earth to enjoy her freedom before ruling alongside me when she turns twenty-one." I know this because everyone knows that the Princess of Hell will rule with her dad. "That is no longer the case." My eyes widen. "You will keep this next part to yourself, do you understand me?" I give him a firm nod. "Abigail has found her mates. Five, to be exact." His jaw ticks, and I'm almost positive I see smoke coming from his nose. "Three, I am not a fan of. One, I'd like to snap like a fucking twig." *Oh, boy.* "But he's not the issue. I just got a call from her. Michael, that slimy little shit, has been up to something. Something big. I always knew he was a fraud. Yet, I'm the one who's made out to be the monster." He rolls his eyes. I mean, I've seen first hand the things he does to those in Hell. He's not innocent by any stretch of the imagination.

"I'm getting off-topic. Long story short, I'm sending you to earth. Your job is to keep a close eye on Abby. Make sure no one is planning to take her by surprise, and keep her mate, Isaac, in line. He's lucky he's not dead," he growls. "I already sent Leo up there, but that boy is so smitten with her, that he's useless in regards to sending information back to me."

"I'm going to earth?" I ask, needing to see if I heard him right.

"Yes. I've enrolled you into Angelic Academy, so you will be able to keep a closer eye on her. Make sure none of those Pure

Blood assholes fuck with her anymore. She acts like nothing can get to her, but I don't like anyone thinking they can fuck with my daughter and get away with it. She might be nice, but I'm not. You are to report anything concerning that would affect her safety. She already plans on telling me anything she finds out about the archangels, but the more eyes the better."

"I thought that school was for Pure Bloods only?" I've been top side a lot in my teenage years, but I've never been anywhere other than Dark Night. I never dared to step foot on Pure Blood soil.

"They have a scholarship program. They have been letting people from other realms into their school. Leo has taken the demon spot, but I've managed to find a loophole. You are a vampire and not originally from Hell. They didn't plan on letting vampires in because of how out of control they are in their realm. But seeing how you've been trained not only by your father but by me, and can control your bloodlust, they have agreed to let you in." I wanna ask how he's managing to get Pure Bloods to do anything for him since they should despise him, but I know when to keep my mouth shut.

"When do I leave?" The idea of going topside excites me. It's been years since I was able to leave Hell. I love my job, don't get me wrong, but I miss the freedom I used to have. In Hell, being on the King's guard is the highest honor and best paying job, but it's also time-consuming and draining at times. This little break is something I need.

But being around Abby isn't going to be easy.

"Today. I'll give you an hour to pack."

He tells me everything he expects of me before dismissing me. As I put my hand on the knob, I know I need to tell him, because if I don't, this could turn into something bigger, and I might get in trouble.

"Sir, there's something I need to tell you about Abby." I

look at him over my shoulder, and my poker face must suck this morning because he takes one look at me and lets out a deep sigh.

"You too? How long have you known?"

"Since she was sixteen."

"Does she know?"

"No." I shake my head. "Because vampires can tell who their mates are through the scent of their blood, I didn't need to touch her to know she was mine. It was by random chance back then. I planned on keeping it to myself, not sure how mating would go with the Princess of Hell. I didn't want to mess with anything you had planned."

"So you were willing to go your whole life without your mate because you were worried about how it might affect me and my plans for Hell?"

"Ah, yeah, I guess." I hate the blush that takes over my cheeks right now.

He smiles. Holy shit, the Devil is smiling at me, and it's not one of those creepy ones that make people shit their pants. "I knew I liked you." He chuckles. "I respect you, Francesca. But no more secrets. Abby is allowed to be with any and all of her mates. I just want her to be happy."

Air leaves my lungs as joy fills me. "You're alright if she knows?"

"I'm gonna hate to see one of my best guards go." He shrugs.

"That's if she even wants me." I chuckle nervously. "She already has some amazing mates."

"Two good mates. The others are questionable, at best. Trust me, I think you will be alright."

"I think I'm going to give her some time though. She already has a lot going on. With her just finding out about her newest mates, I think it's best."

"Already looking out for her. I made the right decision picking you. Go, get ready. Your new adventure starts today, but remember... mates or not, you are still to do as we planned."

"Yes, of course, sir. I won't let you down."

The whole time I'm packing, I'm wondering if this is some kind of joke. *Am I really going to earth? To go to some preppy angel school?* Fuck, that's going to be a nightmare. But I get to see Abby, to be around her. To smell her, to... *no, Frankie, stop.* Not yet, not now. She's already going through so much from what I could tell when she came to Hell not too long ago.

I need to keep my distance, at least from physically touching her. Like I'd be able to stay away from her now that I have the green light to be with her.

This is a one day at a time thing. I might have known who she was to me, but outside of that one run in with her, she has no idea who I am.

Bags packed, I head to the portal, finding my dad waiting for me there. "About time," he says.

"What?"

"That you do something about having a mate."

My brows rise, eyes widening. "How—"

"You think you're sneaky, but I've seen you following the Princess around. It's not just a girl who has a crush, it's a mate who wants to protect."

"You're not mad?" My dad isn't one to show emotion, and when he does, it's never in the open.

"I love you, Frankie. You're my daughter, and I only want the best for you."

"Thank you," I say, my voice soft.

"Now go. Be safe."

"Always."

We don't hug, but I can see the look of love in his eyes.

After stepping through the portal, the first thing I do when I get outside of the building is take in a deep breath of air. Fuck, it's nice to be back here.

Looking around, I start to head toward the parking lot but then remember, I don't know what the hell I'm supposed to do. It's Sunday, are they even open? Do I just show up at the school and say *Hey, I'm your new vampire scholarship student, where do I sleep?*

Instead of wandering around like a fool, I decide to go to the one place I do know.

Remembering the way to Zed's like the back of my hand, and the fact that I use my speed, I'm at my destination in under three minutes.

Smiling, I look up at the house of one of my bestest friends in the whole world. Someone I haven't seen or spoken to in years.

Making my way to the door, I give it a few knocks. "I got it!" I grin at the sound of Libby's voice.

When she opens the door, I can't help but smile like an idiot. "Hey there, small fry."

Her eyes go comically wide. "Frankie!" she screams before launching herself at me.

"My god, you've grown." I chuckle as I hug her tightly.

"That's what happens when you haven't been by in three years," she replies, sassy as ever, as she steps back.

"Who's at the door, Libby?" Zed's voice sounds from within the house, and fuck, it takes everything in me to not launch myself at him. He pops around the corner and looks over Libby's head. Our eyes meet, and he looks like he's seen a ghost.

"Frankie?"

"Hey there, Rock Star. Long time no see."

CHAPTER FOUR

ABBY

"**M**om!" Libby shouts as she rushes into the kitchen, a massive smile on her face. Megan looks over at her from where she's standing at the stove, making Zed's birthday supper. "Mom, guess who's here."

"Who?" she asks, brows furrowing.

"Frankie!" From the look on Libby's face, I guess Frankie is someone to be excited over? I've never heard any of them mention this guy before.

"Really?" Megan gasps, her eyes lighting up.

"Who's Frankie?" Leo asks.

"I don't know." I shrug.

Megan and Libby both rush out of the kitchen.

"Guess we're about to find out whoever this guy is," I say, getting up from my chair and Leo follows.

But when I step into the hallway and look toward the front door, I find out this Frankie guy is in fact *not* a guy, but a tall, gorgeous woman with bright red hair.

Jealousy surges to the surface as my jaw ticks with each passing second that her arms are around my mate.

"Down girl," Leo chuckles.

"Shut up," I mutter. Whoever this girl is, she needs to stop touching my man before I make her.

"Frankie," Megan says her name in a motherly warm tone, making the hairs on the back of my neck stand up.

"Who are you?" I ask, unable to keep the snippy tone out of my question. I'm not one to normally let another woman get to me, but after everything with the guys and the Heathers, I've grown a little testy.

"Little Bird," Zed says, stepping back. "This is Frankie. One of my best friends."

"Really?" I say, letting the question drag a bit. "Funny, because I haven't heard you mention her once."

"She's been gone for years now. I didn't think to bring her up," he replies, looking a little guilty.

My eyes flick over to Frankie, and that's when I realize I've seen her before. "Wait. You're the vampire guard I met when I went home to visit."

I'm unable to stop the blush that creeps up the back of my neck remembering my thoughts of her when I met her. I thought she was attractive in her uniform, but now? It's really hard not to stare. She's stunning; tall, bright red hair, covered in tattoos. She's in a pair of black ripped jeans and a crop top, her cleavage on full display.

"That I am." She gives me a cheeky smile and fuck, it has me blushing deeper. "The name's Francesca, but please, call me Frankie."

"What are you doing here?" I ask bluntly. Her brows go up, but her smile stays in place.

"Right to the point, I see. Your father sent me. I'm here to keep a closer eye on... things." She looks to Megan and Libby, not sure how much she's able to say around them.

"Of course he sent someone," I sigh, shaking my head. "I just called him a few hours ago. He works fast."

"He just wants to make sure you're safe."

"Come in! You came at a perfect time. Supper is almost done. It's Zed's favorite, made it special for his birthday."

Frankie's brows jump. "Oh shit, it's your birthday today? Fuck, I didn't even pay attention to the date. Happy birthday, Rock Star." She punches his arm, and he winces.

"Thanks, Blood Sucker." He chuckles.

My jaw ticks at the little nicknames they have for each other; too personal for my liking.

Frankie follows Megan, giving me a lingering look.

"Fuck, Little Bird." Zed wraps his arms around me from behind, pulling me close to his warm body. "It's so fucking hot when you're jealous." He kisses my neck, making my eyes close, and a shiver runs through my body.

"I'm not jealous," but my protest is weak.

His chuckle has my belly warming. "Yes, you are. And I like it. But you have nothing to be jealous over. If anything, I should be the jealous one."

"What, why?" I ask, twisting my head to look up at him.

"Because..." He nips at the tip of my nose. "Frankie isn't into people who have dicks, if you get what I mean."

My eyes widen. "Oh."

She's into women. That makes the jealousy disappear.

"Also, even if she didn't like girls, it wouldn't matter because..." he spins me so that I'm facing him. "I only have eyes for one girl. One amazing, sexy, badass girl. And the best mate anyone could ask for," he growls, smashing his lips to mine in a bruising kiss. His hand cups the back of my head as his lips devour mine. I moan, unable to hold it in, as his tongue dips between my lips, tangling with mine.

"Ew. Enough of that. We have guests here," Libby gags.

"I don't mind." Leo chuckles.

"You don't count," she deadpans.

Zed breaks the kiss, both of us panting as he looks at me with half-lidded, hungry eyes. "Later. I'm the birthday boy after all, and the one thing I want the most is you, naked, laid out on your bed."

"Okay," I whimper. Now is not the time to be turned on, but can we like speed this dinner up? I'm not really hungry for food anymore.

"Alright, you guys catch up. Libby, help me in the kitchen, please."

"So, Rock Star, I see you got yourself a mate," Frankie teases Zed.

"That I did." His voice is smug as he sits down on the couch and pulls me down into his lap, wrapping his arms around me protectively.

"I bet you never thought that would happen." She chuckles. "And with the princess of Hell, no less."

"What can I say? Only the best for me," he teases back, kissing me on the cheek.

"I'm really confused right now. First, if my dad sent you here, what's your job exactly? And how do you two know each other?"

"You're looking at the newest scholarship student at Angelic Academy." Frankie leans back in her chair, placing her arms on the rests. She looks like a queen.

"Really?" Leo asks. "Are you going to be staying in the dorms too?"

"Ugh." She rolls her eyes. "I really don't want to."

"You can stay here if you want. I'm guessing Abby's dad

sent you here because all of the bullshit going on with my dear old pops," Zed scoffs.

"He doesn't trust Michael. And as much as he knows Abby can handle herself, he's not taking any chances."

"Can you two not talk about me like I'm not here," I grumble. Frankie's eyes flash with guilt.

"Sorry."

"And excuse you for just inviting a woman I've never met to stay at your house with you," I growl, spinning around to face Zed, glaring at him.

"I bet you're so hard right now." Frankie laughs.

"What?" I look between the two of them like they've grown new heads.

"So hard," he confirms with a growl while rocking my ass against his growing cock. *This is weird, but also arousing.*

"What is happening right now?" Leo asks, sounding amused.

"It's okay, Princess. You have nothing to worry about when it comes to me and your boy. He's like a brother to me. I have zero interest in him other than being his friend. And to answer your earlier question, I met Zed, what? About five-ish years ago?"

"Sounds about right," Zed mutters, sounding like he does not want Frankie to continue.

"I'd come topside, mostly for the parties. It was before I started working for the King's guard. At one party, I ran into our boy here." She looks at Zed with a Cheshire Cat grin that has him groaning, sinking back into his seat.

"And what happened?" I ask, finding myself interested, especially if Zed seems so embarrassed about it.

"Well, he hit on me of course," she snorts. "He gave me all his best fuck-boy moves."

"Really?" I ask him, raising a brow.

"I'm not proud of my past before you," Zed grumbles. "You met my ex."

"Don't remind me," I snarl, making his lips twitch.

"His poor ego was hurt when I told him that he didn't have what I was looking for. But the effort was cute."

"Whatever," Zed says. "If you liked dick, I totally would have gotten you to go home with me that night."

"Whatever helps you sleep at night, Rock Star." She laughs. "After she shot me down, we got a few drinks and ended up spending the whole night talking. And that's how our friendship started. Frankie became one of the most important people to me. Then the bitch had to go get her dream job, and I haven't seen her since."

"Sorry, babe." She gives him a sad smile. "If I had a heads up, I would have come to say goodbye."

"If she meant so much to you, why haven't you mentioned her before?" I wonder, because the way he's talking about her, that's something that should have been brought up by now.

"Because..." He blushes. God, he's blushing. It's so cute. "Thinking about her made me sad." The last word is so low it's hard to hear.

"What was that?" Frankie asks, but by her tone she heard him. Vampire hearing and all.

"I said, thinking about you made me sad, okay?" he growls. "You were my best friend, my person, and I never let anyone get close who wasn't family. And you just left."

Frankie's face drops, all humor and playfulness gone. "I know, and I'm sorry. If I could have kept in touch, I would have."

"Hey, don't be mad at her," I say, brushing my thumb against his cheek, kissing his nose. "Once you join the guard, your whole life becomes about it. My dad doesn't let people leave Hell or contact the topside once you're inducted."

"Fine," he huffs. "You're forgiven. You're back now, but for how long?"

"I'm not sure," she answers. "I guess it all depends on how things work out." She gives me a lingering look that I can't decipher.

"Food's ready!" Zed's mom calls.

"I'm starving," Leo groans. I almost forgot he was here. He's been mostly quiet. "Come on, Starbright, let's go get you fed." He pulls me to my feet, saying, "We should give them a moment."

I nod, giving Zed a look. He winks and slaps my ass. "Be right in, Little Bird."

"So, I guess there's always something new to learn about these guys, huh?" Leo comments, kissing the side of my head.

"It's different with them. I know everything when it comes to you," I say.

"Perks of being your number one person." He grins.

"Not a competition."

ZED

I still can't believe she's here. It's been years since I've seen her. She's hardly changed at all, maybe a few more tattoos. She still has her charming personality, that's for sure.

"Seriously, how have you never mentioned you knew a King's guard?" Leo asks, watching Abby and Frankie.

They seem to have hit it off. After supper we came out back

to enjoy some s'mores by the fire. Abby got over her adorable jealousy that still has my cock half-stiff.

It's weird to see them together. Two people who mean a lot to me in very different ways. Frankie is like a sister to me and not having her around was hard. I've missed her like crazy. It'd be the same if Libby just up and disappeared one day.

"I don't know everything about you, do I?" I ask, raising a brow.

"Fair point." He nods, dropping it. "So, another person joining our band of misfits, I see."

"Frankie is good people," I grunt. Not going to lie, I'm happy about her being back. It just sucks that I don't know for how long. But I'm excited to spend what time I do have with her. I just don't want to piss Abby off. She is my number one. I just hope she doesn't get jealous.

As for Frankie, there's something going on with her. I don't think she's lying about what she's here to do, but there's more to the story.

For the rest of the night, I watch the two of them. Frankie hardly says two words to me, unless it's to tease me about something. Her full attention is on Abby.

By the end of the night, I realize two things. Frankie is attracted to her, and I'm the jealous one now and– "Frankie." I pull her to the side as she comes back from the bathroom.

"Hey, Rock Star," she grins brightly at me.

"What the fuck is going on?" I snarl, and her face drops.

"What do you mean?"

"I'm not stupid. I've been watching you all night."

"Don't think your mate would like that very much," she grins.

"You like her." I narrow my eyes.

"Of course, I do. She's a good person, fun to talk to, and I'm not going to lie, she's hot."

"Frankie," I say in a warning tone. "You've kept your distance, making sure not to get too close to her."

"I'm sorry, do you want me to throw myself at your mate, get all buddy-buddy with a stranger?"

"Frankie!" I snarl, getting in her face. I could outright ask her, but I need to hear her admit it. "Is there a reason why you're doing everything you can not to touch her?"

Frankie's eyes flash with panic. "I'm sorry."

"Fuck!" I hiss, running a hand through my hair. "Really? Is she really your mate?"

Frankie nods. "I'm sorry," she says again.

"How long have you known?" I know it's different for vampires. While the rest of us need physical touch to ignite the bond spark to know who our mates are, vampires can smell it in their blood. Frankie has been keeping her distance so Abby doesn't find out. "And why don't you want Abby to know?"

"I've known for a while now. At first, I kept away because of the age gap, and I worried what her father might do if he found out. Now, it's because that girl has had little to no choices of her own the past few months. Out of five mates, she only was able to wrap her head around one of them before her life got turned upside down. And while finding out about you has worked out, the other three, not so much. I don't want to do that to her again."

"Fuck's sake," I groan, scrubbing my eyes with the palms of my hands.

"Are you mad?" she asks.

"No," I sigh. "Surprised as fuck? Yes. Unsure how any of this would work? Yeah. But not mad. Trust me, I'd chose you to be her mate over the other three fuckers any day."

"I see they're not here today. I'm guessing things are still on edge?"

"Yes and no. She's working on things with Luke and Noah. As for Isaac...complicated. *Really* fucking complicated."

She nods, looking out toward the fire where Abby is sitting in Leo's lap, talking and laughing. "That's the main reason why I'm not doing anything right now. I'm going to get to know her, let her get to know me. But the biggest thing is I'm letting her choose. I want her to decide if she wants me, I want to give her the choice she hasn't gotten yet."

"That's not how this works and you know it. You don't get a choice on who you're mated to," I remind her.

"I know," she snaps. "But what if she finds out now, and is so overwhelmed that she wants nothing to do with me? She already has to work on so much with the others, I don't want to add any more to her plate. Please, Zed, just let me be her friend for now. Let her work on things with the others before throwing this at her. She's the only thing that matters."

"Fuck you," I mutter.

"What? What the hell?" she growls.

"Why do you have to go and be all awesome when it comes to Abby by putting her first?"

"Really, fucker?" Frankie deadpans.

"Look, I can't keep this from her. I refuse to lie to her. But because you both mean something to me, and really this has nothing to do with me, I'll keep my mouth shut for now. But if there comes a time when she needs to know, you will tell her. I hate lying to her."

"Just a few weeks, give me until Christmas to at least let her adjust to all the new changes, and then I'll tell her. But Zed, if I feel like me being her mate will only make her unhappy or her life worse, I'm not telling her." Her eyes grow hard, telling me I won't change her mind.

"You're willing to go the rest of your life without your

mate?" I ask her, knowing that there's no way I'd ever be able to be without Abby. I'd rather fucking die.

"If it means she's happy, then yes." Frankie's attention drifts over to Abby again, this look of longing on her face that just doesn't fit Frankie. Frankie is the type of person to go after what she wants. So seeing her hold herself back, means she truly cares about Abby's feelings. And that I respect.

"This is going to be one hell of a life once you join the fold." I laugh. "Seeing you with Abby is going to be weird as fuck."

"Don't be jelly, Rock Star, I can show you a few moves with my tongue someday, give you some pointers on how to rock her world." She wiggles her eyebrows.

"Fuck you." I laugh. "I know how to use my tongue just fine. Trust me, the sounds she makes, pure fucking heaven."

Frankie's eyes flash with heat. "So jealous right now," she mutters.

"As you should be, Blood Sucker. As you should."

Frankie flips me off before joining the others at the fire. I stay back and watch. Abby perks up when Frankie sits back down, and the two of them start talking again. Watching my girl look so happy, I have no doubt in my mind that she would welcome Frankie as her mate, but I understand where Frankie is coming from. Abby has had a lot thrown at her in a small amount of time. I too would like her to adjust to some of it before throwing something else at her. But I don't think adding Frankie as her mate will be as much a hardship as the other guys. Only time will tell, I guess.

CHAPTER FIVE

ABBY

"Little Bird," Zed's voice murmurs in my ear.

"What?" I whine groggily as I shift in his lap.

He chuckles, rubbing his hand up and down my arm. "We need to get you to bed, baby, you have school tomorrow."

"I don't wanna go home." I snuggle deeper into his chest, not wanting to leave his warmth.

"You don't have to." He kisses the top of my head. "You and Leo can sleep here."

"What about Frankie?" I ask, eyes fluttering open.

Zed looks down at me, brows creasing. "Are you alright if she crashes in Libby's room?"

At first, the idea of another woman, one that I just met, staying under my mate's roof filled me with a jealous possession. But as the night went on, and the more I got to know Frankie for myself, it was easy to see that the relationship between her and Zed was more of a best friend or even a brother and sister bond. So that nasty feeling went away.

"I don't mind," I tell him. If she didn't stay, she would have nowhere to go. The admissions office doesn't open until tomorrow, so there would be no way for her to get into her dorm.

I can't believe that my dad sent her here. Not that I'm really upset about it, Frankie is actually a pretty cool person. Maybe it's not a bad thing. Zed seems happy about having his friend back, and I really enjoyed talking with her.

Just wish my dad would understand that I don't need this much protection. But I also see where he's coming from. He seems really worried about everything I told him regarding Michael. I know he wanted to tell me to come back to Hell. He didn't though, knowing I would have flat out refused.

I'm not running from this. I plan on finding out just what kind of sketchy shit that man is up to and put a stop to it.

Michael is a sick, evil man in my eyes. I'm really fucking pissed off he's an archangel because he deserves to be in Hell, just like all the other scum of the earth.

"Come on, Starbright, let's get you to bed." Leo holds out a hand for me, pulling me to my feet.

"I'll go get Frankie settled." Zed stands and kisses my lips softly. "I love you, Little Bird," he growls.

"I love you too." I smile softly up at him.

"How are you doing?" Leo asks, pulling me into his arms.

"It's a lot," I admit, sighing heavily. "I don't know if I want to hate Isaac anymore, but I can't forgive him for what he did. At least not any time soon."

"You don't have to hate him." Leo kisses the tip of my nose. "It doesn't make you weak if you stop hating him. No one said you had to."

"I feel bad, you know? Sure, he's been a royal dick to me,

but he had it so much worse behind closed doors. Some harsh words are nowhere near as bad as being beaten by someone who's supposed to protect you." A tear slips down my cheek. Leo brushes it away using his thumb.

"Tomorrow is a new day. There's a lot that's happened in a short amount of time, and I know we're still all trying to wrap our heads around it. But why don't you try to start over? Get to know the real him and not the persona he's been putting on."

"Yeah. Maybe." I close my eyes, letting Leo hold me closer. "I still can't get over the fact that I have five mates."

"Crazy, yeah." He chuckles. "But I think if you give them the chance to prove themselves, they could make you happy. We both know that the bond just won't go away."

"Don't remind me," I grumble, remembering the pain I've had to endure to reject Isaac. Is that something I plan to retract now that I know the truth of why he's been so cruel to me? I know that it's possible to do so. But if I was to make that decision, I'd have to be sure. I'd have to know that I loved him and accepted him as a forever thing, because I don't think I could handle the pain of rejecting him, or anyone else, again.

Not that I want to reject Noah or Luke. I actually find myself growing to like them. They've changed a lot and it shows. Noah is sweet and understanding, and Luke is funny and caring. I find myself excited to see what it's going to be like dating them.

They're my mates, and I've accepted that. I don't want to hold back anymore. It's not only the bond that wants me to give in and be with them. I want that too.

"You're right. I think it's best if we just start over. I'm not going to just forget what Isaac did to me, but the other two, I... would it be bad that I think I want to forgive them?"

"No, baby." He chuckles. "It means that you're a good person and you're not letting the past control your future.

They've changed, right?" I nod. "And their true colors are better than who they portrayed themselves to be in the past?" I nod again. "Then no," he repeats. "I don't think it's a bad thing."

Leo guides me up the stairs. I can hear Libby and Zed talking in her room, another voice mixing in to the conversion before they all start to laugh.

There's that feeling again, jealousy, but this time it's different. Like I want to be in on the joke. This woman is someone he was once close to, someone who seems to know a lot about him. Maybe more than I do? And what is it with her calling him Rock Star? I know he plays guitar, but is there something more?

"I gotta pee," I let Leo know before we head into Zed's room.

"'Kay." Leo kisses my temple and lets me go.

Closing the door behind me, I step in front of the mirror and my eyes widen. The woman staring back at me looks tired, worn down. This isn't me. I have dark rings under my eyes, like I haven't gotten sleep in weeks.

I'm tired of being unhappy about the things I have no control over. I'm tired of all the pain I have to go through. I'm tired of the lies and the secrets.

Can't I just be happy? Can't I just be with my mates and enjoy life?

Leaning against the sink, I close my eyes and hang my head. "Alright, universe, is there anything else you wanna throw at me?" I mumble. "Because I really don't know how much more I can take. At least let me deal with everything else first."

Turning on the tap, I wash my face, brush my hair and teeth with the toiletries Zed got me for my sleepovers here, and get ready for bed.

When I'm done and step out of the bathroom, Frankie is there, leaning against the wall across from me.

"Hey." She gives me a friendly smile.

My eyes are drawn to her striking bright red ones that match her hair. It's almost like they suck you in, never wanting to let you go. Unable to stop myself, I let my eyes roam over her. She is gorgeous. So damn pretty that if I didn't know with my whole heart that Leo and Zed were madly in love with me and my body, I might be envious of her perfect breasts, her skinny waist, and long, slender legs that seem to go on for days. Her pale skin makes her assortment of colorful and black and grey tattoos pop. There's no fooling myself, I find her very attractive. And that has me filling with guilt.

My eyes flick back up to hers, an unwilling blush growing on my cheeks. "Hey."

Talking to her tonight felt so natural, like we knew each other for years. She was funny, her stories about working in Hell had me full belly laughing.

"Look, I feel like I need to say this. Me and Zed. There's nothing there. There never will be anything but friendship. He's an amazing guy, and I'm sure you find him drop dead sexy, but he is not my type. As in, he has a dick." She chuckles, the husky tone sending a shiver over my spine. Even her voice and her laugh is attractive. "I just don't want you to think that I'm going to try anything with him. He loves you, Abby." She laughs. "He is so head over heels that there's nothing in any realm that would ever be able to rip him away from you."

"Thanks." I smile, her words finalizing my comfort regarding their friendship. "I'm pretty crazy about him too."

"I know it might be a little weird, but I hope we can be friends too." The hope in her eyes is hard to resist.

"Me too."

"Alright, Little Bird. You ready for bed?" Zed steps out of

Libby's room. I nod, letting him pull me into his arms. He looks at Frankie. "Everything should be good to go. Night, Blood Sucker." He chuckles, pulling at one of Frankie's strands of hair.

"Fuck off," she retorts playfully, slapping his hand away.

"No fucking!" Libby shouts. "I need my beauty sleep, and I can't do that with Abby's moaning."

"Oh, god," I groan, feeling mortified as my face turns a burning red.

"Yeah, like that only louder," Libby says, then bursts into giggles.

"I'm gone. Night!" I shout, rushing out of Zed's arms, away from the pretty vampire, and into Zed's room. Leo is waiting for me and must have heard Libby because the fucker is laughing.

"Don't even," I warn before diving under the covers.

"I wouldn't dare think of it." He chuckles.

We all wake up early the next morning. Leo and I need to head back to my place to get showered and in new clothes. Of course, he insisted on showering together, making us really have to rush to get to school on time.

The guys were just leaving as we get out of the shower. I don't have time to do my hair, so I toss it into a messy bun and throw on a clean uniform.

"It would be nice to be able to fly like you," Leo huffs as he closes the car door and starts it.

"Maybe we can get some kind of spell," I offer as we drive down to the gate.

"Ah, no thanks. I'm not messing with that shit. I've seen my fair share of spells and potions go wrong."

"Good point." I laugh. "But, if someone didn't take his time, we wouldn't have to rush."

He gives me this cocky smirk that has my belly boiling. "Oh, Starbright, you loved that I took it slow. So much that you screamed my name—twice."

I glare at him, but he's right. The way Leo's mouth worked my pussy in the shower had me cumming all over his face, then his cock; yeah, there's no complaints here.

We manage to get to school on time, the bell going off just as we walk through the door to our first class.

People avoid me, no one but my friends talk to me. I don't see anyone all morning until a jolt shoots through my body as Isaac pulls me to a stop on my way to the food court for lunch.

"Abby," his voice sounds so broken, so defeated. He doesn't look like the cocky asshole he normally does.

"Hey." My body hums from his touch when he doesn't take his hand off me.

"Can we talk?" he asks, his eyes searching my face as he waits for me to reject his request.

"What about?"

"Everything." He takes a step forward, causing me to take one backward, my back hitting a wall. My heart starts to race as he traps me in place. Only it's not in fear this time. Fuck, this stupid bond and my hormones sure do like to betray my body. "But first, I want to start by apologizing. I know nothing I say can take away what I did to you, how I treated you. But fuck, Abby, I'm sorry." His voice breaks, and I'm starting to wonder if this is even Isaac. *Did someone switch places with him?* "I'm so damn sorry. I let my own bullshit turn me into a shitty person, and I took it out on you. I blamed you for anything and everything I could think of. Whatever made it easier to hate you. The only thing was, I don't think I ever truly hated you. I wanted to. So damn bad. But it was pointless. Then I found out we were mates and that really fucked with my head. Every time I pushed you away, I wanted to pull you into my arms. Every time I called you nasty names, I wanted to tell you how much I wanted you." He pauses looking away from me, his jaw clenching. "You deserve better than me. I'm broken, Abby. I'm fucked up." He looks at me again, and I almost gasp at the emotion in his eyes. "But it doesn't change the fact that you're my mate. I need you. You had every right to reject me. But I'm not lying when I say that it's the worst pain I've ever felt."

That has tears forming in my eyes because, if that's true, if being rejected hurt more than his dad putting his hands on him, then it must have been bad. Did he hurt more than I did? Being the one who was rejected versus the one who did the rejecting, does it change the level of pain?

Guilt hits me with the knowledge that I added to the torture he had to endure alongside what his dad did to him. "I'm sorry." I find myself being the one to apologize.

"No," he says firmly, shaking his head. "You have nothing to be sorry about. I deserved it. Every little bit of it. But I'm promising you now, Abby; no more, I will never treat you like that again." He raises his hand, like he wants to touch me but thinks better of it, and lets his hand fall to his side. "Can we start over? Please?"

My eyes lock with his for what feels like forever as I take in the broken boy before me. "Okay." I nod. "But know this is the only chance you get. If you do something as bad as you've done before, I don't think I could ever forgive you again, for any of it."

His whole face lights up, and I don't think I've ever seen him smile like this. So big, so bright and genuine. "I won't. I promise, I won't. I'm going to show you, Abby. Show you that

I'm sorry, that I can be a better man. For not only you, but for Noah and Luke too. You all deserve better than what I've given you. I don't deserve you, none of you. I will do whatever I can in my power to keep you."

"One day at a time," is all I say back.

He gives me one firm nod. "One day at a time."

"We better get going," I tell him, my stomach growling.

"Right. Food," he says, taking a step back.

As we both walk in comfortable silence, I feel for the first time in a long time that there is a chance everything just might be okay. But the real question is, for how long?

CHAPTER SIX

ISAAC

No more secrets, no more hiding. I need to do this.

I want Abby, and I'm done being a fool. I'm done treating her like shit. That girl has a hold on me, and I was stupid to ever think I could make it go away, to just forget about her.

I don't want to forget about her. I want to pull her into my arms, kiss her until our lips are swollen and we're gasping for air. I want to fuck her until she's screaming my name. The thought of her when she came around my cock makes me adjust myself in my slacks.

No, that wasn't how it should have been. Our first time was amazing and messed up, all balled into one.

Next time I have her, I'm going to fucking worship her like the queen she is.

"Are you sure she won't hate me even more?" I ask Noah. After my talk with Abby a few minutes ago, I walked her into the food court. She's sitting with Leo and her friends.

45

She looks happy, a smile spreading wide across her face before she breaks out into laughter.

"How did I ever manage to hate her?" I whisper more to myself, but Luke and Noah hear me.

"You didn't," Luke snorts with laughter. "That's the thing. You tried, really tried, but in reality, there's no way any of us stood a chance when it came to her. One way or another, she would have consumed us. And I am in no way upset about that now, are you?"

Luke looks to me and then Noah. "Not one bit," is Noah's response.

"No," I sigh. "It's just, fuck," I hiss, running a hand through my hair. "I really don't think she's ever going to forgive me for what I put her through." I shake my head, my stomach rolling at the memories.

"Stop thinking about the past. There's nothing we can do about it. We need to put the time and effort into making things right, now. And that starts with ending things with Heather. You don't have to get up on the tables and yell to the school that Abby is your mate, but Heather is going to come prancing over to you as soon as she sees you. That's when you tell her you need to talk, end things with her, and when she asks why, you tell her the truth. No more–"

"No more secrets, no more lies. I know," I grind out. This is all so weird to me. I've been so filled with hate and pain the past few years–mostly this past year. But now that the truth is out there, I feel like I don't need to hide anymore. I feel more like myself.

A part of me doesn't believe that things will get better. My pride is still wounded because my mates now know that my father has been beating me for years. He's a powerful man, I never stood a chance.

But now, I have people at my side. I guess I always did, but

I was too stubborn to lean on them. Mate bonds are also a powerful thing, and I should have put more faith into the people I love. The people who would never do what my father has done.

That's what I thought about my dad too. That he would never hurt his son—his own flesh and blood—but everything changed after my mom died.

No. I need to stop thinking that way. Luke and Noah aren't my dad, they would never hurt me like that. Ever. I know that deep inside my tainted heart.

"Speak of the devil, and she will appear," Luke mutters.

"What?" I look at him confused, wondering why the heck he's talking about Abby's dad. But then I hear my name, my eyes find Heather heading this way, and I realize he's talking about the saying. "Oh, fuck."

"Good luck, babe." Luke chuckles, slapping me on the shoulder. "You got this."

"I hate you," I hiss with no heat behind the comeback.

"No, you don't." Noah smirks. "Remember who you're doing this for. It's time."

Letting out a heavy sigh, I nod. This might not seem like a big deal. Luke and Noah ended things with their Heathers. But once word gets back to my dad, he's going to lose his shit.

"There you are, baby," Heather purrs when she reaches me. "I've been trying to get a hold of you all weekend. You didn't call me back." She gives me a pout.

"We need to talk," I say.

Her face drops. "No."

"What?" I ask, brows furrowing. "What do you mean 'no?'"

Luke chuckles and Noah groans from their place nearby. The assholes just love watching me suffer. "I said no. You're not doing this to me, Isaac. I'm not letting you end things with me."

47

My brows jump. "That's not how this works. If I break up with you, it's over. I'm sorry Heather, but it's just not going to work. You have to know that I don't have any feelings invested in this, in you. I'm sorry if this hurts your feelings, and I'm sorry for wasting your time this past year, but we won't be getting married. We're not going to be together."

"No," is all she says, looking at her nails. *What the fuck?*

"Yes." My jaw ticks, anger filling me. I'm trying to be a better person for Abby's sake, but I'm also thinking about belittling Heather in a much more public setting if she doesn't get onboard with this breakup. We're in school and people are watching, but I'm about three seconds away from not giving a fuck.

She looks up at me. "I reject your break-up," she declares, her face starting to turn red. "You don't get to do this to me, Isaac. If anyone is to end things, it's going to be me. And I don't want to."

My fist clenches. "Listen here, you crazy bitch. You left me no choice, I've been trying to be nice, but listen to me here and now; I don't want you. I never did. You are nothing but a gold digger. You damn well know you're not in love with me. All you want is power and money. Sorry to break it to you, you're not going to get it from me. Now, fuck off because I have a mate, and I plan on being with her. Not you."

Her eyes widen. "I swear to our God, that if you say you're mates with that demon bitch, I will end you," she snarls.

"Then end me." I smirk. "Because Abigail Morningstar is my mate. The only woman I ever plan on being with is her. So... Fuck. Off. We're done."

"That whore really does get around," she sneers. "You're going to regret this," she warns. "I'm going to make your life a living hell. And when you come crawling back to me, I'll just laugh in your face."

"Okay." I roll my eyes. "You do that."

"Argh!" she screams, stomping her feet like a child before storming off. The other Heathers jump up from their seats and run after her.

"Look at you. Guess you do have a set of balls," someone jests with a laugh from behind me. I spin around to see a girl. A very tall girl.

"Who the hell are you?" I ask. She's not from here. Must be a new student. How the fuck did another non-pure blood get accepted into this school? She's got bright red hair and is covered in tattoos. She doesn't fit in here at all. But then I see her red glowing eyes and my own widen. "You're a fucking vampire. What the hell?" *Did I wake up in some kind of alternate universe?*

"If you don't watch yourself, I'll be your worst fucking nightmare." She takes a step closer, almost meeting me in height. "If you hurt Abby again, I'll end you, Angel Boy. I'll strap you to a chair and pluck every little feather from your pretty set of wings." She grins, her fangs on display. Chuckling, she runs her tongue over them. "I'll sink my fangs into your neck and suck you dry, until you're nothing but a lifeless corpse."

"You're fucking crazy," I grunt, a little in shock. *Who is this woman and why does she care so much about Abby?*

"You have no idea just how crazy I can be, Angel Boy." She laughs. "Just remember what I said." She winks before shoulder checking me as she passes.

I watch as she walks over to Abby's table, taking a seat across from her.

Abby smiles, a small blush taking over her cheeks. *What the fuck just happened?*

"Who was that?" Noah asks as he and Luke come to stand at my side.

"What the fuck did we miss over the weekend?"

"I have no idea." But I plan on finding out.

"So, Heather," Luke starts, looking at me with amusement in his eyes.

"Don't even start," I growl. "Why the hell were your Heathers so easy to break up with?"

"They weren't," Noah mutters. "Mine called me over eighty times and blew up my phone. She went to my dad too. I had to block her on everything. Also, remember them showing up at our place?"

"Yeah, mine stalked me at school for the first few days, threw herself at my feet, and begged me to take her back." Luke chuckles. "Looks like you just got the mean crazy one while we got the normal crazy ones."

"We need to keep an eye on her. I know she's not done, and I'm afraid she might do something to Abby." If she hurts her, I will end her. I don't care if it puts a dent in my perfect pure blood reputation. No one will ever fucking hurt my mate again, especially me.

"Don't worry. I don't think our poor girl is going to get any space any time soon." Luke throws his arm over my shoulder. "Now, let's go get something to eat. I haven't seen her in a day, and I'm going crazy."

"Can we do something tonight?" I ask, not missing the shock on Luke's face.

"Sure. Like what?"

"I don't know." I shrug. "Play some video games, watch a movie..." *Fuck*. But I don't say that. I miss them. I miss kissing them, touching them, the way they feel around my cock as I pump deep inside them.

"I can smell your arousal." Noah smirks.

"Whatever," I scoff. "What do you say?"

"Yeah." Noah nods. "I think we need that."

50

"Good." I nod.

We all get our food and take it over to Abby's table.

She smiles when we sit down, but goes back to her conversion with Penny. Leo greets us with a nod, and I don't miss the evil eye the red haired girl tosses our way. *What the fuck is this girl's deal?*

"So, who are you?" Luke asks, finally.

The red head just glares at him.

"This is Frankie," Abby answers for her. Frankie's eyes flick over to Abby's and soften. *Fucking hell, not this girl too.* Doesn't Abby have enough people interested in her? I'm not competing with some vampire girl. Abby lowers her voice. "She works for my dad. He sent her here. An extra set of eyes and ears for, you know."

For everything that's going on regarding my dad.

"Why does your dad care?" I ask her, eyes narrowing.

Abby raises her brow. "Because he loves me and wants to make sure I'm safe. My mother is married to your dad. And the fact that it's not going to take long before your dad knows I'm mated to you—to all three of you—you think he's going to be happy about that?" I shake my head. "That puts me at risk."

"I'm not going to let him hurt you," I promise her.

"I know." She gives me a soft smile that fucks with my heart in ways I'm not used to.

"She's also Zed's best friend," Leo adds.

"Really?" I ask, looking at Frankie. "How do you know my brother?"

"None of your fucking business," she replies, giving me a sweet smile as she bats her eyelashes.

Leo chokes on a laugh, and I shoot him a glare.

Abby answers for her again, sensing Frankie isn't going to play nice with me. I'd say she doesn't even know me, but if Frankie works for Abby's dad and is also best friends with one of Abby's mates, I can see that it doesn't matter. This girl hates me, and I didn't have to do a single thing to her to cause it. Not that I blame her. If I was her, I'd hate me too for what I did to Abby. "Before she started working for my dad, she would go to Dark Night. She met him at a party."

"I still remember the hurt on his face when I shot him down." Frankie chuckles.

"Why was that?" I ask, trying again.

"Zed doesn't seem like the kind of guy who gets his feelings hurt." Luke smirks.

"Because I don't like men," Frankie says blankly, but looks at Luke when she answers.

Okay, so she only seems to hate me, but not them, got it. *Lovely.*

"Ahhhh." Luke chuckles. "Can't say I agree with you."

My eyes shoot over to his, widening at his admission, but he just winks at me.

Frankie's brows jump. "Really?" Is all she says.

What the fuck is Luke doing? No one but Abby's mates know about us. I look over to Penny, but she's not paying attention, too deep into conversation with Zack.

"Luke," I say in a warning tone.

"Relax, big guy." He rolls his eyes. "She doesn't care, right?"

"Nope," Frankie says, sitting back in her seat. "You can't help who you love." I don't like how her eyes flick to Abby when she says that part.

My big brother better get a leash on his bestie before she becomes a problem.

"Fuck!" Luke shouts, tossing his controller.

"Winner, yet again," I boast with a chuckle, relaxing back in my chair. "Now, I think it's time for you two to pay up."

"Fine," Luke mutters, but his face turns into a sly smile. "How do you want us, Isaac baby?"

Noah places his controller on the table, looking at us both with hooded eyes.

Hoping my request isn't too much after everything we've been through the past few weeks, I answer with, "I think I want Noah on his knees, your cock in his mouth while I take his sweet, firm ass. What do you think?"

"Hell fucking yes," Luke groans, his hand cupping his growing cock. "I've missed this. The three of us together."

"Just think what it would be like with Abby too," Noah says, a soft smile playing on his lips.

"Babe, don't," Luke grunts. "You're gonna make me cum just thinking about it."

Noah chuckles. "Hornball."

"You can't tell me you wouldn't love to be deep inside her sweet, tight cunt while Isaac fucks her ass from behind, and I make her choke on my cock?" Luke raises a brow.

Noah's face flushes. "You have a point." He clears his throat.

That, I want that. The idea not only has my own cock weeping but my heart aching with the need to have her with us, to make us complete. She's just what we all need.

"Someday," Luke sighs.

"I hope so," I mutter. "But for now, Noah, take your fucking pants off and get on your knees for your mate," I growl.

Luke chuckles darkly, quickly ridding himself of his own shirt and pants. His cock springs free, and he grips it, lazily stroking it while he watches with hooded eyes as Noah strips for us.

I watch, my cock aching as I pull off my own shirt, licking my lips as my eyes run over Noah's dark skin. I want to taste him. "Come here."

Noah's eyes flick over to mine. He swallows hard as he walks the few steps, stopping before me.

"I love you," I growl before crashing my lips to his. He whimpers, his hands gripping my hips for support as I fuck his mouth with my tongue in a punishing kiss. I don't stop until we're both gasping for air.

Dropping to my knees, I enjoy the surprised look on his face as I make quick work of his pants. I'm the most dominant one of our group, and while I've sucked their cocks before, I'm more of an ass man.

"Isaac," he whines as his cock falls heavy in my face, tip weeping with pre-cum. My tongue laps it clean, enjoying the salty flavor. "Please," he whimpers.

Gripping his fat cock with my hand, I slowly stroke him, loving the way his knees shake before taking him into my mouth.

"Fucking hell," Luke moans. Out of the corner of my eye, I see him moving his hands faster.

"Don't you cum," I growl, releasing Noah's cock with a pop. "Save all that cum for Noah."

"Yes," Noah says with a heavy sigh as I take him into my mouth again. I suck him, taking him all the way to the back of my throat before pulling back. I get a good rhythm going, bringing Noah to the edge. And when I know he's close, whimpering pleas falling from his sweet soft lips and his hands desperately grasping at my hair, I stop and pull back.

"No!" he sobs, looking at me in horror.

"Shh," I soothe him, getting to my feet. "You will get to cum, baby. But first, I need to fuck you."

"Okay," he whimpers, getting to his knees.

"Such a good boy," Luke purrs, cupping Noah's cheek. Noah leans into his touch, closing his eyes as Luke bends forward, kissing Noah sweetly.

Emotions I normally push down, or are drowned by guilt, hit me hard, and I let the feelings I have for these two men wash over me. I love them with everything inside of me. I'd die for them. And I will never do anything to hurt them again. I don't deserve them, but a selfish part of me wouldn't ever be able to let them go.

Ridding myself of my pants, I grab the bottle of lube hidden under the couch, adding some to my cock. Luke groans, his head resting back on the couch and eyes closed as Noah starts to suck him off.

I watch for a moment, getting my cock ready. "So fucking hot," I growl low. Luke smirks, eyes still closed as he hums in agreement.

I get behind Noah, giving his ass a smack. "Fucking love this ass." I bend over and bite one of his plump globes, earning a moan from Noah. Parting his cheeks, I get a good view of the tight little hole I'm about to fuck.

My tongue brushes over the tight ring of muscles, making Noah gasp around Luke's cock. "You like that, baby?" Luke asks, running his nails over Noah's head. "You like it when our man fucks your ass with his tongue?"

Noah moans again, nodding his head. I play with his ass a little more, giving him just the tip of my tongue before moving away and replacing it with the tip of my cock.

On instinct, Noah relaxes as I start to push inside him. "Fucking hell," I snarl, the tightness of his ass feeling so fucking good.

"That's it," Luke grunts, gripping Noah's hair as he starts to control his movements. "Take that dick."

I don't know whose dick he's talking about, but our mate is taking the both of us so good. Just like he always does.

As soon as I'm inside him, Noah's walls strangle my cock, I grip his hips and start to thrust.

Maybe it's the thought of Abby being with us, or watching these two together, or just the fact I haven't had sex in a while, but I quickly lose control, fucking Noah harder.

Luke is praising Noah as he gets fucked hard, and gags on Luke's cock.

I pump into him, sweat dripping down my back and forehead.

"So fucking good," I growl in appreciation. "Taking my cock like the good little slut you are."

"He loves it, don't you, Noah? Always hungry for our dicks."

"Give him something to satiate that hunger then," I tell Luke, his chest heaving as he gets closer to his release.

"You want it, baby?" Luke asks Noah, his eyes wild and needy. "You want my cum?" Noah nods frantically, sucking Luke harder and bobbing his head faster. "Shit, I'm close. That's it. Fuck, your mouth feels so damn good."

Noah's moans and slurping fills the room, mixing with our grunts and groans. It's so loud in here that I almost don't hear the sudden intake of breath.

My eyes flick up and a primal urge fills me. Abby stands there, a plate of cookies in her hands, eyes wide as she takes in the scene before her.

"I'm gonna– Oh, fuck!" Luke roars, back arching off the couch. I don't watch the two men in front of me, eyes still locked on my girl. Because she *is* mine. Or at least, she will be.

She can't see Noah with Luke's cock in his mouth or Luke's face contorted in pleasure, but she sure can hear every single noise they're making.

Me, however, she can see. And as if she can hear that thought, her eyes lock with mine.

That sets me off. I start to pound into Noah like a fucking animal, hips slapping against his ass, the sounds filling the air with Noah's moans and pleas for more.

Wrapping my hand around Noah's throat, I pull him up so that his back is flushed to my chest.

Abby shifts in her spot, gripping the plate tighter as she bites her lower lip, driving me wild.

My hand wraps around Noah's cock, and I start to jerk him off in tandem with my thrusts. "Our mate needs to cum," I snarl. I'm not just talking to Luke, but to Abby too.

Her eyes flick down to where my hand is gripping Noah's cock. Her breathing picks up, and I can smell just how turned on she is. It's faint, but it's there.

"Yes!" Noah sobs. "Please, let me cum."

I'm close, only a few seconds away from unloading inside Noah.

When Abby's eyes meet mine again, it's like the first time we saw each other. Me fucking into someone, her watching like she wishes it was her.

Only this time, it's with the right people. How it should have been.

"Cum!" I growl to Noah.

He does, letting out a strangled cry. Both Abby and I switch our attention to Noah's cock as he pulses in my hand, thick streams of cum shooting out and landing on Luke's legs.

Quickly, I look back up at Abby, her eyes finding mine again, and I let go. "Fuck!" I roar as my orgasm hits me like a freight train.

My cock violently jerks inside Noah, hot cum filling his tight ass in waves.

The room is thick with the smell of sex and sweat, only the sounds of our breathing left to be heard.

Licking my lips, I smirk at Abby. "Dinner and a show?" I joke, hoping not to fuck this up.

"What?" Luke asks, then looks over the couch. "Well, hello, Spawny," he purrs. "Didn't know you were there."

"Shit," Noah curses, leaning over and grabbing a pillow from the couch to cover his cock.

Poor boy is so damn innocent sometimes. Even after taking two cocks like a champ. Next time, I'd like him to be inside Abby when we do this.

"Little late for that, babe." I chuckle, kissing his cheek. I pull out of him, making Noah hiss.

"And she brought cookies!" Luke cheers excitedly, jumping off the couch butt-naked and hopping over it. He grabs one from the plate and moans as he takes a bite. "Thanks."

Abby just gapes at us. "I—Ah—I made some cookies." She blinks.

"We can see." Luke chuckles, kissing Abby on the cheek before grabbing another one. "They're fucking amazing. I'm going to shower. Wanna watch a movie with us?"

"Ah... sure?" I'm trying not to laugh. But I know for a fact that she's a naughty little thing. Maybe this is a little eye-for-an-eye for the time she was with Leo and Zed in the hot tub.

"I'll be right back," Noah says, standing up and running to the bathroom like his ass is on fire.

"Wait up!" Luke says, running after him. "I'll help."

Abby just stares at the door like she's wondering if she's dreaming or not.

"You're acting as if you haven't seen us all together before." I chuckle, pulling my boxers on.

Her eyes find mine again, clearing from the fog a little.

"True. But I wasn't expecting to walk in on it... again." She blushes, and it's fucking adorable. "Sorry."

"Don't be." I shrug. "I don't mind." I grin and she blushes deeper. "You know, little one." I grip her chin, and her pupils dilate. "You're not the only one who loves some group fun."

Leaning forward, I brush my lips against hers, wishing I could kiss her, but not wanting to push.

When I pull back her eyes flutter open. Taking a cookie off the plate, I take a bite and groan. "Luke's right, these are good."

"Thanks?" she squeaks.

"Stay?" I ask, finding myself not ready to see her go. "We'll be quick. Then we can watch anything you want."

"Alright," she replies, and fuck, my heart almost explodes at the smile she gives me. "Just... I'll go make popcorn. Please have this clean before I get back." She raises a brow.

She means to make sure she doesn't sit in any cum.

"You got it." I smile.

She rolls her eyes, but smiles back, handing me the cookies and taking off up the stairs.

Is this what it feels like to be happy? I'm not saying that I've never been happy with the guys, they are my world, but for the first time in my life I don't feel like there's something lurking around the corner, ready to take everything away from me.

Maybe it's stupid to allow myself to feel this sense of safety, but I can't let the fear control me anymore. If I do, I might lose everything.

And I'd rather be dead than not have every single one of my mates.

CHAPTER SEVEN

ABBY

How do they expect me to concentrate on this movie after what I walked in on? I don't even remember what movie I agreed to. Hell, I don't even think I've had a clear thought since I stopped on the stairs.

Zed was working, and Leo was helping his dorm mate out with something at school, so I had the evening to myself. I got bored and tried to read, but it wasn't holding my attention and there wasn't anything I wanted to watch on TV, so I went down to the kitchen and did some baking.

With all the cookies I ended up making, I thought I'd bring the guys some, knowing they were down here playing video games.

I should have knocked, right? After what I've witnessed down here before, I probably should have.

So here I sit, in damp panties with my clit aching, horny as hell. But I do nothing but stare forward at the TV. A part of me wants to ask one of the guys to take care of it, but none of us are at that point in our relationship. Hell, this is the first time I've hung out with all of them in a normal setting.

Luke has me tucked under his arm, his fingers brushing against my outer thigh, not helping at all with the tingling of the bond. I can feel him at ease, happy, and content, making me the same.

I can also feel Isaac's eyes on me throughout the movie from his place in his chair next to the couch; partly in hunger, but mostly in longing as he sees me and Luke together. Noah is on my other side, my feet in his lap.

Thankfully, he's not rubbing them because I wouldn't be able to keep my laughter in, with being so ticklish. But his hands are on the lower part of my legs, the heat of his touch contributing to the mind fuzz I'm experiencing so badly right now.

Knowing there's no point in trying to watch the movie, I close my eyes and just enjoy being with my mates. Who knew months ago that this would be where we ended up?

I'm going to try my best to not let the past dictate our future. I just hope Isaac shows growth. He's the last piece of the puzzle.

I somehow fall asleep, and the next time I wake, it's in the arms of someone. "Isaac?" I murmur sleepily as I blink up at him through bleary eyes.

"Shhh." He kisses my forehead. "Sleep, baby."

My heart clenches at the endearment. I don't mind the others calling me their nickname, but I'm so damn happy Isaac stopped calling me Devil's Spawn. His words always hurt the most.

Feeling safe in his arms, I close my eyes again and let him carry me to wherever we're going.

"What are you doing in here?" a gruff voice pulls me from my sleep.

"She was watching a movie with us and fell asleep. I didn't want to wake her so I brought her up to her room," Isaac says. "I'll leave."

I don't want him to go. Something inside me, maybe the bond, is loving his touch too much. So without any words, I hold on to him tighter, snuggling in deeper.

Zed, who was the first person to speak, lets out a frustrated sigh. "Stop," he says as Isaac tries to carefully pull away from me. "Stay."

"Are you sure?"

I hear rustling before I feel the bed on my other side dip. "You're her mate. I can't change that. But I'm telling you this now—I don't care if you're my brother, and I feel for you with everything that fucking bastard put you through, but when it comes to her, I don't fuck around. Hurt her again, I will kill you."

"I get it," Isaac replies softly. "I fucked up."

Zed snorts. "That's an understatement."

"I regret it. All of it. I know it's hard to believe, but... I love her." My heart starts to pound painfully in my chest at his admission.

"Kind of hard not to fall for her, I get it. She's my world. My everything. I knew she would be my forever before we even sparked. One look at the pretty girl dripping wet under the gazebo, and I was done for, in the best way." Zed chuckles, warm lips pressing against my temple.

"You're lucky, you know?" Isaac says.

"How so?"

"You grew up with a mom who loves you."

"Yeah," Zed sighs. "She's pretty amazing."

"I'd trade it all. The money, the house, everything to have what you do." I hear the pain in Isaac's voice, and it crushes me. Tears sting the back of my eyes as I struggle to keep faking being asleep.

"I'm fucking pissed. I hate that he did all of those things to you. I hate that you had no one to protect you," Zed responds, sounding angry. "I would have, if I knew."

"You would?" Isaac asks in disbelief.

"I never hated you because you lived this rich life with the fancy house and the nice cars. I never hated you because you were my brother, and he chose you over me. I didn't like you because you thought you were better than everyone. I started to really not like you because you fucked my ex-girlfriend. But I hated you for how you've treated our girl. I would have done something about it a long time ago if I didn't respect her wishes. I came close to breaking my word a few times, though."

"I wouldn't have blamed you." Isaac laughs. "I was awful. I'm sorry about your ex."

"Don't be," Zed scoffs. "She wasn't the one for me. Just a stop on the road to my forever."

"For what it's worth, I never thought I was better than anyone, not really. It was an act to try to make myself feel better because really, I knew I was the worst of them all."

"No, you're not. You were dealt a shitty hand, and you handled it the only way you knew how. It doesn't excuse what you did, but we get it."

"You think she will ever forgive me?" Isaac asks, the pain thick in his voice.

"Yeah, I do. She's fucking amazing. She's kind, loving, and she likes to see the best in people. So, show her something good, and I think you'll be fine. Might take some work, and you should work for it. She deserves to know she's worth fighting for because she is. Also, she felt comfortable to hang out with you and the others, leaving herself vulnerable enough to fall asleep. She wouldn't have done that if she didn't want to be around you guys. *All* of you."

"I know." Isaac kisses the top of my head, and a tear slips free. "She's everything you said and more. I don't deserve her."

"You don't."

"But I can't let her go."

"I get that," Zed says. "I couldn't either."

"I gotta piss, but fuck, I don't wanna move."

I want to hug him tighter, to cry for him, to tell him everything is going to be okay now. I can't forget the way he treated me, but fuck, I can't hold it against him. He was abused by the man who should have been the one protecting him.

While I'm nowhere near being in love with him, I do care about him, a lot. He's my mate, and I need him.

Just being in his arms like this has soothed so much of the pain the rejection left inside me. I know it won't fully go away until I accept the bond back fully, but it already feels like I can breathe so much easier.

Isaac and Zed talk a little while longer. I wait a little bit, so he doesn't know I heard him before I roll over to snuggle into Zed, letting Isaac free to use the bathroom.

"Go." Zed chuckles. "Before she rolls back, and you're stuck here for the rest of the night."

"I'll be back." Isaac gets up. "If that's okay?"

"Yeah, if you don't mind Leo sleeping at the foot of the bed. He should be back any minute."

"I don't think I really get a say." Isaac laughs. "We're going to have to get used to being around each other anyways, right?"

"Yup, my Little Bird isn't going to allow a wall between her mates."

"I'll be back," Isaac repeats, his footsteps heading into the bathroom connected to my room. Yeah, that's right, they finally finished my damn bathroom. It's about time too because I got sick of going down to the guys' floor.

"He's gone," Zed whispers, and my body goes still. Zed lets out a low, deep chuckle. "I know you're awake, baby."

"How did you know?" I mumble, opening my eyes to look up at him.

"I know you well, Little Bird. And soon, he will too."

My lower lip trembles while tears fill my eyes. "I know I should hate him. That I shouldn't even be thinking about forgiving him and move on. But I can't."

"It's okay to want him. No one will judge you. He's your mate. He's done bad things, but I don't think he's a bad person."

"I don't think so either."

"He's my brother. I hate that I couldn't have been there to protect him," Zed growls, wrapping his arms around me tighter.

"The only person to blame is your sorry excuse of a father. Don't beat yourself up over it. It won't do anything but hurt you. He has people who love him, like Luke and Noah, and new people, like me, you, and Leo, to stand by his side. He just needs to let us."

"Yeah." Zed kisses my lips softly. "He better not hurt you again."

"I don't think he will." I shake my head. "I feel it in my heart."

Isaac steps out of the bathroom, pausing when he sees that

I'm awake. "Ah, hey." he scratches the back of his head. "I just brought you to bed. Didn't want you to sleep on the couch. I was just leaving."

"No, you weren't," I deny as he starts toward the door. He spins around, raising a brow. "Get back in bed."

His eyes widen slightly, making me giggle. "You sure?"

"Don't argue with me. I'll always win," I tease.

"She does. Don't bother."

Isaac cracks a smile, and fuck, my heart soars. I know he has Luke and Noah, but I think the more people he sees that are on his side, the more he will see his worth. I just hate that someone went low enough to make him feel like he didn't have any.

CHAPTER EIGHT

FRANKIE

Going back to school at twenty-three is not something I ever planned on doing. But here I am, in my prim and proper school uniform. I'm not sure how Lucifer even got me into this school seeing how most people graduate around twenty-one.

I grimace as I look myself over in the mirror. My tattoos and bright red hair stand out against all this damn white.

I *hate* white; it's too plain, too boring. I love black and bright colors. Sighing, I gather my hair into a pony-tail and accept that this is the best it's going to get. I'm here on a job, I'm here for Abby. What I have to wear isn't a big deal, I can live with it. *I hope.*

Shaking my head, I grab my backpack and head out. School starts in a half hour, and I want to make sure I'm out front to meet Abby.

I've been going crazy not being able to see her. It was easier in Hell, where I had work to keep me busy, to keep me from finding her and claiming her as my own. But now, I have way too much time on my hands.

It's only been a few days since I started school and so far, it's not horrible. The classes I'm taking are random and all the fun courses. When I signed up, the secretary tutted and said I wasn't going to be able to get a good job after I graduate with the type of courses I picked. Little does she know, I'm set for life.

I just smiled and shrugged, took my information packet, and left. Do you know how hard it is to follow all of these stupid rules? The biggest one is no profanity. Swearing is like a second language to me. You think demons in Hell are all classy and shit? No. Also, I *like* the word fuck. Who doesn't? I've had to bite my tongue way too many damn times.

The moment I step outside the dorm, I curl my lip as my eyes fall on the three women who've made my mate's life hell. Who caused her pain and continue to do so.

"It's not fair!" the blonde one whines. "I bet she's using some kind of demon magic. That's the only way she could brainwash them into being with her. I bet they aren't even her mates."

Perks of being a vampire; my hearing is immaculate.

"Yeah, she probably cast some kind of spell to make them feel a spark," the brunette one adds

"Doesn't matter. By the time I'm done with her, they will be ours again," the red haired one smirks. "Isaac will be mine. I'm willing to do whatever it takes."

I'd like to see you try.

Not wanting to start something I know I'll get in trouble for, I continue past them. "It's sad that the administration is letting all the freaks in here. Our poor school is becoming tainted. I should get my daddy to do something about it."

Nope, I can't. I have to. Stopping, I turn around to look at them. They all startle as I lock eyes with the red haired one. "The only thing tainting this school is the rank smell coming from your pussy. Even kitty cats need a bath from time to time. Might wanna think about that," I say, waving a hand over my nose as I give her a sympathetic look.

She gasps before narrowing her eyes at me.

I don't bother listening to what she has to say next because I notice Abby's little punch buggy driving into the parking lot.

An excited rush fills me. I feel like a giddy school girl with her first crush, but it's hard not to. Abby is amazing. During the time I've spent with her, I have only gotten a glimpse of it. I can see her kindness, her love for her mates, the way she treats everyone around her with the respect they deserve.

Her light and smile are something that wraps around me like a spider's web, but it's the smell of her blood that keeps me trapped.

The amount of times I had to stop myself from pulling her into a dark corner and sinking my teeth into her is unhealthy.

Abby gets out of her car, Leo following after her. "Frankie." Abby's smile grows when she sees me.

"Hey there, Princess." I grin, trying not to look too starved for her as I take her in. Her hair is down in long wavy curls today, a coat of pink lipstick coating her lips. "Don't you look good enough to eat?"

"Now, now, don't be flirting with my mate." Leo chuckles as he wraps his arm around Abby. He's a sweet guy, good for Abby. I don't mind him.

"She wasn't flirting with me," Abby argues, her cheeks light up with the sweetest blush.

"Oh, but I was." I give her a slow grin, loving the way her cheeks turn an even darker shade of pink.

"Hey!" Leo says playful. "You're going to make me jealous."

"No need, Sunshine." I pat him on the back. "This girl is

head over heels for you. I'd never be able to get her to leave you for me."

"It's true." Abby laughs.

I might not want her to leave him for me, but I'd very much like to join them. *Down, Frankie. One day at a time.*

"Abby!" someone shouts from behind her.

We all look to see the three royal assholes themselves. Luke gives Abby a grin as he stops before her. "Don't you look yummy."

"Why does everyone wanna eat me?" Abby asks, then her eyes widen when we all start to chuckle. "Oh my god, not like that!"

"I don't know who else wants to eat you, my little Spawny bear, but I can confirm it is just like that." Luke gives her a wicked grin, and Abby's arousal hits me like a train.

Fuck. Get yourself together, Frankie. Her dad trusts you, you can't be losing control around her.

Man, this whole giving her time thing is going to kill me, I just know it.

"Leave our girl alone," Isaac commands, smacking Luke playfully upside the head.

"Oh, come on, you can't tell me you don't want a taste of her too." Luke chuckles, wiggling his eyebrows at his mate. Luke pretty much admitted it the other day and the closer I look at the three of them, the more it's obvious. At least when they are around Abby.

"Save me, Frankie," Abby groans.

"That I can do. Come on, Princess, I happen to know where they keep the cupcakes they have planned for lunch."

Abby perks up. "Cupcakes?" she sighs. "Lead the way."

"Hey!" Leo shouts. "You can't just lure my mate away with sweets."

"Can too, Sunshine! Just did it!"

70

Abby laughs as we take off toward the school. "Thanks for that. Don't get me wrong, I like them all, love some of them, but sometimes there's so much testosterone, I feel like I'm drowning."

"Anytime you want a break, I'm here for you, babe." I laugh as we step inside the school.

"I wanna say I'm sorry," Abby says, looking up at me as we walk down the hall. It's still pretty empty, class not meant to start for another twenty minutes.

"Whatever for?" My brows furrow.

"I was jealous." She shrugs. "When you first came to Zed's place."

"I'm not here to steal your mate, Princess." I chuckle.

"I know that now." She laughs. "But it's kind of hard not to think it, at least a little, I mean, look at you." She waves her hand up and down at me.

"What about me?" I ask in amusement.

"You're gorgeous. I mean, you're tall and sexy, and the tattoos are hot as hell. Your hair is amazing, your eyes are hypnotizing... you could steal anyone's boyfriend or girlfriend if you wanted to."

I stop, grinning so wide that if I felt pain easily, my face would hurt. "You think I'm sexy?"

Her eyes widen as if she just realized what she said. "I mean... I..."

"It's okay, Princess," I say, lowering my voice as I step closer to her. I can hear her hearts picking up alongside her breathing. "I think you're fucking stunning."

She swallows hard, her throat bobbing as her eyes flick back and forth between mine. She's caught in my eyes, something that easily happens when you look directly into them. It helps when you want to compel someone. I won't do that to her, ever, unless she asks. I'm down for a little dom and sub control some day. But for now, I would never.

Before I look away, breaking the contact, I want her to understand something. "I would never try to take anyone from their lover. If anything, Abby, the only one of the two of us who has the power to bring someone under their spell is you, sweetheart." I lick my lips, my fangs aching to taste my mate's sweet blood.

The voices of other students nearby has me looking away. "Come on, Princess, let's get you that cupcake."

"Okay," she breathes out, looking a little dazed. Pink looks good on her, it looks better on her cheeks.

Stopping outside one of the entrances to the kitchen, I look around to make sure no one is watching. "Wait here." Using my speed, I'm in and out in ten seconds with two cupcakes in hand.

"Chocolate with blue frosting or vanilla with purple?" I ask, holding up the cupcakes.

"Blue, please." She laughs, and I carefully place it into the palm of her outstretched hand, making sure I don't touch her. But damn it, it's like my body knows. Just a millimeter from her, and I feel the hum inside me.

For a moment, I think Abby can feel it too, but then she's digging into the cupcake, pulling off the wrapper and taking a bite. She moans and my pussy aches at the sound. "So good." She sighs. "The chocolate are always gone by the time I get to them."

"No more missing out now that I'm here." I grin, biting my lower lip as I smother a laugh at the blue frosting on the tip of her nose. I want to pull her into my arms, lick it off, then chase the taste with her lips.

I'm no better than Zed when it comes to her. She's addicting, and I have yet to even taste her.

The bell rings, and I curse it for taking the only alone time I've had with Abby so far. I miss her when she's gone, finding myself using any chance I can to talk to her. I'm whipped, fallen hard already, and I don't care. I'm hers.

"We better get going," she says, wiping the frosting off her nose. "Thanks for this, by the way." She holds up the half-eaten cupcake.

"Anytime, Princess." I grin. "We better get you back to that mate of yours before he loses his mind."

She rolls her eyes, a smile playing on her lips. "He would die without me."

I'm sure he would.

I hate school. I hated it when I was in Hell, and I hate it even more now. Sitting in a classroom for an hour at a time while people whisper about you, not knowing you can hear every damn thing they're saying, isn't how I want to spend my time. I should be in all of Abby's classes, because how the hell am I going to keep an eye on her if I'm not? But none of her classes had openings.

I'm going to have to see who I can... *convince* to change classes.

"Done," I say, adding the last stitch of the dress we're making in fashion and apparel class.

"Already?" my teacher asks as she walks over to my station. "My, my. It's very... black," she comments, giving me a tight smile.

I repress my laugh as I smile brightly at her, pretending the very gothic looking dress didn't stand out from all the pale pink and champagne-colored ones the others are working on. "Thank you. I'm thinking of making of a pair of stockings to go with it next class."

"Don't you think maybe something more... school appropriate would be better?"

"Why?" I ask. "We're not allowed to wear these inside school anyways."

"Very well." Her answer comes out overly reluctant.

The bell rings, and I quickly put my mannequin away in the back before grabbing my backpack and rushing out the door. I try not to use my speed, another thing I don't like, as I head to the bathroom.

Just as I'm about to go in, I hear Abby's voice. "Look, I don't know what kind of crazy bullshit you three have concocted in your head, but I don't want to hear it anymore. I didn't steal your men. They are mine. My mates. I didn't ask for it, but it doesn't mean I'm just going to give them up."

"They don't want you. They don't even like you." I recognize the red headed Heather's voice. Isaac's ex, I've come to learn. "Whatever witches' powers you're using on him, you better stop now. Or you're going to regret it."

"I'm a demon." I smile at the dull sound in Abby's voice. My girl is sick of their crap, and so am I. "And mind control isn't one of my powers. Lighting your ass on fire is one, however."

"I'm not afraid of you," the red haired Heather says in a dangerous tone that has me on edge, the smile falling from my lips. "But you're going to fear me. Give them back," she demands.

"They're not some kind of toy I can just hand over when I'm done," Abby's voice rises, her patience with them running thin. "But I am done with this conversion."

"You're going to regret this. Isaac is mine! Luke and Noah are theirs. We will get them back."

"Fuck you," Abby spits.

I hear feet pounding against the floor toward me. Ducking behind the corner, I wait until Abby is out of the bathroom and heading down the hall before I use my speed to get inside the bathroom, locking the door behind me.

It's just Isaac's ex in here, standing in front of the mirror as she applies a coat of red lipstick.

She sees me in the mirror as I step forward. "What do you want, freak?" she sneers.

My smile grows, slow and eerie, making her sneer drop as I stalk toward her. "You know, you have a pretty mouth. Shame about the amount of shit that comes out of it."

"Watch how you talk to me," she snarks, lifting her chin. "I can have you kicked out of here before you can blink."

Before she can blink, I'm rushing forward, wrapping my hand around her throat. She gasps, her eyes filling with a satisfying amount of fear as I slam her against the mirror, making it rattle. "And you better fucking watch how you talk to me." I show her my fangs, making her whimper. "I don't like you. I think you're a sad little girl looking for love in all the wrong places. It's pathetic, if you ask me. Working so hard for a man who clearly doesn't want you. Who belongs to someone else. Where is your self-respect?"

"He doesn't belong to her!" she struggles to speak, anger flashing in her eyes. "He's *mine*."

"He really isn't though." I sigh, shaking my head. "Here's the deal. You're going to leave Abby and Isaac alone. Your friends are going to leave Luke and Noah alone. Find another poor man to leech off of because they are no longer an option."

"A-and if I d-don't?" she manages to get out. I let go of her, and she slumps forward, her hand reaching for her neck as she coughs.

"Then I'll kill you," I say simply, giving her a shrug.

She looks at me with tear-rimmed eyes. "You're fucking crazy."

"Oh girl, you haven't seen anything yet." I chuckle.

"I'm reporting you to the school board. You need to go back to Hell where you belong and take the devil bitch, while you're at it."

I didn't use compulsion last time, but gripping her chin painfully, I look her in the eyes and use it this time. "You will not tell anyone about what I've said to you in this bathroom, but you will remember my warning, so I suggest you act wisely. If not, I won't hesitate to follow through."

Giving her a shove into the mirror, the glass cracks. "Until next time." I give her a promising smile before turning around and leaving her coughing before she starts to cry.

I will do anything to protect Abby, and if that includes killing that Heather bitch, then so be it.

Looks like Michael isn't the only one we have to worry about.

CHAPTER NINE

LUKE

Why am I so nervous? I've never been like this before. I feel like an idiot as I stand in the foyer, waiting for Abby to come down.

"I feel stupid," I mutter, tugging at my tie, cringing at myself in the mirror.

"Stop that," Isaac huffs, grabbing my tie to straighten it. "You don't look stupid, you look hot as fuck, and if you weren't about to go out with our mate right now, I'd be bending you over and showing you just how *not stupid* you look."

My cock stirs at his words, and I grin. "Do I make you horny?" I tease in my best Austin Powers voice.

He snorts out a laugh, and the smile that forms on his lips makes my heart soar. He's changed a lot since the big confession about his dad. I've seen him laugh and smile more than he has in a very long time.

And a lot of it has to do with Abby. I want to thank her for easing up on him, for giving him a chance to prove himself. She doesn't have to be nice like she has been, but my man is so damaged that it changed him. Noah and I forgave him for how he treated us, for everything he did that hurt. I don't care anymore after finding out what he had to go through.

I still see the pain in his eyes when he's away from Abby for a long time. Just being in the same room with her does wonders. Now that I know about the rejected bond, I see it more clearly.

I'm hoping Isaac is able to win her over and Abby takes back the rejection, because the idea of him hurting any more than he already has, hurts to watch. I'd never ask Abby to rescind it. He deserved it. But he's also not that person anymore. None of us are who we were when we first met her.

I'm just glad things are changing.

It's crazy to think she's my mate. This stunning, sexy, smart, and strong woman is mine. But the cherry on top is that she's also theirs.

"Don't you look handsome?" Abby's voice has both Isaac's and my attention snapping up to where she stands at the top of the steps.

"Holy shit," Isaac whispers.

"Fuck me," I breathe as I take her in. She's in a dark green dress that hugs her body perfectly. There's a slit that goes all the way up to her hip, and fuck, it's really going to be hard to keep my hands to myself tonight.

As she descends the stairs, I get a good look at her cleavage and now my cock is hard because her tits look phenomenal in that dress.

"What are you doing?" Isaac grumbles as I step behind him.

"Adjusting my boner," I hiss.

"What?" he laughs.

"You do see her with your own two eyes, right?" I scoff, tucking my cock into the waistband of my pants.

"God, you really do get stiff over a light breeze." He chuckles.

"Fuck off," I grumble.

"Ready?" Abby asks.

My eyes snap over to hers, and my breath catches in my throat. Her hair is styled up, showing off a neck I want to bury my face in as I fuck deep into her tight—

"Luke?" Abby asks again as a snort of laughter sounds, coming from behind me where Zed stands.

"Sorry, what?" I blink up at her.

She's grinning at my lack of subtlety. "Real smooth," Zed says, shaking his head.

"I said, are you ready to go?" Abby laughs.

"Yeah, totally, for sure." I clear my throat. "You look... Fuck, Abby, you look amazing."

"Thank you." She does a little spin, showing off, and yeah, my eyes fall to her ass. "Hope it's not too much."

"It's perfect. You're perfect. Marry me?"

"Watch it," Zed growls, stepping closer to Abby.

"She's his mate too," Isaac says a little defensively.

"I know that," Zed huffs. "But if anyone is marrying her, it's me."

"Why do you get to be the one to marry her?" Isaac argues.

"It's not gonna be you," Zed snaps.

"Hold the fuck up," Abby says, putting her hands up at the both of them. "No one's getting married. Can't I just go on a damn first date? Relax. And if we ever get married, I can just marry all of you."

"No, you can't," I say, confused.

"Why not?" Abby asks, raising a brow.

"Because it's not legal. You can only marry one person."

"Maybe here you can't." She crosses her arms. "But in Hell, you marry however many people you want. There's no rule on that, just like there's no rule on how many mates or people you can love."

"Okay, so, Hell sounds fun," I say, looking at Isaac.

"Alright. That's enough," Noah interjects, stepping out of the kitchen. "You two have a date to go on. Let's stop planning the poor girl's future and just take her out to dinner."

"Thank you." Abby giggles, leaning up to kiss Noah on the cheek. And fuck, the blush he gets is so damn adorable.

"Fine," I huff. "I'm going to show our girl a good time because we all know Noah is planning a date that's gonna top what any of us can do. But I'm still going to try."

"Maybe." Noah grins, giving a little shrug.

"I can't wait," Abby says, then turns to me. "But first, it's me and you. Let's go, big guy. Show me what you have planned."

"Yup, this food is amazing." Abby moans around another mouthful of food. It's taking everything in me not to cum in my pants. Dinner was a bad idea. I forgot how much Abby loves food, and the sounds she's been making are enough to keep me hard this whole time.

"I'm glad you're liking it." I grin, taking a bite of my steak.

"I love meat. And this is so juicy."

No, Luke, you are not going to crack a joke telling her you have some juicy meat she can try. Save it for later.

"It is." I shove another bite into my mouth to keep me from saying it.

"So." She puts her fork down. "Tell me about yourself."

"Oh." I blink at her. I haven't had anyone ask me that in a while. "Well, you know my name, where I'm from, and my age."

"Yes." She laughs. "Tell me, what does Luke like, what makes you happy, sad, excited?"

"Well... I like music. No specific kind really, a little bit of everything." I laugh. "It drives the guys crazy. I could be listening to Skrillex one song and then Spice Girls the next."

She grins at that. "You like Spice Girls?"

"Yup." I give her a cocky smirk. "Who doesn't?"

"I was going to say I didn't know you listened to that kind of music because a lot of the pure bloods look at you like you're committing some kind of crime if you listen to anything to do with sex, drugs, or swearing, but then I remember you've never been like them. At least, not really." She raises a brow.

"It might seem hypocritical, but we've never really pushed that kind of stuff. At least, not after we found out we were mates. We kind of went along with it, didn't argue with people about it." I lower my voice so no one around me hears. "But when you realize you're in love with not only one man but two, and everything you've been taught says you're going to get sent to Hell for it, you don't wanna preach everything that is against you."

She gives me a sad smile. "I'm sorry you had to grow up this way. I'm sorry God made these kinds of rules."

"That's the thing," I tell her, leaning in closer. "I don't think he did."

"What do you mean?" Her brows furrow.

"We've been looking into what you overheard our dads talking about. While I do believe God doesn't want people to kill, to cause harm, to hurt others or do bad things, I don't think a lot of the things we're led to believe are wrong."

"Like what?"

"Well, for starters, I don't think God would tell people to love and respect one another only for pure bloods to turn their nose up at them for not being as good as they are."

"That always made me wonder. Pure bloods are always preaching to treat each other with love and respect. Unless you're someone outside their kind."

"And there's other realms with so many different customs and rules, right? It's my understanding that he watches over all of those."

"Not Hell," Abby says.

"No, not Hell, but the fairy realm, the vampire realm, even the dragon realm. I don't know much about those places, but I'm assuming they don't have a crazy amount of rules like we do. I don't know. We need to keep digging, but there's something bigger going on, and I'm not convinced God knows much about it."

"I don't think so," Abby agrees, looking like she's in thought. "I know Hell doesn't but that doesn't count because Hell is where anyone who's too evil to be around others goes."

"Is everyone in Hell evil?"

"No," she snorts. "Am I?" I shake my head. "Is Leo?" I see her point. "There are different sections in Hell. A lot of places run just like earth, only a lot hotter and the sky is a gloomy thing. We have schools, businesses, houses, hospitals, all that kind of stuff. But we also have a fuck ton of magic." She grins. I throw myself back as her hand lights up with fire.

"Holy fuck. I forgot you had powers."

"Maybe I can show you all of them someday." She smirks.

She's so fucking hot. "You done?" I ask, dying to get out of here and really enjoy the night with this girl. I've made myself hold back from being around her, and now all I want to do is have her next to me; to hear her laugh, to make her smile.

"What did you have in mind?" she asks, grinning excitedly.

"Come on, Spawny. I wanna have fun with you tonight." I wiggle my eyebrows.

She shoves a fork full of food in her mouth. "Done," she mumbles, making me chuckle.

Getting out, I toss a few hundred dollar bills on the table and hold out my hand.

She takes it and the contact makes my body come alive. I pull her through the restaurant in a hurry.

"What's the rush?" She laughs breathlessly as we stumble outside the building.

I look at her, the moonlight bright in her eyes, her face happy and carefree. She gasps as I push her up against the tree on the sidewalk, my hand cradling the back of her head as I crash my lips to hers.

It's like fireworks as our lips move together. She parts her lips, letting my tongue slip in and over hers. I feel like I'm high and she's my drug.

She moans, her hands reaching out to grab onto my dress shirt. "Fuck," I pant, breaking the kiss as we both suck in air. Putting my forehead to hers, I close my eyes and just enjoy the moment with her. "I've been wanting to do that all night. No, that's not it, since the moment I laid eyes on you."

Opening my eyes, I pull back enough to look at her face, keeping my body pressed into hers, not ready to lose this closeness. "I'm sorry, Abby, for everything I did to hurt you. I know I've said this before, but I'll say it again. I'll say it every day for the rest of our lives if it means you stay mine."

Her smile is sweet, tears making her eyes glassy as she reaches up to cup my cheek. "I forgive you, Luke. I want to keep the past where it is. Be in the here and now with me. You're my mate."

I bite my lower lip painfully to keep my own tears in check. "I don't deserve you."

"How about we let me decide what I deserve?" She guides my face closer to her so that she can kiss me again. This time it's slow, but the emotions within the bond are enough to cause the tears to fall. "I'll say the words, you know. Someday."

My eyes widen in shock. "Really?" I whisper. When you bond with someone, you don't have to cement it by making those official vows. We already wear the same mate marks. Something I'm still not used to but love. So for her to be willing to make our bond as strong as it can ever be, it means the world to me.

"Someday," she repeats, a sweet smile playing on her lips.

"I wish I was a werewolf," I growl, too damn turned on right now.

"What?" she snorts out a laugh.

"So I can sink my teeth into you and leave my mark."

She gives me a sexy little smile. "You don't need to be a werewolf to bite me, Luke."

I groan. This girl. She's perfect for me, for us.

CHAPTER TEN

ABBY

Tonight has been perfect. Spending this alone time with Luke has shown me a whole new side of him. A side that I very much enjoy being around. He's his regular, cocky, funny self, but more sweet and attentive.

He kept finding reasons to touch me all night, and I found it adorable. Every time he does, the hum I get from the bond settles something in my soul. That this is right where I'm meant to be, and I'm with who I'm meant to be with.

Supper was amazing. I may have laid it on thick with the enjoyment sounds, but not by much. The food *was* really tasty.

The heat in Luke's eyes every time I made a noise was worth it. I want him, bad. But I held off taking anything further until I could get this time alone with him.

The kiss just made me want him even more. I feel comfortable to do whatever feels natural when it comes to what's next between us. I won't run.

"You know, I don't think I've ever really just enjoyed a walk along the beach before," Luke says as we walk hand in hand, barefoot in the sand. He's looking up at the sky, the stars shining bright tonight. "It's nice. Peaceful and the stars are... wow."

"Yeah," I sigh, a smile forming on my lips as I admire the beauty of the night sky. "It's why this is my favorite place to be; to go for a run or just escape." Actually, it's my second favorite place—the gazebo at the graveyard takes the number one spot. I'm not ready to share that bit with him right now, though.

"Do you come here often?" He gives my hand a little squeeze as he looks down at me.

"I used to." I shrug. "Before I met Zed, I was here a lot. Needed to get out of the house pretty much as soon as I got there." I give him a guilty smile, and his eyes grow dark.

"I'm sorry, Abby, about everything."

"I know you are." I hug his arm, laying my head against this shoulder. "It wasn't a hardship. I really do love the beach. Places like this, we don't have anything like it in Hell. Someday I wanna see it all, you know? Travel the world. Some place with mountains would be the next place I wanna go."

Luke chuckles, murmuring something under his breath that sounds a lot like 'Might be sooner than you think.'

"After Leo came topside, I've only been here a few times. And well, the last time didn't end so great." That night with Isaac and the Heathers will be one I forever want to forget.

"Well, I hope when we leave here tonight, you only have good memories of this place again."

"Don't think you're going to have to worry about that. This night has been amazing. Thank you, Luke."

He stops me, wrapping his arm around my waist and pulling me into his arms. "I'm excited to get to know you better, Abby. Not just because you're my mate, but because you're just an amazing person. I want to show you that you mean as much to me as the others do."

"I'd like that." A small part of me feels like because he's been with Isaac and Noah for so long, I'd never have something with him that's as strong as what they have. But I know I need to build something with each of them on my own as well as something with them together because they are mine, but they are also each others.

Also, I'd be lying if I said watching them together isn't something I'd very much like to experience first hand. Again.

He kisses me on the forehead. "I don't think I've ever wanted a girl as much as I want you."

"Awe, you're so sweet," I say playfully.

"Really." He looks me in the eyes. "Honestly, I don't think I've ever wanted anyone outside of the guys. I've been with girls before, as have the others, in whatever ways that suited them, but you're the only one I've wanted more from. With them, it fell into my lap, something that's always just kind of been there, you know? With you, I enjoy working for what I want." He grins.

"Oh, really?" I laugh. "Well, how about we make you work a little bit harder?"

His brows jump. "What do you mean?"

With a grin that takes up most of my face, I say, "Catch me and find out." I don't give him any time to process what I've said before turning on my heel and sprinting away from him.

I burst into giggles as he shouts at me to wait up, pumping my arms and legs faster. Being a demon, my speed is a little more than most people. Nothing too crazy but it's why I haven't bothered joining track and field. It wouldn't be fair.

But I guess I'm not as fast as I thought, because a few moments later, arms wrap around me. I shriek, bursting into a fit of giggles as we hit the sand, rolling as we land.

"Well, look what we have here," Luke purrs, both of us panting as we catch our breath. "I caught me an angel."

"You did." My eyes flick back and forth between his, heat forming in my lower belly. My dress has risen up to my hips, the slit on the side making it easier for me to widen my legs, allowing him to fall between them easily. He growls as his hard cock meets the heat of my covered pussy. "What are you going to do with me?"

A part of me knows we're on a public beach, so there's a chance someone could stumble upon us. Thankfully, this part of the beach is hardly used, with it being private property. It's owned by a sweet old lady, so I don't think we have to worry about her.

"There are so many things I want to do to you, Little Mate." He bends forward pressing his lips to mine. I moan as I wrap my arms around his neck, pulling him into me, forcing him to kiss me deeper. He bites my lower lip before pulling back, making me chase him for more. "But a lot of it I can't do here."

The naughty grin he gives me has my pussy pulsing with need. "But some you can." I lift my hips, grinding my pussy against this rigid length.

He hisses, his eyes searching mine. "Here? Are you sure?"

"At least I can say I've had sex on a beach." I wiggle my eyebrows. He lets out a playful growl before nipping at my nose.

"You're a dirty little angel, aren't you?" he mumbles against my neck, his voice thick with want as he rolls his hips.

"Only where it counts," I breathe out, the feeling of his hardness against my clit sends a wave of pleasure through my body.

"Fuck, Abby. I don't know. I don't want you to feel like this doesn't mean something to me. You deserve flowers, candy, candles, and all that romantic stuff."

"No, I don't... I mean, I do, but I don't always need that." I shake my head, playing with the blond strands on the back of his head. "I just need you."

He growls out a low rumble as he dives forward, capturing my lips in a searing kiss.

I whimper and moan as his tongue dances with mine. Hands grab at clothing, both of us filled with a desperate need. I free his length, giving it a stroke.

"Abby," he moans, breaking the kiss and putting his forehead to mine. He closes his eyes, his breathing labored as I drive him wild with each movement of my wrist. "I need to be inside you."

"I'm all yours." My dress is already up over my hips, only a thong in the way, but not for long. He quickly rids me of it, leaving my core bare for him.

"So wet," he moans as he rubs the tip of his cock against my folds. "Next time, I plan on getting comfortable between these thighs and eating this pretty pussy for hours until it's weeping for me. But right now, I just need to feel you wrapped around me, to suck me in and never let me fucking go."

I gasp, eyes widening as he pushes inside me. It doesn't take him long before he starts to lose control. Our bond hums to life, filling both of us with this euphoric feeling, like we're a live wire of energy.

"Luke," I moan, clinging to him as he pounds into me. He doesn't look away, his eyes locked on mine as his hips snap into me, forcing me to take every inch of his thick cock.

"So perfect," he grunts. "Too damn good. Mine. Fucking mine."

He kisses me again, and I whimper against his lips. He holds me tight, fucking into me in punishing thrusts. I lock my legs around him, using the heels of my feet to push him forward.

The burning in my belly grows rapidly. I want to cry at how perfect this is, how everything feels so amazing. That's when I know what I'm about to say is right.

"Luke," I pant out.

"Such a good girl. That's it, baby, God, I... fuck."

"I know." Tears fill my eyes as he looks at me with this frantic look. "I feel it too."

"I– I love you, Abby." A tear falls as his thrusts slow, his body trembling in my arms. "And I'm so sorry for ever hurting you."

"Shh." I brush his hair out of his face. "I forgive you. And Luke?"

"Yeah?" he asks. His eyes flick between mine, and with this boyish look in his eyes it makes me hurt for him and everything he's lost with his mother, with having to hide who he is with his mates.

"I love you too." I smile.

The grin on his face makes my heart pound painfully in my chest.

"God, hearing you say that." He shakes his head. "It's everything."

"Luke," I say again, his eyes meeting mine. "I, Abigail Morningstar, accept you, Luke, as my mate."

His eyes widen in shock, looking like a deer caught in headlights.

"What?" he whispers, more tears flowing.

"Are you going to just leave me hanging or what?" I laugh out.

"Are you sure?" he asks hopefully, and I nod. "Fuck, Abby... fuck." He takes a shuttering breath. "I, Luke, take you, Abigail Morningstar, as my mate," he says it with no hesitation.

And just like that, it's official. As we speak the words out loud, we're hit with a wave of ecstasy. I cry out while Luke moans as pleasure fills our bodies. Luke starts to pound into me with savage thrusts once again.

We both watch each other, unable to look away as our orgasms build. I can feel Leo and Zed in the bond, curiosity and concern on their end. But I can feel something else, it's faint, but I think I can feel Isaac and Noah as well. There's a feeling of longing, but I can feel the pure joy in there too.

"I'm gonna cum, Abby. I can't—I can't stop it."

"Cum," I sob out, as my own orgasm crashes into me. "Luke, oh fuck, yes!"

My nails dig into his back as I shake and shudder in his arms.

"Abby!" he roars, tucking his face into my neck, biting down on the sensitive flesh. I moan as his cock jerks inside me sending ropes of hot cum, filling me up.

I feel drunk off of happiness as we lay here in the sand, locked together as we come down from the high.

"I can't believe we just did that," Luke whispers.

"Do you regret it?" I ask, praying he doesn't, but it was the heat of the moment.

"No." He kisses me. "Never. You're mine, Abby. And I'm going to show you everyday just how much you mean to me."

"It's weird, you know." I laugh, running my hands through his hair. "To say I love you."

"You don't have to."

"I want to. It's just, we went from hating each other to loving each other in what seems like a blink of an eye."

"Yeah." He chuckles. "But I'll be honest, I never really hated you. I did, however, want to fuck your brains out the moment I locked eyes on you."

"Pig." I roll my eyes, but the smile stays on my lips.

"But I'm *your* pig," he counters.

"Yeah," I sigh happily. "You are."

"Ah, Abby, not to ruin this moment, but I think we should get up. There's sand in places there shouldn't be."

I cringe. "Yeah, I don't think we really thought through this whole sex on the beach thing," I huff out a laugh as he pulls out of me.

He stands up and holds out a hand for me. Grabbing it, I let him pull me to my feet.

"Your hair." He laughs.

"Yeah, I'm going to be washing sand out of it for weeks." I groan, giving my head a shake. Sand falls out of it like crazy.

Luke does the same, hitting me with the sand, and I burst out laughing. "Stop."

"We're a hot mess." He chuckles.

"Worth it." I bite my lip as his eyes heat.

"So worth it," he chuckles.

"And Luke?"

"Yeah?" he looks back at me, pure happiness in his eyes.

"That mate mark looks good on you." I give him a beaming smile.

His hand goes up to his neck, realization hitting him as a ghost of a smile forms on his lips. *My mark looks good on all my men.*

We walk back to Luke's car, hand in hand and I try to ignore the itchy feely of the sand as it shifts with each step I take. *Yeah, I'm checking this off my bucket list and never doing it again.*

The whole car ride back, we keep catching the other sneaking glances or just plain watching. It's a comfortable silence, our hands laced together.

"You know how hard it is not to pull this car over and take you into the backseat?" Luke huffs as we turn down the corner onto our road.

My belly heats at his words. "As much as I wouldn't say no

to that, I think I need to shower this sand off before anything else goes inside me." I laugh.

"Fair enough." He grins, kissing the back of my hand and making my belly erupt in butterflies.

We pull into the garage, and as I'm about to get out, Luke grabs me, pulling me into his lap. "Luke!" I giggle, staring at him with wide eyes.

"Shh, now. Let me carry you," he demands, opening his door and taking me out with him.

"You could have just taken me from my seat," I point out, raising a brow as he carries me into the house.

"Yeah, but that would have been too long of a time with my hands off you." He grins, wiggling his eyebrows.

"I'm guessing I'm sleeping with you tonight?" I ask, not at all upset about that.

"You're cute if you think I'd be able to be away from you just after we made things official. You're mine for the night, Spawny. Tonight and the rest of our lives."

"You're adorable."

"Don't let the others hear you say that, they wouldn't let me live it down," he growls playfully.

"My lips are sealed." I wink, making him laugh.

We enter through the kitchen doorway, and as we step in, a voice has us stopping. "Look who's home," Isaac states.

We both look over at him, finding him standing there in his sleep pants and nothing else. Noah is sitting on the counter next to him, eating from a tub of ice cream.

Isaac isn't mad though, there's a small smile on his lips as he takes in his mate holding me.

"Best night ever." Luke kisses me on the forehead. "Hey, is that the last of it?" Luke gasps.

"Yup." Noah grins, shoving a spoonful in his mouth. "All gone," he mumbles.

Still in Luke's hold, he rushes us over to Noah. "Like that is going to stop me," Luke taunts with a wicked grin before kissing Noah, deeply

Their lips part, tongues tangling together. Heat fills my core as I watch them together. My eyes look to Isaac, but he's watching our mates with a hungry look.

"Yum. Chocolate," Luke comments, licking his lips as he breaks the kiss with Noah. He looks down at me. "Want a taste?" I don't get a chance to answer before Luke kisses me next. I moan as I taste the sweetness on my tongue.

"I'm going to guess from the very powerful feeling we were both hit with not too long ago, you two accepted one another?" Isaac asks, leaning against the counter, looking at the both of us.

"Is that going to be an issue?" I ask him. I don't feel bad, I don't feel like I did anything wrong. Luke is *my* mate too.

"No. I'm glad."

"Oh." I blink.

"You're up next, big boy," Luke teases Noah, and shit, he's so cute when he blushes.

"Ah, Luke, babe, can I go shower?" I ask, remembering all the sand.

"Right." He chuckles, shaking his hair and sending sand flying everywhere.

"What the hell?" Isaac shouts, flinching away. "Is that sand?"

"Yup. We can now say we've had sex on the beach."

"Ouch," Noah says more to himself.

"It's not so bad." I giggle. "But I really need that shower."

"Yes, baby, let's go get you cleaned up. I'll help, of course."

"Of course." I roll my eyes, grinning.

The rest of the night is just as perfect. Luke and I spend a long time in the shower, and he makes sure I'm very clean.

Then he takes me to his room. We don't have sex again, but we do kiss until we both drift off to sleep in each other's arms. I can feel Leo and Zed checking in via the bond, and I let them know I'm okay.

Because I am. There's still a lot of things we don't know, but something I do know is that I'm going to be okay. That for once, I feel like my life is going how it was meant to. No more heartache, no more tears. Just... love? Yeah, that's what I feel. I'm at different stages with all my mates, but the one thing they all have in common is I want all of them.

CHAPTER ELEVEN

ABBY

"You know, I kind of came at the perfect time." Frankie laughs as we walk down the street to go meet Zed. Today was the last day of school before the holiday break, and there's a party tonight that we all plan on going to. Even Luke, Noah, and Isaac. Not sure how that's going to go, but a part of me is excited to hang out with all of them at once.

Since finding out about what Michael has been doing to Isaac, the whole dynamic of how we treat each other has changed. Isaac and Zed still have snarky arguments. Luke still makes his sexual jokes, which has only gotten worse since we've solidified our bond, but I love it. And I love him. It really is weird. But in a good way.

Leo has been a sweetheart through everything. I can tell he misses me, but he's been so supportive in giving me the time I need with the guys. But that doesn't stop him from sleeping in my bed every night. He technically still has a dorm room, but he never sleeps in it.

"And why is that?" I ask Frankie as we reach the garage Zed works at.

"Because I've only been here for a week, and I already get a week off." She grins. I smile, shaking my head.

"The whole holiday stuff is new to me," I tell her as we lean against Zed's car. "We don't celebrate Christmas in Hell, as you know. The Dark Night community celebrates it like the people do on TV with the tree, presents, and decorations, while the Pure Bloods celebrate it more toward God's birthday. Luke and Noah said they just hang out at home and are forced to go to fancy events by their dads and my mom."

"I'm excited that we get to do it like it's done on TV." She gives me a child-like smile that has my heart beating a bit faster.

The more time I spend with Frankie, the more confused I get. I've always been attracted to women, I like boobs and butts, what can I say? But I've never blushed, or felt like butterflies were dancing around in my belly when one looked at me.

Do I like Frankie? Like, have a crush on her? Fuck, the more I think about her, the more I think I do. *It's wrong right?* To like someone else when I already have five mates? Would they be pissed if I had a thing for someone who wasn't my mate?

Before coming up here, I wouldn't have cared. It's a part of Hell's customs to be with whoever you want, as many people as you want—mates or not.

But I'm still getting to know my mates, whom I just found out about and working past the hurt one has caused me. I shouldn't be thinking about anyone else but the guys.

Yet, as she looks at me with her bright red eyes, the tilt of her smile, the way she licks her lips as she talks to me, I realize I'm fucked.

"Abby?" Frankie asks, amusement in her voice.

"Sorry, what?" I ask, looking away. "Got lost in my own mind for a moment."

"I asked if Zed is doing anything for Christmas?"

"Oh. Ah, yeah. I think so. He mentioned something about his mom doing a big dinner and inviting everyone on Christmas Day. I'm thinking of inviting my dad." I look at her with a big smile.

"No way." she bursts out laughing. "You think he'll come?"

"Maybe." I shrug. "He is my dad, after all." I lean in closer, like I'm going to tell her something top secret, but I guess in a way it should be treated like that. "My dad might be the king of Hell, but when it comes to me, he's a big teddy bear." I wink.

Her smile grows just as big as mine. "You know what, I could believe that. The man on his own scares me enough to piss myself, but with you? Yeah, he would burn the whole world, all the worlds, down for you."

A warm feeling settles over me. My mom might not have been a mom to me at all, but my dad... he's been there for me since day one. That's right, the devil changed dirty diapers, sang lullabies, and had tea parties when I got older.

He's an amazing dad, and I'm glad he's mine. "I'm going to invite him. Zed's mom said Christmas is about family, so..."

"Couldn't hurt."

"I said fuck off!" Zed's booming voice comes from inside.

Frankie and I give each other *what the fuck* looks before pushing off the car and heading into the shop.

"Grow the fuck up, Zed." My stomach drops when I see his ex standing there before him. "If this is about me fucking your brother, I didn't know."

"I couldn't care less whose dick you let inside you." He steps up to Tilly. "We are over. I have a mate. And it's not you. And if you don't leave me the hell alone, I'll tell her that you've been bothering me and let her loose on your ass."

"Sounds like you're keeping secrets, Zed. Why haven't you told her I've been coming by? Is it because you like it when I bring you coffee? When I show up dressed like this, watching you work on cars? How does she like the fact that I fucked both of her mates? Hope she's enjoying my sloppy seconds."

I feel sick, and I hate that tears fill my eyes. He's been keeping this from me. How long has this been going on? I thought he would never lie to me. Not Zed.

"Yeah, Zed," I spit his name out as I step forward. His eyes snap over to mine. He goes pale, horror filling his stunning blue eyes.

"Abby, it's not what it looks like."

"Don't listen to him, Abby. It's exactly what it looks like," she purrs, putting her hand on my mate.

Yeah, fuck this shit.

Zed goes to remove her arm, but I'm faster. My hand grips hers in a punishing hold as fire envelopes my hand. "Touch my fucking mate again, and I will kill you. You will go straight to Hell and I'll follow after. Then I will enjoy the fuck out of torturing you however I please. You're here bragging about fucking my mates, but do you know what that makes you sound like? A whore, because all you've ever been was a warm hole to fuck. Me? I'm their fucking Queen!"

"Please," she sobs. "It hurts, my hand!"

"Your hand is the least of your worries. I mean it, stay away from Zed, from Isaac. There won't be a next time."

"Okay!" She's ugly crying now, snot dripping down her face.

I let go, and she cradles her hand to her chest, letting out screaming sobs. "Might want to go get that checked out. Looks like some pretty nasty burns."

There's murmuring around us, and I look over to see other people in the shop watching. "Anyone helps her, I'll give you matching burn marks," I snarl. They all look away, going back to what they were doing as Tilly runs off, her whines of pain following behind her.

"Abby, Little Bird. Nothing happened, I swear." I've never heard Zed sound so desperately broken in his life as he pleads his innocence.

I spin to face him, chest heaving as I use every ounce of willpower not to go full demon on his ass. The fire from my hand recedes. "I know that, you fucking asshole. I know you would never cheat on me. It's not that I thought you would, it's the fact that apparently she's stopped by here more than once, and you never once mentioned it."

"I didn't want to upset you because of some sad girl who can't take rejection well," he grabs at his hair. "I tried to get her to leave me alone. I used every nasty name in the book. I did everything apart from physically harming her to try to get rid of her."

"Then after the first time, you should have told me. I'd have come down here and done exactly what I just did, ending this a lot fucking sooner."

"You've been dealing with so much lately, I didn't want to stress you out more. I hate seeing you in pain. I hate seeing you hurt!"

"It is not your place to decide for me when something is too much for me to handle. We don't lie, we don't keep things from each other!" His eyes flick up to Frankie so fast I almost miss it. That just pisses me off more. *Is there something else he's keeping from me?*

"I know, baby. I'm sorry. Fuck." He punches the car next to him. "I wasn't thinking."

"Yeah, I'd say," I huff out a humorless laugh. "I'm pissed. Really fucking pissed. And honestly, a little disappointed. I need air."

"Don't walk away, please," Zed begs.

"We're okay. But I need some space before I kick your ass. Then you can grovel like crazy and make it up to me."

"Well, she might want to stop herself from kicking your ass, but I don't." Frankie steps up to him. "I love you like a brother, man, but what you did? Yeah, that's not right."

"I know," he hisses at his best friend.

"Therefore, as your best friend, I think you deserve this." Zed looks at her confused, and I watch with wide, shocked eyes as Frankie uses her full vampire strength and punches Zed in the face.

"What the fuck?!" he screams, his hands flying to his face. I heard the crunch, and now I'm seeing the blood. Then Frankie brings her knee up and nails him right between the legs. Zed lets out a strangled sound as he falls to the ground.

"Sorry, man." Frankie shakes her head.

"I deserved that," he groans.

"Yeah, you did. But don't worry, I'll take good care of her while you sit here and suffer for a while." She reaches into his pocket and pulls out a set of keys.

He looks up at me with fear and sadness in his eyes. "I love you."

My whole body deflates. A part of me hates to see him hurt like this, but he's right, he deserved it, and being a dark angel, he's gonna heal within the hour.

"I love you too," I say, stepping close and kneeling down to kiss his bloody lips. "We'll talk more tonight."

"Okay," he groans, rolling onto his back.

"What do you say about taking a drive?" Frankie asks, dangling the keys in the air. "I got to warn you, I like to drive fast." She wiggles her eyebrows.

"You know what?" I look over at Zed's McLaren F1 he repaired himself. "I could use a ride. Windows down?"

"Only way to ride." She gives me a wicked grin.

Leaving Zed there on the ground, I follow after her toward the car.

"Keep her safe," Zed growls out.

"Always, Rock Star," Frankie calls back.

We get in and the moment we pull out of the parking lot, the tears fall.

"Hey," Frankie says softly, getting my attention. "You know he loves you. I can promise you, that bitch didn't get her way. He didn't touch her, didn't do shit with her."

"I know," I sniff, wiping my eyes. "I know he wants me and only me. It's the fact he kept it from me. Am I overreacting?"

"No," Frankie says. "But don't be too hard on the guy after this. I think he learned his lesson. You don't need protecting, and these guys need to see that. You're a badass demon princess who doesn't need anyone to treat her with kid gloves."

"Thank you!" I say, tossing my arms in the air. "Someone who gets it."

She laughs, the sound making me smile. "Come on, let's go for a ride, get some wind in our hair. Then I'll bring us back to Zed's place to get ready for the party with Libby. We will make you look so mouth watering, then make Zed watch you dance with all your mates before he finally gets his chance."

"Deal."

Today has been one crazy day. First, I've been getting nasty glares from the Heathers all day, now this. I really want to enjoy tonight, I've been excited about it all day. I'm not going to let it ruin my night. But first, I'm going to hang out with my new best friend. The drop dead sexy vampire who's making me rethink way too damn much.

I'm fucked. I know it. But I can't seem to stop.

CHAPTER TWELVE

ABBY

"How are you feeling?" Frankie asks as we lay in the long grass by some forgotten headstones.

"Better," I sigh, rolling onto my belly and picking at the grass. "I think I overreacted."

"No, you didn't." Frankie rolls over too, laying across from me so we're facing each other. "I trust Zed. That man would never cheat, never hurt you on purpose, but I can tell he cares too hard sometimes. He was trying to protect you, but only ended up hurting you. When you love someone so much, it's hard to realize that they just might be able to hold their own. And in your case, you're a lot stronger than they give you credit for sometimes."

"So, what do I do?"

"I say we head back to Zed's, get ready with Libby, and meet the guys at the party. Then you pick one of your mates and enjoy your night with them."

"Okay?" I narrow my eyes. "But how's that going to fix anything?"

"Because." She gives me a wicked grin. "He's going to be forced to watch you be all sexy and dirty dancing with a mate who isn't him. Make him sweat it out for at least the night; then, if you want to let him off the hook, go for it."

"I do like that idea." I grin, biting my lower lip. I don't miss how it attracts Frankie's attention, making her lick her lips. "Leo has been giving me too much space, and I hate it. He's trying to give me time to find my way with the others, but he's only around during classes and at night to sleep. I'm going to have a talk with him tonight."

"Then demon boy it is. Give him all the love and attention, let him know that you appreciate him giving you time with those bad boys, but you need your sex machine back."

"Stop." I snort out a laugh, smiling wide enough to make my face hurt.

"How is it being with a sex demon?"

I give her a look, raising a brow. "It's fun. He was shy with his powers at first. He didn't want to be like his parents and have it become his whole personality. But after we mated, I got him to open up to us. He uses his powers here and there, but it's mild. He likes knowing he makes me feel good on his own without the help. But..." I wiggle my eyebrows playfully. "He has used it on Isaac to get back at him for me."

"No way!" Her brows jump. "What did he do?"

"Leo would give him boners at the most inconvenient times, like in the middle of a class presentation."

"Fuck, I would have died to see that." Frankie bursts out laughing.

"It gets better." I chuckle. "There were a few times Leo made him cum in his pants; moans and groans and all."

Frankie rolls onto her back, holding her belly as she dies laughing. I can't help but join her. Maybe I should feel bad after finding out what Isaac was going through, but I don't. In the end, he was still cruel to me and he deserved what Leo did to him.

"Ahh." Frankie sighs as she catches her breath. "I think we need to get going, the sun is going down."

"Yeah." I get up and dust myself off. "Thanks, by the way." Frankie gets up and does the same thing as she gives me a curious look.

"Thanks for what?"

We start walking back toward Zed's car. "For being there for me today, for kicking Zed's ass in my defense, for just hanging out with me and being someone I could talk to." I give her a half smile. "Zed's your best friend, but you had my back. So, thank you."

"Of course." She looks a little shocked by what I said. "Zed might be my best friend, but you're my friend too, Abby. And I'm not going to let him, or anyone else, get away with hurting you."

I shouldn't enjoy how protective she sounds right now, but damn it, I do.

Not sure what else to say, I smile again as we get into the car.

When we get to Zed's, Megan tells me Zed left with Leo to go to my place to get ready with all the guys. I was shocked, to say the least, that he went there without me. But I guess that's a good thing, right? Maybe there's hope for all of them to get along. Maybe even become friends someday. One can only hope.

"Abby. Do you think you could ask your other mates to come over for Christmas?" Megan asks as she hands me a cup of tea.

Frankie is curling Libby's hair, and I'm already dressed, so I came downstairs to hang out with Megan.

"I could ask what they have planned. I know my mom said something about a Christmas Eve supper with the guys' dads and me. I don't want to go, but I don't want the guys to face their dads on their own either."

"It's bad, isn't it?" The dark look she gives me... it's like she's haunted by her past.

I chew on my lower lip, wondering what I should tell her. She is Michael's rejected mate and has a child with him. I think she has the right to know.

"He's not a good man. I know he puts on this whole 'holier than thou' persona, but he's evil."

She swallows hard, tears filling her eyes. "I was afraid of that. Once I got over the shock of being rejected, I started to see how things really were between us; I finally saw it clearly. He was very controlling, would do anything to make sure no one knew about me. I was glad to see him go, you know? I didn't care that I was a single mom. I'd rather have done it alone than with him in our lives." A tear slips free. "Sadly, I didn't want to be alone forever and found comfort in another man who turned out to be even worse in some ways. I don't regret it, because I got my sweet Libby out of it, but... thank you. You have no idea how much it means to me what you did for us."

"Of course." I take her hand, giving her a comforting smile. "No one deserves to be hurt. People like your exes need to be in Hell with my dad." I sigh, leaning back in my chair as I let go of her hand.

"What did he do?" she asks, her voice low and filled with fear of what's to come.

"He hurt Isaac. Bad. And often."

Megan gasps, raising her hand to her mouth. "Oh, no. That poor boy."

"Yeah." I nod, biting the inside of my cheek to keep from crying. "It messed him up. He turned into someone that I now know wasn't who he truly is. He hurt me, not physically, but in a lot of other ways. He's my mate, I rejected him, and well... we both paid the price."

"Don't give up on him," she says with pleading eyes. "I can't even imagine what he's been through. While I don't agree with how he chose to vent his anger and pain, he wasn't in a place where he had any control."

"I know." I give her a sad smile. "We're working on it. It's going to take a little more time, but the more I get to know the real Isaac, the easier it is to accept that he's my mate."

"Are you going to rescind the bond rejection?"

"Yes," I say, admitting it to myself for the first time. "But not anytime soon."

"I understand that." She sighs heavily. "I hope Zed and Isaac can put their differences behind them. I think Isaac could use a good big brother."

"I think they're on the right track for that." I grin, remembering their conversation. "He's already protective of his little brother."

"Good." She giggles. "Family means the world to Zed."

"That's something we have in common."

"Ready to go?" Libby asks, bouncing into the kitchen.

"Damn, Libby. You look both sexy and adorable at the same time. Zack is going to have to pick his jaw up off the ground," I compliment, taking in her outfit for the night.

"Thank you," she says, giddy as she does a little spin. She's in a corset dress that flows a little bit at the hips. Her hair is down and curled but there's two little buns at the top of her head and two curled pieces of her bangs hanging down.

"Maybe I should have put a little bit more effort into my look." I laugh. My hair is similar to Libby's, up in messy space buns, my bangs like hers. I'm in a tight black dress with a slit that goes up to my hip, and my boobs look fantastic too.

"You look perfect." Frankie steps into the room, and my mouth goes dry. If anyone was to look like Jessica Rabbit, it's Frankie right now. The way that dress hugs her curves has me sweating.

"Thanks." I swallow thickly. Libby gives me a look, and I have to turn away to hide my blush. "Thanks for the tea, Megan. I'll see you in a few days for Christmas supper. I'll ask the guys about coming. Oh, and also, would it be okay if my dad comes?"

Her eyes widen. "Lucifer. Here? In my house?"

"If it's not okay, that's fine—"

"No, no, it's fine, it's just my house... it's not meant for someone of his... status."

I can't help but giggle. "Your house is lovely, as are you. He won't care about stuff like that."

"Are you sure?" she asks with a furrowed brow.

"I'm sure." I smile.

"Then yes, of course."

"Thanks." I give her a hug, lingering for a moment. Her hugs are the best, a motherly touch I've never known. I could easily call her mom, and have caught myself a few times almost letting it slip.

I let Libby take the front seat with Frankie. Mostly because I need a little space from her. The more I'm around her, the more I feel things that have guilt eating me up inside.

I'm drawn to her; there's this pull, a lot like the one I've felt for the guys. It terrifies me. It's crossed my mind that maybe if I touch her, she will end up being my mate.

I don't know if I could deal with that right now. With everything going on with Isaac, getting to know Luke better, and starting to share moments with Noah—who I still haven't had my date with yet—it's a lot.

But then again, I'm probably overthinking it, and I just have the hots for her. Is that wrong of me? To be into someone who isn't my mate? Yeah, I'm going to need to talk to Zed about his best friend. It might be a little weird. I feel like Leo wouldn't mind, he's always been on board with anything as long as I'm happy.

There I go again, overthinking because who even knows if Frankie would want anything more than friendship with me. Sure, I can tell she's attracted to me; I see the way she looks at me. But something more? While I'm mated to five guys? Would she want to share? Would she ask to have me all to her self? Would—

"Abby."

I jump in my seat and shake my head out of my thoughts. "Sorry, what?"

Libby laughs. "We're here, babe. And there's a group of guys waiting outside for you."

My head snaps over to the window to see Zed leaning against a car, Leo standing next to him. Luke, Isaac, and Noah are not far behind, standing close to another car.

Zed is eyeing up his car as he waits for us to get out.

"What did my brother do?" Libby asks. "Frankie mentioned something about him being in hot water."

"His crazy ex tried shit with him."

"Fucking bitch," she snarls. "He didn't do anything, right? I can't see him doing that."

"No, he didn't. But he kept it from me, and I don't like that."

"I don't blame you. You should give him hell."

"Frankie already did that for me." I laugh.

"Really? What did you do?" she asks Frankie.

"Punched him in the nose and kneed him in the balls." I look over to see Frankie with a smug look on her pretty face.

"Nice!" Libby laughs, raising her hand to high five Frankie.

"I guess I better go over there and let him know I still love him," I concede, looking at the broody face of my sexy angel.

"Remember what we talked about," Frankie reminds. I look back over to her and grin.

"Yeah, it's still the plan."

She gives me a wink. "Good girl."

Fuck me. Nope, we are not going to let that one sink in. I am not turned on. *Maybe if I keep telling myself that, it will become true.*

Getting out of the car, I close the door behind me and walk over to Zed.

"Hey," he says, his face changing from a brooding man to a worried one.

I walk into him, wrapping my arms around him tightly as I place my head on his chest. "Hey." I inhale his leather and tobacco scent, holding on to the lingering mint.

He lets out a relieved sigh as he wraps me up in his arms. "Fuck, Little Bird. I'm so sorry," he murmurs into the top of my head before kissing the spot.

"I know. And I forgive you. But I don't want you keeping things like that from me, okay?"

"I promise. I love you so damn much." I pull back to look at the storm waging in his eyes.

"I love you so much too."

He leans down and gives me a punishing kiss. I moan, melting into his touch.

"Alright, you two. Let's not fuck out here for everyone to see." Leo chuckles. I giggle, smiling up at him. He smiles back, shooting me a wink. Fuck, I love him too.

"Why not?" Luke sounds from close by. "I wouldn't mind watching."

"Of course, you wouldn't," Isaac mutters as he passes by. "I'm heading inside before I end up seeing my brother fuck our mate."

"It's gonna happen one day, little brother!" Zed shouts with a chuckle. "Our girl likes to play."

"Zed," I groan, burying my face into his chest.

I suck in a breath as lips that aren't Zed's brush the shell of my ear. "I like to share too, sweet girl," Luke purrs before stepping away. I look over my shoulder to see him walking away with Isaac, shooting me a wink over his shoulder.

"Ah, Abby?" Noah asks. I look over to see him standing close by looking awkward. "Would you... Would... You know what, never mind." He has an adorable blush that makes me smile. I break out of Zed's hold, a grumbling sound of protest from him, and walk over to Noah.

"What were you going to ask me?" I ask, giving him all of my attention, just in case he didn't want to say it in front of Leo and Zed.

"I was wondering if you would save me a dance?" he says it with this bashful look on his face. *Ugh, this man is just too cute.*

"Of course, I will." I give him a beaming smile. I can see his worry melt away at my words. "I'll find you later, okay? I'm going to hang out with Leo for most of the night. He's been really good about me spending time with you guys, but I can tell he needs me."

"Of course." Noah nods. "I understand. It's a lot to deal with and a lot of changes."

"Thank you for being so patient with me." I lean up on my toes to kiss him on the cheek. "I'm excited about our date, you know."

"Me too." He gives me a soft smile.

"When is that exactly?" I laugh.

"I wanted to wait until after Christmas, if that's alright?"

"I can't wait." I kiss him again, and I love the face he makes as I catch him off guard. "Your mates are waiting for you." I nod toward the door where Luke and Isaac stand.

"Our mates." He chuckles, giving me a kiss on the cheek this time. His lips are warm and when he moves away, the feeling lingers on my skin.

Turning around, I go back over to Leo and Zed.

"Ready to head inside?" Zed asks.

"Yup, only not with you." I grin.

"Why not?" he growls.

"Because, I'm with him tonight," I say, pointing to Leo.

"Me?" he asks, brows rising.

"Yup. Be my date for the night?"

"Hell yeah, Starbright." Leo grins. "My sexy mate all to myself tonight. I sure do like the sound of that."

"Don't get too comfortable," Zed mumbles.

"Whatever, Angel Boy." Leo chuckles as he tosses his arm around my shoulder. "I got myself a hot date. Which, by the way, Abby, you look fucking amazing." Leo gives me a heated look as he stares down at me. "But, that's nothing new."

Yeah, I think this is going to be a fun night after all.

CHAPTER THIRTEEN

LEO

I'm not one to get jealous easily. I'm confident in my love and relationship with Abby. She's not only my mate, but has been my best friend, my person, for pretty much my whole life.

When Zed came into the picture, I could see how much he wanted her. It was easy to accept him into the fold because we both craved Abby's happiness and pleasure before all else.

Finding out that Isaac was her mate made me mad for her, not at her, because at the time, he was the worst option to be hers. As only pain followed, none of which Zed or I could take away no matter how much we tried.

Now, she has Luke and Noah. As much as I don't like how they treated her in the past, I can see how much they've changed, and that they care for Abby. I've been doing my best by giving her the room she needs to build her bonds with them, not wanting to overwhelm them, but fuck, I miss her. I've had way too much free time on my hands.

I tried hanging out with our friends, but I just end up thinking about Abby the whole time. When we're not in school, I've just been spending my time walking around the island while she's with one of them until it's time for bed. That's when I come back to the house and slip into her bed. It's the only time of the day that I feel at peace.

"Leo," Abby moans as her ass grinds against my painfully hard cock. Her fingers tangle in my hair at the back of my head, and I groan as she tugs at it.

We've been dancing for an hour now, just me and her. *I'm in heaven.* A part of me loves how the other guys are watching her, hunger in their eyes like they wish it was them she was grinding against. But she's all mine for tonight.

"Fuck, Starbright." I suck at her neck, leaving little kisses and bites. "I've missed you."

She moves until she's turned in my arms, facing me. Cupping my face, she locks her eyes with mine. "I love you for the space you've been giving me, but it needs to stop. I can find time to connect with the others without missing out on time with you or Zed, okay? I miss you too. Please, stop spending so much time away from me."

I lick my lips and nod. "I'm sorry, baby. I just wanted to take as much stress off you as I could."

"I know, and I appreciate it, but I'm starting to get more stressed with you being away." She pouts, and it's adorable. She's a little tipsy and a lot horny. I can feel the sexual energy radiating off her. It's driving me wild, and I can not get my cock to go down. I miss being inside her, to feel the way her sweet hot cunt grips my cock.

"Okay." I nod. "No more space. I'm going to be so far up your ass, you'll get sick of me."

"Never." She giggles, and the sound warms my heart. Her

eyes grow hooded, and I groan as I'm hit with a wave of her arousal. "Follow me," she breathes, licking her lips.

Swallowing hard, I follow her, my cock throbbing in my pants as she leads me through the crowd.

This house is big, but it's also packed with dark angels. I think I see a few demons too.

"Where are you two going?" Zed asks as we pass him and the other guys who've been sitting on a couch looking like they would very much like to be in my place. I've seen Luke and Noah dance a few times, but Isaac has been sitting with Zed on the opposite side of the couch. While Zed's been drinking, Isaac has not. Good for him for keeping away from the alcohol. I'm sure being at a party surrounded by alcohol can't be easy.

"I'm taking Leo up to one of the empty rooms, and I'm going to ride him until I'm nothing but a boneless heap from cumming so much," she announces with so much sass that it bleeds out into her movements and has her jutting her chin out at Zed. I choke on a laugh, grinning as he glares at her.

"You're drunk," he accuses her.

"Am not," she scoffs. "And so what if I am? Drunk sex is fun, it feels good. I want it, and you do too, right?" she asks me. I nod eagerly. "See. So, shh. You're just jealous you did something stupid, and it's not your dick I'm riding."

"I like drunk Abby." Frankie snorts a laugh as she sits next to Zed on the arm of the chair. "She seems fun."

"Thank you. I am fun. You should test it out sometime." She giggles. Frankie's brows jump, and my eyes dart to Zed.

My stomach swarms with guilt. Zed told me about Frankie, and I hate keeping this from Abby. This is making a decision for her and look what that got him into today.

I only found out the day before yesterday after bringing up the fact that Frankie and Abby seemed to be getting close. I saw the look on Zed's face and knew something was up. They managed to convince me to keep my mouth shut for now, because it's not my business. I do agree Abby still has stuff with Isaac to work through, and she hasn't connected with Noah yet like she has Luke, so adding on another mate would be a lot.

But unlike Zed's opinion, I think Abby has the right to know. Although, it seems like things are working out on their own and it makes sense as to why Abby and Frankie have been hitting it off so well.

The vampire isn't so bad. I like how she puts Isaac in his place. She's nice enough, and I can tell she cares for Abby. Her reasoning for keeping this from Abby is, in it's own way, considerate. Frankie wants to let Abby get to know her, connect with her, and make the decision to be more than friends without the pressure or the knowledge of being mates.

"I got to pee," Abby blurts. "Be right back." She takes off toward the bathroom down the hall, and I spin around to glare at Frankie. "You two need to tell her."

"Not yet," Frankie says. "Things have been going good. She seems to be connecting with me on her own. I don't want to rush things, to feel like she doesn't have a choice."

"I hate lying to her. Look where that got you." I glare at Zed.

"This has nothing to do with you." Frankie stands up, getting in my face. "This is our connection, our bond. Not yours."

"Abby is my business. She's my mate too. She's *my* best friend, and I will not stand by and watch someone else hurt her more."

"I'm not hurting her!" Frankie hisses, flashing me her fangs. "I would never."

"How do you think she's going to feel when she finds out you both knew and kept it from her?"

"She will understand once I explain," Frankie growls.

"You better hope so. And I'm going to be pleading my ass off for keeping my mouth shut. You better hope she forgives me for that too, or it won't be pretty. If I lose Abby, I'll make sure you all do too."

"What has gotten into you?" Zed asks, narrowing his eyes. "You're acting like we're scheming behind her back."

"What's gotten into me is I've seen my mate hurt, felt her pain. And it kills me every time, changes a piece of me with each passing day. If I could go back and take all her pain away and put it onto myself, I would have."

"And you don't think I would?" Zed shoots up off the couch.

"I'm not fighting with you, that would hurt her more. We just need to get in a place where everything is out in the open and go from there. Because all this is doing is fixing one thing at a time, while other things break in the background."

With that, I push past him and go in search of my mate. I'm worked up, pissed off, and still fucking horny.

When I see her coming out of the bathroom, she smiles up at me. "Oh," she gasps as I push her up against the wall. She looks at me with wide eyes filled with desire.

"I need you, Starbright. It's been far too long since I've been inside you," I growl before diving forward and pressing my lips to hers in a bruising kiss.

She moans, wrapping her arms around my neck as my tongue slips past her parted lips. Our tongues tangle in a desperate dance as I grip her hips, picking her up. She locks her legs around my waist, whimpering as she grinds her pussy against the bulge in my pants.

I can feel her wet heat through my pants. *Fuck, I need to be inside her.*

Still in my arms, we kiss as I carry her to the first room with an unlocked door. "Out!" I bark to the couple kissing on the bed. They jump up and scramble out of the room. Slamming the door behind us, I lock it and stride over to the bed.

Abby giggles as I toss her onto the mattress with a bounce. "Naked. Now."

"Fuck," she moans, rushing to rid herself of her dress. "I love this side of you. Please tell me you're going to use some of your powers on me tonight."

I stop, hands on my belt as I look at her. "You want that, Starbright? Do you want me to help you lose control? To cum so hard everyone in this house can hear you scream my name before you pass out?"

"God, yes! Please," she moans as she falls back onto the bed. She pulls her panties off as I finish undressing.

She looks so gorgeous right now, sprawled out on the bed before me. Her hair fanned around her head, her body flushed pink as her chest rises and falls. Her eyes watch me with need, waiting for me to take her.

I'm all incubus right now, my demon side taking over. I like it. I don't feel shy or awkward. I don't think I've ever felt more confident than I do right now as my mate lays bare, legs open, showing me the feast I'm about to have.

I prowl toward her, a wicked promise in my eye as I move between her legs. She yelps as I grip her thighs and pull her toward me.

"Leo!" she moans as I dive for her center. Running the tip of my nose up her slit, I inhale, letting out a feral rumble from deep within my chest as her sweet arousal fills my senses. Needing to taste her, I get to work. First, I lap up her juices, which are already dripping for me.

She pants and moans beneath me, writhing on the bed as I start to eat her pussy like the starved man I've been this past week.

Thrusting my tongue in and out of her, I let the first wave of magic hit her at the same time I do something I've never done before. My tongue starts to grow longer, thicker, pushing its way deep inside her. "Leo!" she screams, grabbing my hair in a painful grasp as she starts to grind her hips against my face, fucking herself on my tongue.

Using my powers, I add a feeling of pressure to her clit, sending little shocks with it every few seconds. She gasps, her back arching off the bed. I move my tongue inside her, reaching her sweet spot. With the tip, I rub back and forth. With the thickness of my tongue thrusting in and out of her like a cock, the magic on her clit, and the way I'm working her sweet spot, she loses it.

I'm hit with a wave of powerful pleasure as she screams my name, cumming so hard she gushes, covering my mouth and tongue with her juices until it's running down my chin. I look up to see her body writhing on the bed as she struggles to breathe.

Pulling back on my powers, seeing that it's a little bit too much, she sucks in a breath as she falls back onto the bed.

For a moment, I think I went too far, but when I move up to look at her face all I see is a blitzed out grin.

"Holy fuck, Leo," she sighs, her voice raspy from screaming. "What the fuck was that?"

"It was my tongue." I chuckle, moving up so that my weeping cock is pressed against her folds. "Did you like it?"

"I fucking loved it. Do that more often, please."

"Anything for you, Starbright." I brace myself over her before entering deep inside her with one thrust. We both moan as my cock fills her. Sliding my arms under her, I pull her to me and roll us so that she's on top. "You said you were going to ride me, baby. So get to work."

She licks her lips and rocks her hips, her hands on my chest for support. My eyes roll back as she starts to move on top of me. At first it's slow, and I can feel my cock drag against her inner walls with every roll.

Sitting up, she starts to move faster. My hands find her hips, and I give her some help. She starts to bounce on my cock, tits moving with each one. "Fuck, Leo. Yes," she moans, tossing her head back as she takes her pleasure from me. It's hers, all hers. Anything she wants. My little demon queen.

"That's it, baby, fuck. Look at you on your throne where you belong." I grunt thrusting up into her. She looks at me with this sexy little smile, biting her lip as she reaches up to grab her tits.

My heart pounds in my chest as my balls tingle with my pending release. I could hold off, fuck her all night if I wanted to, but we are not in a place that will allow that. So I need her to cum again so I can, because fuck, this woman drives me insane.

"Your cock feels so good," she whimpers, pulling at her nipples. "Can it do what your tongue did?" she asks with doe eyes.

It takes me a moment to understand what she means. Fuck, I didn't think of that. It is something an Incubus can do. I just have never tried.

Letting my powers take over, I watch her eyes widen, her mouth falls open as my cock thickens inside her. Not only does it grow in length but in girth too.

"Oh, shit," she whimpers as I move her faster on my cock. "Oh, oh, yes! Oh god, Leo."

"Cum!" I shout, ready to blow my fucking load deep inside her tight cunt.

She falls forward, her hands landing back on my chest as she digs her nails into my skin. I hiss at the bite of pain as she leaves behind red lines that bubble with blood. My cock twitches as she lets out a screamed moan mixed with a whimper. Her pussy clamps around my cock, pulsing as she cums for me like the good girl she is.

Unable to take it anymore, I flip her on her back and start to pound into her while she's still cumming. I look down to see my cock stretching her pussy good, her cream covering my shaft. "Mine!" I snarl as my own release takes over.

With one last thrust, I pause and spill inside her, my cock jerking with each wave of hot cum. It feels like it goes on forever, until my cum is leaking out of her.

"Leo," she whimpers, chest heaving.

"You did so good, baby," I murmur the praise as I kiss her sweetly. "So damn good."

My cock goes back to its normal size, and I pull out of her, a gush of cum coming with me as I lay down on the bed next to her.

"I'm dead." She sighs happily. "I have to be."

"Killed by cock?" I joke.

She looks over at me with a smile so wide my heart soars. "You've been holding out on me, Leo."

"You want me to start doing more stuff like that?" I ask, reaching up to brush her hair behind her ear.

She moves so that she's leaning on her arm. "I want you to feel comfortable with being yourself. If something ever becomes too much, or I don't like it, I'll let you know."

I smile. "I'll keep that in mind." Leaning up, I give her a kiss, and she moans against my lips. "We need to get cleaned up and back out there before they come in here to make sure I didn't kill you with all the screaming you did."

She blushes, groaning and covering her face as she falls back on the bed.

"No." I remove her hands. "No being embarrassed. It was

so fucking hot, and I know they wish it was them in here with you. Own it."

"Okay," she says softly. I help her up and over to the attached bathroom. For the Dark Night side, this is one of the nicer houses. Zed told me there are people here with money, I just haven't seen any for myself.

We clean up and get dressed. Abby stops me before we head outside. "I love you, Leo. All of you. No more space, no more hiding who you are. You've shown me it's okay to be a demon, and I'm telling you the same."

"Okay." I kiss her forehead. "I love you too, Starbright. So fucking much."

I would die for this woman. I would kill for her too. There really isn't anything I wouldn't do for her. She's my everything, and that will never change.

CHAPTER FOURTEEN

ZED

I've been in a miserable mood all fucking day. Knowing I hurt Abby has been eating away at me. I was stupid; I'll admit I was wrong. I didn't think Tilly would be an issue, but I should have known better.

She's always been crazy and lives for drama. It's why I wanted to try and handle things my way. I knew Tilly wouldn't shy away from being rude to Abby. I've seen her make people cry just from her words. *Fuck, I really can't believe I ever dated her. She's a horrible person.*

I also should have known Abby can handle herself, but I guess the thought of seeing yet another person throw insults at her made me want to protect her like I couldn't do while she was at school.

"What were you and Leo arguing about before?" my brother asks me. He's been sitting there the whole night and hasn't said a word.

"Fuck off," I mutter, taking a swig of my bottle of beer. My cock twitches in my pants as I hear Abby scream again. Some people can hear her over the music, and I snarl, giving them a death glare. "Mind your own fucking business!" I shout. They snap their heads away from the direction Abby is and go back to dancing.

"Okay," Isaac sighs and tries for something else. "Wanna tell me why you showed up to my place covered in blood?" *Because I fucked up.* I don't have to be a dick. He's trying, and I should be too.

Taking a drag of my joint, I look over at him. "I fucked up," I say, and blow the smoke right in his face. He doesn't move, just glares at me. "I kept something from her when I should have trusted her to be able to handle it."

"What was it?"

I look back out to the crowd, my eyes finding Frankie dancing with my sister and her mate. "My ex, the one you fucked." I shoot a sideways glance at him, waiting long enough to see him cringe. "She came sniffing around. Thought she could win me back or some shit." I put the joint out, feeling it hit my system and pull out my pack of smokes, lighting one up. Taking a deep drag, I sigh, closing my eyes. "Waste of her time because the moment I found out Abby was mine, all other women became dead to me."

"So, what did Abby do? Beat you up?" he snorts.

I shoot him a glare. "No, that was my blood-sucking best friend who did that honor."

"I don't like her," Isaac says, looking over at Frankie. As if she can hear him, Frankie looks over at Isaac and gives him a toothy smile, fangs and all, before raising her hand. She does this cranking motion with her other hand—her middle finger slowly rising until it's flipping Isaac off.

"I fucking love her." I cackle as Isaac mutters something about her being crazy. "She doesn't like what you did to Abby."

"She seems pretty protective over someone she just met a week ago."

"Frankie has been working for Abby's dad for years now. Frankie has always known who Abby was."

"But Abby only found out about her this week," Isaac points out. "I've overheard their conversations at school."

"And your point is? Frankie is my best friend; she's up there as one of the most important people in the world to me."

"My point is, Abby looks at Frankie like she looks at you or Leo." He narrows his eyes.

"Leave it alone," I growl. "It's none of your business."

I can tell he wants to say something, but he doesn't. He runs his tongue over his teeth, sits back in his seat and brings his attention to where Luke is practically fucking Noah on the dance floor.

"You know, I bet she's going to enjoy the three of you at once." I chuckle.

"What?" Isaac's head snaps over to look at me again.

"Our girl likes to be taken by more than one person. You've seen it with your own eyes." I raise a brow, remembering the hot tub. "And I'm sure the three of you would love to add her into the mix."

"I mean, if she would want that, I could see her being with them at the same time, but not me. I fucked up too much to be anything more than I am right now."

"Abby is an amazing person, and she forgives, if you're worthy of it. Just keep showing her you are, and I think you're going to be okay. Remember what we talked about."

He nods then his eyes glance behind me. Turning to see what he's looking at, I groan. "Done, Little Bird?" The look of her screams *just got fucked*. Her hair is a little messy, make-up smudged, and her dress looks like it was put on in the dark. She's fucking gorgeous.

"Oh, yeah." She gives me a dreamy blissful smile. Abby moves to stand in front of me before tossing herself in my lap. I chuckle, wrapping my arms around her. She reeks of sex, and it has my cock twitching.

"Hey," Leo says with the biggest grin on his face as he takes a seat next to me, pulling Abby's feet up into his lap.

"Lucky fucker," I grumble, kissing the top of Abby's head as she snuggles deeper into me.

"Did anyone happen to hear me?" Abby asks sleepily. I shoot a look to Leo and nod my head as I tell her not really. It's not a lie. Not *everyone* heard her.

"I don't even care," she sighs contently. "I got fucked by Leo's magical lizard tongue and then by his inflatable dick."

My brows shoot up, and Leo blushes, looking away. I lock eyes with Isaac, and he looks just as confused as I am. "Lizard tongue?" he mouths, and I just shrug. Maybe she's still drunk, or maybe Leo has some powers we don't know about. I'm not sure I want to know right now.

Noah comes over, looking at Abby with a bit of a sad look. "Is she asleep?"

"Nope!" Abby's head pops up as a new song comes on. "I owe you a dance." With a little fumbling, she manages to get to her feet after I give her a little help. I chuckle as Noah smiles, looking at our mate adoringly. As much as I hate the part he played, I can see he really does care for Abby.

Luke manages to get Isaac to dance, and Leo ends up hanging out with my sister and Frankie for a song or two before Frankie comes over to sit down next to me.

"Once she connects with Isaac and Noah, I'll tell her."

Taking my eyes off my girl, I look at my best friend. "Are you sure?"

Frankie sighs, crossing her arms as she settles back into the couch. Her eyes find Abby as if our mate was a magnet. I don't blame her. I could stare at Abby for hours. I don't care how creepy it would be.

"It sucks always being so close to her and never being able to touch her. I want to hug her, cuddle her–"

"Fuck her. Suck her," I add playfully.

"Okay. Yeah, that too, but it's not just sexual."

"I know. I can see how much she means to you." I bump her shoulder with mine.

"I want to tell her before I touch her."

"What do you mean?" I raise a brow in question.

"I want to let her know that I know she's my mate. But if I don't touch her, don't ignite the spark, it gives her the chance to say no. Or at least let her have more time to decide if that's something she would want. I don't want to take her choice away."

"Fuck," I sigh. "You're so damn good for her. I just hate that everything has to be so complicated."

"You're telling me. Not only does she have the stress of new mates, she has the bullshit with your dad. And speaking of dads, aren't they coming back tomorrow for Christmas?"

"Damn it. I forgot about that," I groan, scrubbing my hand over my eyes. "Yeah, I think they are. I mean, Isaac hasn't said anything for sure, but I know Abby's mom is putting on a supper. I'm assuming they're going to be there too."

"You going to the supper?" We plan on having another one after theirs is over. We talked about just showing up to avoid the drama and partly to see if there's anything else the guys can dig up on their dads. We've planted a few bugs in the places they would mostly open up in.

"Yeah. Can't wait. Going to be quite the family party," I deadpan.

She snorts. "Sorry, I'm going to have to miss it."

"Just help Mom and Libby make an amazing turkey supper. That's what I'm most excited for."

"I got her a gift," Frankie says, looking a little nervous.

"Really?" I smirk, raising a brow. Leo and I went to the shops in town the other day and spoiled the fuck out of her. But we plan on giving that to her at my place.

"Yes, but I don't know if I'm going to give it to her yet."

"What is it?"

She covers her eyes and says, "A glass heart necklace filled with my blood."

"Wow." My brows raise in surprise.

She peaks at me through her fingers. "Too much, isn't it?"

"Isn't that like a big deal to vampires?"

"Yeah." She nods, lowering her hands. "Vampire blood is worth a lot. It's sold on the black market in some realms for its ability to get people high fast. And it has healing properties. But it's also the highest honor a vampire can give to their mate."

"Don't you want to wait until you can tell her what it means?"

"You're right," she sighs. "I'll wait."

"I mean, Frank-and-beans, that's an amazing gift."

"Fuck off." She snorts as I grin, the nickname she hates the most is something I love to tease her with.

"Ah, I think it's time to go," Noah says, walking over with a sleeping Abby in his arms. I chuckle and stand.

"What happened?"

Noah looks down at her sleeping face affectionately and kisses her temple. "We were slow dancing, and she fell asleep."

"Oh, boy." I laugh. "Yeah, we need to get her home. She's had a long night."

"Yeah, getting railed good and hard does that to a person," Luke teases, popping up on Noah's left side. "Right, Noah?"

Noah's cheeks heat. "Yeah, sure."

Rolling my eyes, I let him carry her out to the car. Frankie gets Leo, Libby, and Zack, joining us a minute later.

I take Abby and Leo home while the guys offer to take Libby and Frankie back to my place.

As we all get settled into bed, I turn the light off and snuggle up to my mate.

"Leo," I murmur into the dark.

"Yeah," he grunts.

"Do you have a lizard tongue?"

Groaning, I roll over and almost jump out of my damn skin when I open my eyes to see Abby staring at me. "Jesus," I breathe out, my heart racing. "What the hell, Little Bird?" I growl.

"Sorry," she whispers, giving me a little smile. "It's morning, and it's my first Christmas. I couldn't sleep."

I have no idea what her mother plans on doing for Christmas because there's not a single decoration in this house, not even a tree. It's kind of sad to know that the guys have never woken up on Christmas morning and ran down to see what Santa left.

My family loves Christmas, and my mom goes all out. We wake up, open gifts, eat breakfast. Then we take the gifts we collected down to the homeless shelter for the children. We read them a story and help set up for their supper before going and doing some fun things around Dark Night. After that, we come back to the house and have our own supper. We're doing things a little differently this year. Abby didn't want to leave the guys alone here, knowing their dads were coming.

My mom invited the guys too, from what I heard. I'll have to see if they want to come later on.

"Don't be sorry." I smile and lean forward to kiss her. She puts a hand up to cover her mouth.

"Morning breath," she mumbles behind it.

Gripping her wrist lightly, I pull her hand away. "Fuck morning breath," I growl before kissing her. She moans against my lips, reaching up to pull me closer.

I move so that my body is pushed up against her and grin against her lips when I feel my girl's fully naked body under the blanket. "Naughty Birdy," I groan as my hand trails up her bare leg and over her ass cheek. I give it a squeeze, and she whimpers against my lips.

"I got hot last night." She licks her lips, her pupils dilated. They flutter closed as I move my hand from her ass to her pussy, dipping two fingers in and finding her soaked.

"Dirty little mate. Are you wet for me?" I growl, biting her lower lip.

She whines, nodding eagerly. I pump my fingers in and out a few more times before removing them. She whines again at the loss of my fingers as I bring them up and press them to her lips. "Taste how wet you are."

She opens her mouth like a good girl, and I push my fingers that are shining with her juices into her mouth.

My cock throbs as she locks her pretty pink lips around them and sucks, her tongue tracing my fingers and licking them clean.

"Fuck," I breathe, needing to be inside her. It's been days and I'm going mad.

"Between you touching me, and Leo's cock poking me in the ass, I'm horny as hell."

That makes me grin, and it grows wider as Leo moans out Abby's name in his sleep. "At least we know what's got him hard." I chuckle.

Abby sits up with a giggle, the blanket falling to reveal her perfect tits. "I want to fuck these," I purr, leaning forward and taking one of the stiff peaks into my mouth.

"Zed," she moans, her fingers tangling in my hair.

"Abby," Leo moans again, making both of us laugh.

"Want to have some fun?" I ask her, giving her a mischievous smile.

"What did you have in mind?" she asks, smiling as she bites her lower lip.

Pulling the blanket back off Leo, I find that he, too, is naked. "Well, that makes this easier." I chuckle, looking back to Abby. "How about you wrap those pretty little lips around Leo's cock. Suck him so good he wakes up cumming down your throat. And while you do that, I'll fill your wet, tight cunt up with my cock." I grab her hand and place it over the bulge in my PJ pants.

"Okay." She nods, eyes lighting up.

I stand to rid myself of my pants as Abby gets onto all fours, sticking her delicious ass right in the air. She rocks it side to side like a red flag to a bull, teasing and tempting me.

Kneeling back on the bed, I get behind her. "Grab his cock, Dirty Girl," I murmur against her ear, making her shiver. She reaches over and wraps her hand around Leo's cock. Her hand looks so small and dainty; I have to admit, he has an impressive cock. "Test it out, give him a squeeze and see what he does."

She does, stroking him slowly. He mumbles in his sleep, his cock twitching in response.

Gripping a handful of hair, I shove her face down over his

cock. "Now, take him into your mouth. Choke on it while I fuck you."

Abby moans as she wraps her sinful lips around the head of his cock. I watch as she bobs her head up and down a few times. Leaning back on my heels, I grip my own cock. She moans again around his cock, her sounds alone have me leaking pre-cum as I rub the tip of my cock against her entrance.

"Such a good girl. Deeper," I growl, pushing her down to take his whole cock. She gags, and I pull her back to let her get some air before doing it again. "Fuck, you take him so good."

My eyes flick over to see Leo watching, looking half asleep. Looking to me, he opens his mouth to speak, but I raise my finger to my lips, and smirk. Still looking at him, I grip Abby's hips, holding her still as I thrust deep inside her. Abby cries out around Leo's cock, and he bites his lip to hold back his reaction.

I slowly drag my cock in and out of her, loving the way her walls suck me back in every time I pull away. She's dripping, my cock already coated with her juices. Smirking, I gather some and bring it to Leo's lips and smear it over them.

He licks his lips as I go back to fucking into Abby, his eyes are wild as he watches her take him over and over.

I don't rush it, I don't go hard and fast like I normally do. Instead, I just enjoy the immense amount of pleasure I'm feeling right now.

She's so wet, warm, tight, and perfect.

"Make him cum, baby. Make him blow his load deep down your throat, and I want you to swallow it all."

I pump into her, wishing I could feel this forever. I would fucking live inside her pussy if I could.

"Oh, fuck," Leo groans groggily, becoming fully awake now. "I'm gonna cum, Starbright. Fuck, yes! Just like that."

"Make her take you, Leo. Guide her, take what you want. She fucking loves it, don't you, our dirty little mate?"

She moans, her pussy fluttering around my cock. Leo's eyes roll back for a moment before he reaches over and grabs a handful of her hair. "So good," he grunts as he starts to take control. "Just like that."

I'm trying to not lose my control and fuck into her as I watch Leo's body tense. He's going to cum soon. Abby whimpers as he picks up the pace. She tries to match his movements, eager to pleasure her mate. "Oh shit, fuck yes, oh—" he lets's out a long groan as he thrusts up into her mouth. His hips twitching as he cums.

"Don't swallow," I tell her, slapping her ass.

Leo slumps back into the bed, looking pleased and ready to go back to sleep.

"Were you a good girl?" I ask Abby, and she looks over at me, mouth closed as she nods. "Show me." She sticks her tongue out, showing me a pool of Leo's cum on her tongue. I know she likes it, she's told me that an Incubus' cum has a pleasant taste, causing people to have a craving for it.

That's why I enjoy doing this next. "Such a good girl, doing as she's told. Now crawl over there and let Leo have a taste."

Leo's eyes widen in surprise, but he says nothing as our temptress of a mate crawls her sexy ass over to him, my cock falling free from her cunt.

"Open your mouth, Leo," I growl. I guess he's a dirty little freak like Abby because he opens it.

I stroke my cock, growling in pleasure as Abby looks down at Leo, allowing his cum to fall from her lips and into his mouth.

"Now swallow." She does, and holy shit I'm about to lose it if I don't get control of myself right now.

"Leo, move down here and let our girl ride your face like

she rode your cock last night. It's time she chokes on my cock next."

"I'm not into dudes, but fuck, this is hot," Leo groans and moves down the bed, laying down so that he's looking up at my dick.

"Come here," I command my little bird who looks fucking sexy with her messed up hair, flushed cheeks, and her body covered in a layer of sweat.

Biting her lower lip, she gives me hooded eyes as she takes my hand. I help her to hover over Leo's face.

"Fuck me, she's dripping," Leo growls.

"I bet she is." I chuckle, rubbing my thumb over Abby's lip. "Are you wet, my dirty little bird?"

"Yes," she answers in a breathy tone.

"What has that pretty pussy all messy?"

"You," she moans. "And Leo."

"Why don't you be a good girl and sit on his face, let him lick that kitty until it purrs," I growl. She looks hesitant, and my eyes flick down to Leo so we can have a silent conversation.

"He said to smother me, Starbright, so fucking do it," Leo demands as he grabs her hips and pulls her down to his mouth.

She gasps, reaching out to brace herself on my chest. Leo wastes no time getting to work as he starts to devour her cunt.

I watch my girl lost in pleasure, puffs of breaths leaving her swollen lips. Cupping her face, I look deep into her eyes. "I love you, Abby. You're my everything. I'd die for you in a heartbeat."

"Zed," she whimpers, tears filling her eyes as she rocks her hips on Leo's face.

"Shh. No crying, Little Bird. The only tears I want to see falling from your pretty blue eyes are when you're gagging on my cock." I chuckle as I step back, pushing her shoulder down so she's on all fours, her mouth level with my cock. "Now open your sinful lips and show me just how much of a cock-hungry little demon you are."

She parts her lips, opening wide for me. Gathering her hair into my fist, I yank her head where I need it before guiding my cock to her mouth. "I can't wait for you to come apart for us, sweet girl. I know you're going to look so stunning when you do."

I shove my cock into her mouth, pushing it all the way to the back. She gags, but I don't give her much of a chance to get used to my cock in her mouth as I start to thrust my hips. "That's it, baby. Take that dick like a good girl."

Her mouth feels so warm, the vibrations of her whimpers and whines from Leo feasting on her below makes my cock throb with need. As much as I'd like to go for hours, we don't have long before someone comes looking for us. And I'd much rather it not be Abby's mom who catches her daughter with a cock down her throat.

Abby won't take long to cum again, not with the way Leo is driving her wild.

She sucks me, hollowing her cheeks. "There we go. Fuck, look at you. So pretty with my cock in your mouth. I bet you would look better with my cum too."

I'm so madly in love with this woman it's not even funny. She's perfect. She really is the best thing to ever happen to me.

My thrusts start to grow quicker, my balls tingling with my pending release. "Are you going to cum for us, Dirty Bird?" I ask her as she gags and moans for us. She's close, I can tell when my girl is ready. "Yeah, you are, aren't you?" I chuckle, brushing the hair from her face as I slow my thrusts. "Shatter for us. Do it now."

I can feel it when Leo sends a little shock of his magic into her, and she lets out a muffled scream as her orgasm rips through her. She's sobbing, tears falling down her cheeks, as Leo holds her to his mouth and eats her through it.

"Fucking hell!" I roar as my orgasm rips through me without warning. I thrust into her and hold her so that my cock is down her throat as it jerks violently, sending jets of cum down it. "Swallow it all, Dirty Bird," I grunt, my abs contracting with every word.

I cum even harder as her throat works around me with every swallow. "That's it. Fuck, you're such a good girl. A fucking good, dirty girl."

Finally, after my balls are drained and Abby has taken every last drop, I pull free. She sucks in a big breath before breaking out into a coughing fit.

"Deep breaths, baby. I'm so proud of you." She gives me a watery smile, the praise pleasing her. "You did so damn good." I cup her cheek, brushing it with my thumb. She sighs, closing her eyes and leaning into my palm, her chest still heaving.

"I'm fine, thanks," Leo says, his words sounding muffled.

Abby gasps and quickly moves off Leo. "I'm so sorry!"

"Don't be." Leo grins like a fool, his face soaked with her release. "I would have died a very happy man."

Abby bursts out laughing, Leo and I join her. "Come on, my little mate," I say, scooping her up. "We have to get dressed. It's Christmas, after all."

"Merry Christmas, baby," she murmurs, her eyes closed as I carry her to her bathroom.

"Merry Christmas, Little Bird." I kiss the top of her head. I'm not sure how this day is going to go, but I'm going to try my hardest for my Little Bird to have the best first Christmas. At least with what I'm able to control.

CHAPTER FIFTEEN

ZED

"Do I have to?" Abby whines as we get to the bottom of the stairs.

"We only have to be here long enough to please the parents, and then we can go to my place."

"I wish one of my powers was to speed up time." She gives me an adorable pout. I chuckle and suck her lip into my mouth, giving it a little nibble. She sighs, leaning into me.

"Come on, you two." Leo laughs from behind us. "Any more of this and we will be going for round two."

"I don't mind." Abby gives us a sassy grin.

"I love how naughty you are." I grin, wrapping my arm around her. We head into the kitchen, following an amazing smell.

"Hey," Noah says when we walk into the room, giving Abby a big smile.

Abby detaches herself from me and heads over to Noah. "Merry Christmas," Abby says, leaning over to place a kiss on

Noah's lips. When she pulls back, Noah looks stunned. I've never seen a man blush as much as he does, it makes me wonder how he was ever one of Abby's tormentors. He doesn't seem to have a mean bone in his body.

"Get over here." Luke snatches Abby around her waist, pulling her down into his lap. He wastes no time pulling her in for a kiss. I roll my eyes, a small smirk finding my lips. I ignore the two of them going at it like animals, and Leo sits next to Noah, starting up a conversion.

"Hey," I say to my little brother as he flips pancakes.

"Hey," he murmurs, not looking up at me.

"How are you feeling about today?" I ask, knowing it must be bothering him.

"Can't wait to be stuck sitting at a table with the man who loves to beat me behind closed doors," he huffs out a humorless laugh, giving his head a shake.

"Hey." I place my hand on his shoulder. He looks up at me, and I hate the pain I see in his eyes. "He won't hurt you. We won't let him. One of us will be with you at all times."

"He's not going to be happy. I'm sure he's found out about Heather by now. And I'm sure she told him about Abby being my mate."

"Doesn't matter if he has. Hell, we can tell them all at lunch just to get it out there. They can't do shit."

Isaac plates the last few pancakes and turns to me, a haunted look in his eyes. "The thing is, he can if he wants. Zed, next to God, he's the most powerful being. As are the guys' dads. If he really wanted to make my life Hell on Earth, he can, and no one can stop him."

"We'll find a way. Maybe one of the cameras we set up will pick up something useful. We can use it against him."

"Well..." Isaac grabs a plate and a few pancakes. "I'm not

putting my hope into anything. I've learned it only hurts more when everything comes crashing down around you."

My heart breaks as anger rises. I should have been there for him, I should have protected him. He's my fucking brother, and while I was living my own life, he was being abused by our sperm donor. Isaac might not have faith, but I do. We might not be able to fight him, but we can blackmail him. We just need something on the fucker.

Isaac brings a plate of pancakes topped with whipped cream, strawberries, and sprinkles and places it in front of Abby.

Abby breaks her kiss with Luke, her lips red and swollen. She looks at the plate, eyes going wide, then up to Isaac. "Thank you," she says softly.

"You're welcome." Isaac smiles back.

This isn't the guy I'm used to. Before we found out, he was this arrogant asshole who had a mouth to back it up. Now he looks so broken, so defeated.

And by the looks on Noah and Luke's faces as Isaac walks back over to the stove, they see it too.

We eat breakfast, everyone making small talk. It doesn't feel like Christmas here. There's not a single decoration. A part of me is a little jealous of Libby, Frankie, and my mom right now. I know she's going all out for them. It's what Mom does.

I know we could have slept at my place, ate there, then come here, but Abby was so worried about what time the dads would show up. She didn't want to be gone and leave them open targets, especially Isaac. I agreed, I didn't want Isaac to be alone when they arrived.

The other two dads might seem reasonable, but Michael isn't. He would have found a way to get Isaac alone, but not with me around.

We don't end up seeing any of them until noon. It's weird

because all three of them, as well as Abby's mom, come in together. Abby's mom is normally here before the men, getting everything perfect.

"Show time," Isaac mutters as we shift our attention away from the TV to look at each other.

Abby take's Isaac's hand. "We got you."

Isaac relaxes a little. "Thanks."

Getting up, we head into the foyer. My brows furrow as I see Luke and Noah's dads talking to each other, but what has my hackles rising is how Michael is with Abby's mom. She looks like she has fear in her eyes as Michael whispers angrily to her.

"Merry Christmas," I say in a booming tone.

All of their heads snap over to us.

"What are you doing here?" Michael asks, giving me a dirty look.

"Didn't you know, dear old Pops, I pretty much live here now?" I give him a wicked grin as I wrap my arm around Abby's shoulder.

Michael shoots daggers over to Isaac. "So, you're letting him stay here now?"

"I'm letting him," Abby speaks up. "This is my house too."

"No, little girl, this is *my* house." He chuckles. "And you're only here because I allow it."

"Michael," Abby's mom says, placing a hand on his arm.

He throws it off him, not even bothering to look at her. She winces at the force, and I swallow a growl. *Fucking dick.*

"Isaac, can I talk to you alone?"

I can feel the tension in the air as everyone goes still. "No," I answer for him.

Michael looks at me with pure hatred. He's really not bothering to hide much of who he is anymore, is he? From the looks on Gabriel and Raphael's faces, they look worried about what

Michael might do next. *Oh, how the mighty have fallen.* This will be interesting. I wonder how much I can get them to break.

"I didn't ask you. I asked my son," he snarls.

You know, if it was anyone else, that might have hurt. "And this *son* is answering for him. No. You won't be talking to him. You have something to say, say it to me."

"Isaac," he shouts.

"No," Isaac says. I can hear the shaking in his voice. "I don't want to talk to you. I don't have anything to say to you."

"Boy." Michael takes a step forward.

"Okay, Pops, let's just get this out there and save everyone some time." I clap my hands, taking a step forward, putting the rest of them behind me. I look to Gabriel and Raphael. "You see that stunning, blonde, badass, demon princess behind me?" It's a rhetorical question. "She's mine and Leo's mate, as you well know, but she's also your son's mate. Both of your sons."

Their eyes go wide as they look at their sons. "Really?" Noah's dad asks.

He clears his throat. "Yes. Abby is our mate, and we're happy about it. She means everything to us."

"Just fucking amazing." Michael lets out a cruel laugh. I'm sure we are all surprised right now because I don't know that this man has ever swore before. At least, not in front of other people. "So, the three of you share a mate?" He shakes his head. "How could you, Son? I'm so disappointed. Why couldn't you do the right thing and just marry Heather? Her parents called me furious that you broke things off with her, and then they told me they heard the demon trash was your mate," he spits.

Abby's mom's eyes widen, and Abby grumbles *fucking asshole* under her breath, making me smirk. I'm about to tell him not to talk about my mate like that, but my little brother beats me to it.

"Don't fucking talk about her like that!" Isaac shouts,

taking a step forward. "I don't care anymore." I look over and see the dark circles under his eyes. "I don't care what you want for me. You never once thought about what might make me happy. Heather is a gold-digging bitch."

"She loves you! You will call her back and apologize. And you will move the wedding up to next month. They might be okay with their sons' disloyalty, but I will not allow it!"

"She doesn't love me." Isaac shakes his head. "She loves my money and the power that marrying into our family comes with. She's a heartless bitch. You teach about God's kindness, and how we should be good people. She, as well as the other Heathers, have been bullying and tormenting Abby for months. We weren't any better. But while we've realized how messed up it was, they are still out for blood. So no, I won't marry the cruel woman whose only goal in life is to have everything handed to her."

Michael is fuming, his body trembling with anger as he takes another step forward. "Do it, I dare you," I snarl.

He pauses for a moment before storming upstairs.

"I'm so sorry," Abby's mom says, her voice trembling as she looks at her daughter with pain in her eyes before turning around like the coward she is and taking off toward the backyard.

"Boys," Luke's dad says. "I'm sorry about all of this. We just want you to be happy. We love you, we are proud of you. And if Abby is your mate, and you're happy, that's all we care about."

"Thanks, Dad." Luke and Noah hug their dads. I look down at Abby who's watching. She has a watery smile on her face. My eyes find Isaac, and I can see the longing there. I know how he feels, having a father who doesn't love you. He doesn't have an amazing mom like mine to be on his side. I think I'm going to have to share her, I know she would accept him with open arms. It's the type of person she is.

"We're going to go," Raphael states. "Just, stay out of his way. He will be like this for a while."

"Dad, what's going on?" Noah asks.

The dads just give them a sad look before turning around and leaving.

"What a fucking shitshow." Luke lets out a breath.

"Tell me about it." I look at them. "Wanna go for a swim? Then we can head over to my place?"

"Are you sure it's okay for us to come?" Isaac asks.

"Yeah, man. Christmas is for family." I wink.

He smiles at me. And damn it, I'm starting to like my little brother. Who would have thought?

We all hang out in the backyard for a while, Abby's mom nowhere in sight. She must have gone back into the house at some point.

"I'm going to go get some more bottles of water," I tell everyone, leaning over to kiss Abby on the lips as she sun-tans. "I love you, Little Bird."

"Love you too." She smiles.

When I get inside, I hear the doorbell ring. I make it to the fridge and hear it again. "Guess I'll get it," I mutter to myself and head to the door.

"What are you doing here?" a snarky voice greets me.

"Heather, what a horrendous surprise. To what do I owe this very unwanted visitation?" I smirk, leaning against the door frame.

"I'm here to see Isaac, where is he?" she asks, looking behind me.

"He doesn't want to see you."

She glares at me. "How do you know?! He doesn't even know I'm here."

"Because, Heather, no one wants to see you. You're like an unwanted growth that everyone wants gone."

She gasps. "You are so rude! Let me talk to Isaac."

"No," I say blandly.

"Isaac!" she shouts, and I roll my eyes.

"Listen, he doesn't want you. He has a mate. When will you get that through your head?"

She gives me a disgusted look. "He can do so much better than her."

"Really, like who? You?" I snort. "Bitch, please."

"I am better than her!" She stomps her foot like a child. "If he would just let me show him, I could make him forget all about her."

"Stop, it's getting sad. Go find someone who wants you and stop chasing after someone who doesn't. It makes you look desperate."

"You're mean!" she shouts, turning around and stomping away. "I'll be back!"

"Please don't!" I shout after her.

Closing the door, I let out an exhausted sigh. "What the fuck was that? No wonder they were all assholes. I'd be one too if I was expected to marry that."

Grabbing the bottles of water, I head back outside. "What took you so long?" Abby asks.

"Isaac's ex-bride-to-be was at the door."

"What?!" Abby shoots up.

"Please tell me she's not still here," Isaac groans from his chair. He pulls his sunglasses down, eyes filled with dread.

"Don't worry, I sent her packing."

"Thank God," he sighs.

"It's sad." Abby shakes her head. "She should just try and find someone who will make her happy; not for their money, but for how they treat her."

"I know, Little Bird." I place my hand on her thigh. "Sadly, some people are just like that."

We hang out for a while before everyone heads back into the house to get ready to head to my place.

As I'm heading down the hall in search of some more shampoo because Abby is out, I hear noises.

"Yes. Oh, yes, right there. Harder." My brows shoot up. *Is Michael fucking Abby's mom while we're all in the house?*

"That's it. Take it, you stupid whore," Michael growls. "You're so desperate for my cock, aren't you, Heather?"

Holy shit. Holy fucking shit. He said Heather. No fucking way I'm hearing this shit, right?

The sounds get louder, and I'm standing there frozen, not sure what to do. He's cheating on his wife... with his son's ex. *What the hell?*

This, fuck, this is what I've been looking for. The perfect thing to blackmail him with. A grin so damn wide takes over my face. I'm way too excited as I grab my phone out of my pocket. Bringing up the camera, I hit record and walk toward the room the sound is coming from.

Raising my phone, I slowly open the door, just a crack but enough to be able to see in.

I regret it right away because what I'm seeing will never be able to be scrubbed from my mind or my eyes.

Michael has Heather bent over his desk, both recognizable from this angle, as he plows into her. One hand is wrapped around her neck while the other fists her hair. Both are butt-ass naked. Her tits sway as he fucks her. She looks like she's really enjoying it.

"That's it, take it," he growls.

"So good, your cock is so good. So much better than Isaac's would have been," she moans.

He chuckles. "Of course. Why have a boy when you can have a man?"

I roll my eyes so hard I'm surprised they don't get stuck in the back of my head. I record for a little bit longer, then stop, wanting to get the hell out of there. I close the door carefully and turn to leave.

"Are you going to use that against him?" I almost have a heart attack as Abby's mom scares the crap out of me.

"What the hell?" I breathe.

She looks behind her, worrying her lower lip. She grabs my arm and pulls me toward a door. She shoves me into a room and closes the door behind her. "What are you doing?" I growl as she turns the light on. I look around to see we're in the maid's supply closet.

"Are you going to use that against Michael?" she asks again, pointing to my phone.

"What's it to you?" I narrow my eyes suspiciously, wondering why she's not getting mad at me for snooping.

"If you do..." Her eyes fill with tears, confusing me more. "Can you make me a part of whatever deal you make?"

"What?" my head shoots back, brows furrowing. "I'm so confused."

"I know why you need that. I know what he's been doing to Isaac," she sniffs.

"Then why the fuck haven't you done anything about it?" I growl.

"The first time it happened, I saw him so broken and beaten that it killed me. I love that boy like he was my own. I lost it on Michael, asking how could he ever be like that toward his own son. He didn't like me making him out to be the bad guy, said I didn't understand. Then he..." she looks away, tears falling from her eyes.

"He did the same to you, didn't he?" I ask in a low deadly tone.

"Yes." She looks back at me. "I'm a coward, okay! I should have done more to protect Isaac. I did the best I could. I made sure he was always working, spending the least amount of time at home. It helped slow down the amount of beatings, but it didn't stop. Last year, I tried again, after finding Isaac bloody and almost dead." She lets a sob break free. "He pinned me down and told me to mind my own business, to be the good wife I was meant to be. Then he... he forced me to do my wifely duties and take it."

"He raped you?" I ask, my body shaking from anger. I feel sick. I want to kill him. I'm fucking going to.

"Use that video against him, demand him to leave Isaac alone. But please, can you tell him to leave, not to come back? To let me go too? I've wanted to leave for so long, but the idea of what could happen to Isaac if I wasn't here kept me from leaving. I knew I couldn't stop the beatings, but what if it got bad to the point he was going to die if no one got him help? I needed to be here to help him."

"Shhh." I pull her into my arms as she breaks down. This is so fucked up. This house is full of so many dark and fucked up secrets.

"I didn't want to leave her," she sobs. "I loved Abby from the moment I found out I was pregnant with her. I went home to tell my parents, and they filled my head with so many things. I let them talk me out of being with Lucifer, to leave Abby with him and come to earth. I was young and stupid. Afraid of losing my parents. I thought Abby would be better off with her dad because I knew this world would never accept her. This island isn't as it seems, Zed." She looks up at me with haunted eyes. "Michael isn't what he seems."

I've seen enough of that with my own eyes.

"Why didn't you go back? How did you end up with Michael?"

"I wanted to for so long, even tried once, but the portal guards were told to never let me down there again. I never stopped thinking about her, never stopped loving her. My sweet baby, Abigail." She wipes her eyes. "As time went by, I threw myself into all the community groups and committees, anything to keep myself busy. That's when I met Michael. He lost his wife a year before, and I felt so bad for him and his son. I offered to help watch the boys, then it turned into something more. For a small time, I thought I could love Michael. But my love for Lucifer never allowed it. Lucifer is my fated mate, and you can't just wish something like that away. It sticks with you for the rest of eternity. As Isaac got older, I saw how he treated him, and I knew I could never love a monster like him."

My head is spinning. Way too much hitting me at once. "Why would you bring Abby here if you knew what Michael was like?"

"Because when her father contacted me, I was so happy. I wanted to see my girl, my daughter, I wasn't thinking. Michael is rarely around, I didn't think they would cross paths. He didn't hurt her, did he?" she asks, eyes widening with fear.

"No, he didn't. But his son did."

"What do you mean?" she asks, brows furrowing.

"Isaac has been tormenting her for months. It got pretty bad at one point. Never physical, but it was messed up. His friends went along with it. We didn't find out until just recently why Isaac was such a fucking dick."

"Don't blame him, please. I know it was wrong of him, but Zed, what Michael did to that poor boy..." She covers her mouth, smothering another sob.

"Abby found out they were mates, and she rejected him," I state, and she sobs harder. "But Abby is an amazing woman. She tries to see the good in everyone. She's working to forgive him, as well as the others."

"Everything is so messed up." She sucks in a deep breath. "She hates me, doesn't she?"

I don't say anything, just give her a pitying look. "I do plan on using this. I'll make sure he leaves Isaac and you and never comes back, but I want you to tell Abby everything. Let her know and give her the chance to choose for herself if she wants to have something more with you or not."

"Thank you." She gives me a bone crushing hug. "You are a good man, Zed. I'm glad your mom, and you, got away from his poison."

"Me too." *Me fucking too.* One thing I know for sure, I'm *going* to find a way to kill an Archangel. I'll ask the devil himself to do it, if I have to.

CHAPTER SIXTEEN

ABBY

"Zed, I can't see." I laugh as we stumble our way into his house.

This morning started off amazing. Being with Zed and Leo like that meant everything to me. And when I came downstairs to eat, I couldn't help wondering what it would be like to be with Luke and Noah like that, maybe even with Isaac too.

Then of course, the parents had to come and ruin everything, like always. Michael didn't even seem to care that his cruelty was showing.

I was so damn proud of Isaac for sticking up for himself, although I know none of us would have let him be alone with that monster.

After that shitshow, we went to hang out around the pool. Zed told us that Heather stopped by to see Isaac. I knew she wasn't going to just go away now that Isaac is with me. If anything, it's making her want to try harder.

"I want it to be a surprise," he chuckles before stopping. "Alright, open your eyes and see what Christmas is really supposed to look like." He removes his hands from my eyes and I open them.

"Oh my gosh!" I gasp, eyes widening as I take in the room. It looks so magical. Reds, greens, silvers, and golds fill the living room. Little Santas and snowmen everywhere. *And the tree!* "It's so pretty," I breathe, stepping up to the tree that's brightly lit. My foot knocks into something, and I look down. "Holy shit." I laugh at the insane amount of gifts tucked underneath the branches.

"Leo and Zed went a little crazy," Frankie admits. I look over and smile at her outfit. She's dressed in reindeer PJs, matching with Libby. "Don't worry," she holds up some clothes. "We have a pair for you too."

Biting my lower lip, nodding my head and bouncing on my feet, I smile as she tosses them to me. "Go change and we can open gifts."

"This is so exciting!" I squeal, not even caring how I look right now as I run upstairs to put on the matching pajamas she picked out for me. When I come back down, I snort a laugh as I see all the guys in matching Christmas sweaters. And the adorable thing is, none of them, not even Isaac, seems to care.

Isaac is the first one to spot me. He gives me a crooked smile as he takes in my PJ's "Don't you look cute, Angel."

"Why thank you." I laugh. The others turn to look at me.

"So damn cute," Luke confirms, shooting me a wink.

Things with him have just become so natural. I'm not sure if it's because of the bond, or if it's just who he is, but we've already settled into this comfortable rhythm—like I have with Leo and Zed.

Noah and I have had some alone time, but Noah is so quiet and keeps to himself. I think we need this official date night to open up to each other and really get to know one another. I already know I like him a lot and wouldn't say no to bonding with him officially, if the moment was right. I think I'm already in love with him too.

Tomorrow Noah plans on taking me somewhere. I'm not sure where exactly, but he told me to pack an overnight bag. The look Luke had given me had me feeling that it was something big, and I was going to like it.

"Come, sit, let's open gifts," Frankie urges.

Grinning like crazy, I rush over, and we all sit around the Christmas tree.

For the next hour we all open our gifts, talking and laughing. Zed got my gifts for everyone out of the trunk, and they opened them up too.

"I don't think he's coming," I sigh, leaning back against the couch between Zed's legs.

He plays with my hair, the feeling so relaxing that I close my eyes. I could fall asleep like this.

"I'm sure he will," Zed replies, leaning over to give me a Spider-Man style kiss.

"Who is coming?" Luke asks, playing with one of the nutcrackers he got.

"My dad," I answer, opening my eyes.

"What?!" he drops the nutcracker, eyes filling with fear. "You're telling me the king of Hell is coming here for Christmas?"

"Yes," I grimace, remembering that I forgot to tell the others, outside of Leo and Zed.

"Oh, man. We're all going to die on our first Christmas together, aren't we?" Luke groans.

"Don't be so dramatic, boy," a booming voice I recognize sounds, making us all jump. "I know better than to kill my daughter's mates."

"Daddy!" I can't help feeling like a little girl as I jump up and run over to where he appeared behind the couch, almost stepping on Zed's crotch as I do.

My dad catches me with a chuckle. "Hi, Gale."

"I hate that name," I murmur as he gives me the best bone-crushing hug. "But I don't care, I'm just glad you came." Happy tears fill my eyes as he puts me down on my feet.

"I told you I'd come." He grins, wiping away the tears. "So, you want to introduce me to everyone?"

When I turn around, I huff out a laugh. Everyone is standing at attention like my dad is some kind of drill sergeant, all with different levels of fear in their eyes.

"You already know Leo and Frankie," I say. "This is Libby, Zed's little sister."

"Hello, Sir." Libby nods, not making eye contact.

"Nice to meet you, Libby," my dad says in a soft voice, making Libby look up. She gives him a small smile.

"This is Zed."

"Hello, Sir." Zed steps forward, holding out his hand.

"Yes, Zed. The dark angel who has mated with my daughter." My dad glares at him before cracking a smile. "Your drill sergeant attitude and obsessive need to love and care for my daughter wins you points in my book."

"Your daughter is my world. I'd die for her."

And there goes the tears again. Ugh, I love that man.

"As you should." My dad nods.

"This is Luke and Noah."

Luke looks about three seconds away from pissing his pants, his cocky confidence long gone. Noah has caution in his eyes, but he's doing a good job at keeping his cool without coming off like he doesn't care.

"Right, the little shitstains who thought it would be fun to fuck with my daughter."

"Dad," I chastise, stepping in front of them as Luke lets out a scared squeak. "You said you were not going to hurt them."

"I say a lot of things," he snarls.

"Daddy!" My powers come forth, the need to protect my mates makes my eyes glow and my hands burst into flames.

He looks at me with surprise. "I don't think I've seen you use your powers before."

"She's a fucking badass all the time, but damn, when she uses them..." Zed trails off. I look over to see him biting his knuckle, arousal in his eyes. I shoot him a glare before looking back to my dad, who seems to have forgotten I'm standing right here.

"I have no doubt about how powerful she is. I am her father, after all," my dad chuckles. "Fine, fine. I'll let them live," he sighs, waving a hand. Then he spots Isaac, and I sense the shit is about to hit the fan. "Him, on the other hand."

He takes a step toward Isaac, but I grab my dad's arm, pulling him back. "I need to talk to you—right now, please!" I shout, knowing he really is about to kill Isaac, not giving a fuck about what we talked about before. "Daddy, please."

His eyes are black, his demon side seconds away from being on full display.

I manage to pull my dad out into the front yard. "I know, I told you I wouldn't hurt him, Abby, but I don't think I can keep that promise."

I look at him with pleading eyes. "I know Isaac has done some shitty things to me. Things that hurt more than anything I've ever felt. But Dad, Michael... he's so much worse than you thought."

That gets his attention. "What do you mean?" he snarls.

"Michael has been beating Isaac for years. In some really fucked up ways," I sob. "Some things that make Hell look tame. Dad, Isaac isn't a bad person, he just made some bad choices."

"Fucking hell," he growls as he paces back and fourth. "After what you told me, what you overheard those three fools were up to..."

"We still don't know much more than what I told you, but Michael is a monster. Isaac was hurting, deflecting from his pain. Dad, he thought you were the reason their moms died."

"What?!" he shouts. "I didn't kill their mothers!"

"I know that. My guess is some demons killed them, and Michael put the blame on you."

"Wouldn't surprise me," he scoffs, shaking his head. "So, Isaac hated you for something he thought I did?"

"I know it's wrong, and I shouldn't make excuses for what he did, but Dad, he's messed up. Broken. All I want to do is put him back together, to make sure no one hurts him again. I have you, an amazing dad who would burn down all the worlds to protect me. Daddy, he had no one."

Dad deflates and pulls me into his arms. "Don't cry, love. You know I can't stand to see you sad. Fine, I won't kill him."

"Thank you." I laugh.

We head back into the house and everyone is on edge. My dad walks right up to Isaac. For a moment, I think he's going to say fuck it and snap his neck.

"You hurt my daughter again and I will kill you, do you understand me?"

Isaac gives him a firm nod. "I would rather die than ever hurt her again."

"Good," he snarls.

"Cookies are ready!" Megan cheers, stepping into the dining room with a big smile on her face, just now joining the party. Her eyes widen, smile dimming to something more shy.

My dad goes stiff, the look on his face has me shaking my head.

"No. No, no, no!" I protest, my heart pounding in my

chest. I know this look, had this look a few times myself. "Dad, no." I groan as he ignores me and strides over to Megan.

"Holy shit, is this really happening?" Zed mutters, but I say nothing as I watch my dad cups Megan's face—and there it is, the shock.

Megan gasps, her eyes filling with tears. My dad leans forward and whispers in her ear, too quietly for any of us to hear.

"Damn, your dad really is a sweetheart, isn't he?" Frankie asks. For a second, I wonder what the heck she's talking about, and then I remember she has vampire hearing.

"Did we just watch our parents reveal as mates?" Libby asks.

I say nothing, still looking at the two of them in shock.

"Little Bird, relax," Zed soothes, wrapping his arms around me.

That snaps me out of it. I spin in his arms and gape at him. "Relax! Are you kidding me? Our parents are mates! *Mates!*"

"I can see that." He chuckles.

"How are you so calm?!"

"Because," Zed starts, gripping my face softly and guiding my head back in my dad and Megan's direction. "My mom has been suffering for years with heartache and pain, and I know your dad has too, in some way. My mom was rejected by her first mate, your dad was left by his. You know what it feels like to be away from yours, the hurt you feel. They don't have to feel that anymore."

"Shit," I sigh, realizing he's right. I watch as they whisper together, my dad wrapping an arm around her waist as he looks down at her with... damn it, he's totally smitten with her. "It's like looking at you with me."

"Yup." He chuckles.

"He's totally head over heels for her at first glance, isn't he?" Zed hugs me from behind, kissing my neck.

"He would burn the world for her too now."

"So, he's like your step brother now too?" Luke asks. "Your mom is with his dad and now his mom is with your dad. Trippy."

"Don't even start." I warn him, and he raises his hands, smirking.

"Kids," Megan says, her face flushed pink as they walk over to us. He doesn't take his hand away from her, a grin so wide on his face, I can't even be mad. I've never seen him this happy. "I'm going to go ahead and assume that you all know what just happened."

"That Abby's daddy is my new daddy?" Zed chuckles, grunting when I elbow him.

"Here's the deal. Megan is my mate, she's coming back to Hell with me, so we can get to know each other. She is, however, worried about you two."

"Don't," Libby says, sounding like she's about to cry. Her mom looks at her with panic. "Dont worry about us," Libby sniffs. "I'm eighteen, I'll be fine. I have my mate and Zed, as well as Abby and Frankie."

"Libby, honey, are you sure?"

Libby steps up to her mom and places her hands on her shoulders. "I saw what my dad did to you for years. All I wanted to do was help you every time he laid a hand on you, but I was too little. Zed knew if he did anything, you would have gotten it worse when he wasn't around. We love you so much, Mom, and we just want you to be happy."

"Oh, baby," Megan cries as she pulls Libby into a hug. I look at my dad, knowing he's ready to snap his fingers and find Libby's dad at any second. He's pissed, really pissed.

"I should go pack a bag," Megan says.

My dad is about to follow her when Libby grabs his arm. "Mr. King of Hell... Sir. Can you find my dad and kill him?"

My dad gives her a smile that freaks even me out. "Oh, love, I already planned on doing that."

"Good." Libby nods. "Thank you. You won't hurt her, will you?"

"Never," he replies with so much emotion you can't take it as anything other than a promise. I can't help but smile.

"Thank you."

My dad nods and follows after Megan, like even just those few passing moments were too much time away from her.

"So, that happened," Frankie says. I turn to see her taking a bite of one of Megan's cookies.

"How is this even my life?" I sigh.

At this point, I'm just expecting new shit to pop up. Would it be stupid to think otherwise?

Now, how the hell am I going to process the fact that my dad is mated to Zed's mom? I don't think this is what they meant by "keeping it in the family."

CHAPTER SEVENTEEN

NOAH

"Everything is going to be fine," Isaac reassures as he hands me my bag.

"How do you know? What if she hates what I have planned? It's too much, isn't it?" I look at him with worry in my eyes. I'm so nervous to go away with Abby. I have a weekend planned in another realm, and it was not easy to pull together. There are perks to being the son of an archangel, and I'm not ashamed to use them.

Isaac chuckles. "Babe, she's going to love it. Not just because of where you're taking her, but because it's you who is taking her."

My eyes narrow. "You've become so sweet lately. I like it, but it also kind of freaks me out."

"Get used to it." He grins. "I'm not the angry asshole I was before. Sure, I'm still depressed as fuck at times; but with all of you at my side, I know I'll be okay."

"You will." I step into him, putting my hand behind his head and pulling him in for a kiss. "It's us, forever."

Placing his forehead to mine, he sighs. "I want Abby to be a part of that."

"I know you do. We all do. It will happen in time. I already see things changing between you two."

He groans. "It's so weird being around her. Most of the time I want to just get down on my knees, telling her over and over how much I'm sorry and beg her to forgive me. And then there are other times where I want to slam her up against the wall, spin her around, and fuck her until she's screaming my name. This bond shit really fucks with your head."

"Damn, baby, stop," Luke groans, stepping up behind me. I can feel his hard cock against my ass. "With that kind of dirty talk, Noah won't be leaving any time soon."

"Oh, don't you worry, I'll be taking care of you once he leaves." Isaac gives Luke a cocky smirk.

"And I'm going to miss it." I chuckle.

"Babe." Luke kisses the side of my neck. I sigh happily and lean back into him. I'm going to miss these two, but I know I'm going to have fun with Abby... I hope. "You're the luckiest of the three of us. A whole two days away with our girl."

"Are you sure it's not too much?"

They both chuckle. "No! Now get going." Luke slaps my ass making me laugh.

After two very long goodbye kisses, I head upstairs with my bag.

I can't help but stop and watch Abby for a moment when I see her standing by the door, the sunlight streaming through the window, making her glow.

She's gorgeous. I'm so lucky to be one of her mates, and I hope I get to show her that on this trip.

As if she can feel me watching, she looks over at me and my heart starts to race as her lips form a smile. "Hey. All ready?"

"Yup," I say, holding up my bag and walking over to her.

"I didn't know what to pack, so I packed for all types of weather."

"Sorry about that." I blush as I run a hand over my short curls. "I just wanted it to be a surprise as much as I could. If there's something you need but didn't bring we can get it there."

"Okay." She smiles. "And where is there?"

"Nice try." I laugh and open the door. She follows after me, down to the packed Jeep.

I open her door, taking her bag and tossing it in the back with mine.

When I get in and start up the car, Abby bounces in her seat.

"Sorry. I'm just so excited." She grins as we head down the driveway.

"Really?" I ask, casting a look over to her.

"Yes! Of course, silly. I've been dying to get you alone and do this, just us."

"Me too." The nervous feeling inside me settles at hearing that.

Turning on the music, I smile as Abby hums along to what-ever song is on the radio. When we pull up to the portal ware-house, Abby stops and sits up, looking around. "We're at the portals?"

"Yes." I pull up and into the warehouse.

"We're leaving earth?"

"Is that okay?" I can feel the panic within me starting to rise again.

"Yes!" She laughs. "Oh my god, what realm are we going

to?! I've only been to Earth and Hell, this is going to be so exciting."

I let out the breath I was holding and chuckle. "Thank god you're okay with that."

We pull up to one of the portals. A security guard approaches the window.

"ID please."

I give him my ID, he looks it over then at me, back at the ID again. "Destination and how long will be you gone for?"

"The Empire of Falerin and for forty-eight hours, starting when we get there," I state. He nods and waves us through.

"You're taking me to the fairy realm! For two days!" She's bouncing in her seat as I drive us toward the portal. "I'm going to the fairy realm. This is so cool! You're the best!"

I'm shocked when she leans over and kisses my cheek.

This girl, she's everything. And now I'm not so worried about this being a stupid idea. The smile on her face right now is everything.

"A few things before we enter. It takes a little while longer to pass through with a car. When it's just you, it takes seconds, but with a car it's minutes." Abby nods. "And, you're going to need this." I grab a winter coat out of the back seat and hand it to her. "It's going to be pretty snowy this time of year."

Her eyes widen, filling with tears, and I pray it's happy tears. "I get to see snow?"

"Yup." I smile as she quickly puts on the jacket. I wait until her seat belt is on again before driving into the portal. Everything is dark, but I don't think Abby minds as she talks away.

"I want to go skating and snowboarding and skiing and make snowmen. Oh, and we can go sledding! Oh my!" she gasps as we drive out of the portal and into Falerin.

Right away, this place looks nothing like home. Normally,

everything is green, but with the snow, it's a winter wonderland.

Without stopping, I drive out of the portal compound and down the main road. Thankfully, where we're staying is in the first town, only a few miles down the road.

Abby watches out her window, taking in all the snow-covered trees. "Noah, this place. It's amazing!"

"It is." I smile. It doesn't take us long before I'm pulling off onto the road that leads to the cabin where we're staying.

"I know I said this before, but oh my god, this is amazing!" Abby gushes as she takes in the cabin. "It's so cute!"

"This is my family's cabin. My mom bought it long before I was born. She and my dad would come here for special occasions. I remember them taking me here a few times when I was little. We never came back after she died, but I know my dad has been paying someone to look after the place. Mom left it to me, and I guess I never really thought to ask the guys to come with me. Not that I think our fathers would have allowed us, anyways. At least, not back then."

"I'm honored." She grabs my hand, lacing her fingers between mine. "I would have loved to meet her."

I smile. "She would have loved you."

"Show me around?"

I nod, deciding to be the one to make the next move. I go to kiss her on the cheek... only she moves her head at the last second and our lips meet. My body instantly heats up, and I pull her closer. She parts her lips and I waste no time slipping my tongue in and over hers. This is our first real kiss. I've been too nervous to try anything more than a peck on the cheek or head before now.

With the guys, everything is natural, comfortable. We've been together for years, but with Abby, it's all new, and exciting. Don't get me wrong, it's exciting with the guys too, but this is different, but in an equally good way.

"We should go inside," Abby says panting as she breaks the kiss.

"Okay." I nod, panting just as hard. Speaking of hard, my cock is painfully stiff right now.

"But I want to do more of that later." She pulls back, biting her lip.

"Yes, please." I nod, making her giggle. Fuck, that sound is music to my ears.

Abby gets out and helps me bring the bags to the door. The place should already be unlocked and set up with everything we need for our stay.

"I love it," Abby says, placing the bags on the ground as we enter the cabin.

"I do too. I know we have money, but Mom wanted something small and cozy."

"It's perfect," Abby agrees, taking off her sneakers. I'm glad I bought her boots, because I don't think she would have packed any.

"I was thinking we could get settled here, then we could get bundled up and take a snowmobile into town and grab some supper. Tomorrow, I have the whole day planned."

"Sounds perfect." I can't get enough of that smile. I like seeing her happy. Knowing I'm the one who's making her that way, fills me with pride.

"Let me show you around," I offer, my eyes widening as she grabs my arm and hugs it. It takes me a moment before I start moving. "The living room and kitchen you saw when we walked in. This is one of the bedrooms." I show her the spare one. "This is my parents room." She takes a moment to look. "This is the bathroom."

"Oh my god! A stone bathtub."

"Thought you might like that." I chuckle. "There's also a hot tub out back."

"We need to use that." She gives me a cheeky smile.

"We will." We continue to the end of the hall. "And this is my room."

"This is very... you." She laughs as we step inside. The room has thankfully been updated. I had someone do it a few years ago, just in case I wanted to come and stay. From what I remember, it was a room fit for a little boy, not a grown man.

"This is the first time I've been in it since I had someone update it."

"Oh." She looks over at me as she runs her hand along the dresser. "And how do you like it?"

"It's nice." I nod, taking the room in. The walls are a dark army green. The dresser and side tables are light gray with a comforter to match. There's nothing on the walls or dressers. No personal touches.

Now that things are going good with Abby and the guys, I'll have to bring everyone here another time. I feel like this place would be perfect if we need to just escape our lives for a little bit.

Honestly, a part of me feels like just telling the others to come here, and we forget about our problems. Sadly, that's not how life works.

I'm not sure what my dad or the others have been up to, but I can say I'm glad he's being open-minded with not wanting me to be with Heather and having Abby as my mate.

Maybe some day I can tell him about Isaac and Luke. But I don't see that day being any time soon. Not until we find out what Michael is up to.

"It needs a few things in here that shows this is your room," Abby comments, sitting on the bed with a little bounce.

I smile, walking over to her until I'm towering over her. I

cup her face, brushing her cheek with my thumb. "Our room." I lean in and place a soft kiss on her plush lips, loving the little hum she gives me as she kisses me back. I could easily become addicted.

I'm not like Luke and Isaac when it comes to sex. I mean in the way that I don't always think about it. I love sex, I love having sex with Isaac and Luke, to get lost in the moment and give myself to them. I trust them with my life and my body. But sex isn't always on my mind. It's just something I'm used to with the guys, so I don't feel the need to always think about it when I'm getting the attention I need regularly.

But it's not like that when I'm around Abby. I crave her, need her, and never in my life have I thought about sex as much as I do when she's in the same room with me. Actually, even just the mention of her has my mind wandering to some pretty dirty places.

I've heard her with Zed and Leo before. I didn't go looking to overhear, it's just, I don't think Abby knows how... *vocal* she is.

It's so sexy. Her moans and cries are on repeat in my mind. I want to make her feel good, to have her making those sounds for me.

"Noah," Abby says with amusement in her voice. "Lost you there for a moment."

"Sorry." There goes that stupid blush again. Another thing I never really did before meeting Abby. There's something about her that turns me into this ball of nerves and I find myself caring way too much about what she thinks of me. Not that her opinion of me doesn't matter, it does. It's just... the thing is... I've never cared about what anyone thought of me.

But I want her to like me. Part of me is afraid she will let the past overrule the present; that she'll tell Luke, Isaac, and me to get fucked before walking away with Zed and Leo. Not that we wouldn't deserve that.

"Do you want to unpack anything?" I ask her.

"Sure."

We head back down to the front room and grab our bags. I watch as Abby puts her clothes in piles. "I guess I won't be needing these." She laughs, putting her shorts, dresses, and t-shirts back into her bag. "But I'm glad I brought these." She picks out a sweater and a pair of jeans from her clothes and leaves them on the bed before putting everything else in the dresser. "I know we're only going to be here two nights, but it's easier than digging through everything every time." She gives me a playful smile. "Also, if I leave anything, it gives us a reason to come back here."

She doesn't need to make up a reason to come back here. All she has to do is say the words and I'll make it happen.

I'm starting to see that I'd do just about anything she asks of me, as long as she's happy and I get to see that smile.

As I finish putting my things in the dresser, something in the mirror over the dresser catches my eye.

My heart starts to race and my breathing picks up, my palms growing sweaty as I watch Abby pull her shirt off. My eyes fall to her breasts almost spilling from her bra, down her belly to where her hands meet her shorts.

Licking my lips, I watch as if it's slow motion while she undresses. My throat bobs as I swallow, my thoughts immediately going to touching her, feeling her soft creamy skin under my hands.

"Noah." Her voice has me snapping up to look her in the eyes, still watching through the mirror.

"Y-yes."

"Just checking that you're still here with me." She grins as she grabs her sweater and pulls it on, her pants following.

I let out a shaky breath as I will my cock to calm the hell down.

"You know," she walks over to me and I spin around to face her. "If any of the thoughts going through your handsome mind were for you to come over and touch me." She leans up, her hands on my chest as she whispers in my ear. "Next time, don't hesitate to do it."

I groan as she sucks my ear lobe into her mouth, giving it a little nibble. A full body shiver takes over me as I forget how to breathe.

"Now, how about we head into town, so you can feed your hungry mate?" she asks, stepping away from me. I miss her as soon as she's gone and wish I had wrapped my arms around her, carried her to the bed, and had my way with her.

But that will have to wait until later, because my *mate* is hungry.

"Right," I breathe out. "Let's go."

Abby follows me back downstairs where I give her the new boots I bought her. "Noah!" she gasps. "Thank you. You didn't have to do that."

"I assumed you didn't have any, and seeing how you will for sure need them here, I felt like I should." I shrug.

"Good point." She nods. "Well, thank you, I love them."

"You're welcome." Her approval makes me so damn happy. "I'm glad you like them."

She slips on her winter coat. "Do you think I'm going to need snow pants?" she asks, looking down at her legs.

"I don't think so. It doesn't get too cold here, just enough to keep the snow on the ground, but if you think you need some, we can pick some up." I curse myself for remembering a coat but not the snow pants. "Oh!" I remember the other stuff I got her. "I did get you these, though."

I grab the brown paper bag from one of my backpacks and pull out a pink hat and mittens set.

"Oh, they are so cute!" she laughs. "Thank you."

Taking the hat, I pull it on over her head and kiss the tip of her nose. I almost pause to think about what I did, but let it go. This feels right; I shouldn't be second guessing everything I'm doing with her.

I help her into her mitts before getting my own hat and gloves. With the keys to the snowmobile in my pocket, we head outside.

"So, we have a shed where we keep all the smaller things, like lawn mowers and leaf blowers, but there's also a garage around back that houses the quads and sleds."

"Wow. You have it all, don't you?" She chuckles. "We should come back here when the snow is gone so we can experience the different things this place has to offer."

"I agree with that." I smile over at her. "I think that can be arranged." Abby waits while I go in and grab the snowmobile. "Hop on," I say, patting the seat behind me.

She excitedly rushes to me and swings her leg over the seat. Wrapping her arms around me, she snuggles close, and then we're off.

The whole way into town, Abby is so adorable as she points everything out, telling me to look each time. I can understand her excitement. It's not just because she hasn't seen much outside Hell and the Island. This place is a real work of beauty.

"Although Falerin allows people from other realms to visit, they have rules that must be met. It's one of my favorite things about the fairy realm" I tell Abby as we start to walk down the main street in the little town we're staying in. "No violence. The fae are peaceful and kind people. The crime rate is next to nothing here. No littering, either. The people of Falerin thrive on having a clean environment. Only certain things use power, and the ones that do run on solar panels or batteries. Even the snowmobile is run by a big battery. But the biggest rule is respect. Everyone here is friendly and open, so they expect the same treatment."

"I knew I liked this place as soon as we went through that portal, now I know this is my new favorite place. I hope you like it here because I'll be making you bring me back."

"Anything you want, Hellcat."

"Careful, Angel Boy, those are powerful words to a girl like me." She winks.

We pick a cute little pub and as soon as we walk in, people turn to stare. But it's only for a minute before everyone goes back to doing what they were seconds ago.

"Hello, welcome to Finnegan's! Table for two?"

"Yes, please." I nod.

The waitress brings us over to a booth away from everyone else. Abby takes the spot across from me.

"Here are your menus. What can I get you to drink?"

"Just water for now, please," I tell her. Abby looks at me like she wants to ask for something but the waitress leaves too quickly and the look on her face makes me chuckle. "I know you wanted to order a soda, but they don't have that here."

"What?!" Her eyes go so wide they almost bug out of her head. "Why the hell not?"

"One, it's bad for you." I smirk, and she rolls her eyes.

"Shit like that doesn't kill us, Noah."

"I know." I'm really trying hard not to laugh. "But it could here. That's all processed garbage. We might not get sick and can put anything we want into our bodies without worrying about side effects, but here, they don't live forever."

"Oh." She sits back against the booth. "Sometimes I forget it's not only the humans who die eventually."

"While the fae live longer than most mortals, they still can get ill, still die of old age."

"That's shitty," she mumbles, looking over her menu. "I was about to say maybe I'd rather be a fairy than a demon princess, but nevermind. The thought of leaving you and the others behind makes my stomach do weird stuff that I don't like."

She's not even looking at me as she says it, being so open it's like she's not even aware of her words. Maybe she doesn't mean to, maybe these are things that feel right in her mind. But I smile, loving the fact that she included me in that. That the idea of not having me makes her feel sick.

Because I feel the same way about her.

"Abby?"

"Yeah?" She looks up at me with her bright blue eyes.

"You're not going to lose me... or them. We're with you for life."

CHAPTER EIGHTEEN

ABBY

Supper was amazing. The food was unlike anything I've had before.

As we walk hand in hand down the street of Moss Meadows, I can't keep the smile off my face. Noah isn't a chatty person, but I don't mind. Just being here with him like this means the world to me. And it hasn't stopped him from planning some fun and thoughtful things for us to do.

"Tomorrow we can go to the ski resort about a half hour away from here. I thought we could leave after breakfast so that we could have a whole day there, seeing how today is half over."

"I think that's a good idea. What did you have in mind for tonight?" I ask, smiling up at him. His cheeks are a little rosy from the cold.

Thankfully, it's not cold enough that I'm freezing my butt off, but any time I see Noah look like the cold might be getting to him, I send a wave of heat through his body. I had to hide my laugh when I did it the first time because the poor guy looked so confused. It didn't take him long to realize what I was doing, and he looked grateful.

"You mentioned you wanted to go skating and sledding. There's a skating rink just at the end of this street. We have some sleds back at the cabin and a hill not too far from it. Just the two of us. If that's okay?"

I stop in front of him and lift my arms up to wrap around his neck. "More than okay." I pull his head down so that I can kiss him.

He moans against my lips, and I deepen the kiss. My body heats and not because of my powers. I'm about to say we should just head back to the cabin when someone clears their throat.

We break the kiss, both of us panting and look over to see an older lady. She has pointed ears and an amused grin.

"Sorry." I blush, then burst into giggles as I grab a mortified Noah by the hand and pull him toward the end of the street.

"Is that it?" I ask, pointing to the place where some people are gathering.

"Yup." We walk over to a booth. "You wait here, and I'll go get us some skates." He kisses the side of my head and leaves. I watch the families on the ice. People are laughing as they try not to fall.

"Here we go." He holds up a set of skates. "I got you a size seven. Is that right?"

"It is." I take them from him. "Thank you." I already know he knew my foot size, seeing as he got these amazing snow boots for me, but it's sweet of him to check to be sure.

Taking a seat on the bench, I hold my hands out to him for the skates, but he just gives me a lopsided grin as he kneels down before me.

I watch, biting my lip as he takes my foot and pulls off my

boot, replacing it with the skate, then does the same with the other.

"Thank you. You didn't have to"

"I know, but I wanted to." He stands up and kisses the side of my head before taking a seat on the bench next to me to put on his own skates.

When he's done, he stands back up and holds his hands out to me. "Ready?"

It's only now that I remember that I have no idea how to skate.

"Ahh," I cast a worried glance over to the rink.

"Don't worry. I got you."

Taking his hand, I let him pull me to my feet. It feels weird standing on skates, my legs wobbling as I hold onto Noah. "Have you done much skating before?"

"Nope." He grins down at me. "Haven't since I was five."

My eyes widen. "What? Then how are you going to keep me from falling on my ass?"

"I'm not." He chuckles. "I'll just be joining you."

I pause for a moment before belting out a laugh. "Alright then, we will fail together."

"As long as you're by my side, I'm winning," he says with a wink.

Oh, I like this cheeky side of Noah. "Smooth, hot stuff."

"Sometimes I try."

Together we walk to the entrance of the rink. We aren't even on the ice yet, but it already feels like we're baby deer walking for the first time.

"Ready?"

"Good thing we don't feel pain for long." I laugh, taking the first step.

The moment we're both on the ice, we lose our balance and fall on our asses with a grunt.

Flat on our backs, we turn to look at each other and burst out laughing. Not sure how eventful this skating is going to be, but I already know it's going to be memories worth making.

"I know we heal quick, but it doesn't really help when we can't stop falling long enough for it to kick in," I grumble as Noah helps me up from the ice for the millionth time. He got the hang of it after a few minutes—I, however, did not.

"Come on, Hellcat." He chuckles. "Let's get you and your sore ass back to the cabin. We can build a snowman, have some hot chocolate by the fire, and relax for the rest of the night."

"I like the sound of that," I say, eagerly trying to move toward the exit.

"Hold up." He laughs harder. "You're going to hurt yourself again."

We're in the middle of the rink, and I'm not planning on falling on my ass again. "Help me down."

"What?" Noah asks, raising a brow.

"Help me." I start to let my knees bend, and he helps me to sit back on the ice.

"What are you doing?"

Quickly, I unlace the skate and pop them both off before jumping to my feet. "Ahh, that's better."

"Abby," he calls after me as I start to slide my socked-feet against the ice. He skates his way over to me. "You're crazy," he sighs.

"Crazy smart." I shoot him a grin, ignoring how my feet are now wet and freezing.

When we get off the ice, I rush over to my boots, pull my socks off, and slip my feet back into the warmth of the fur-lined boots.

"Let me bring these back," he says, taking my skates from me.

Once we're ready to go, I start to walk the way we came from, but Noah stops me.

"Walking will take too long," Noah states. "Come here."

I give him a funny look but step into his outstretched arms. He wraps them around me, and I sigh happily, the bond humming to life.

"I'm all for cuddles, but can it be at the cabin, on a couch, in the warmth?" I murmur against his chest, making him chuckle.

"Yes, love, just wait." With my eyes closed, I hold on to him and wait for him to say or do something.

When I open my eyes to ask, I gasp when I see that we are no longer on the ground. My eyes snap over to Noah's stunning, pure white wings. "Wow. I've never seen your wings before."

Come to think of it, I don't think I've seen any of their wings outside the fight Isaac had with Zed, and the first time I saw Isaac pull the black feather from his wings.

"We don't use them much. Not really sure why. I miss it." We fly over the buildings, and I grin at how tiny everything looks.

"They're so white," I comment as we land in front of the cabin. Reaching out, I run my fingers along the softness. Noah groans, his whole body shivering, and I grin, forgetting that wings are a sensitive body part. "Noah."

"Yes?" His voice is thick with need and my heart starts to pump a little faster.

"Have you ever plucked a black feather before?"

His body goes still. "No."

"Isaac has."

His eyes widen slightly before nodding. "I know. Isaac... he's done some hurtful things. Some things that were deemed so wrong that his feathers would turn. At first, he freaked out because he thought his dad would lose his mind if he found out. But one time, I saw Isaac watching his dad through the crack in the office door. Michael had his wings out, and we watched as he grabbed a black feather and pulled. I was horrified because losing a feather by force like that is like ripping fingernails off. Later, when all the adults left again, I was awakened in the middle of the night to Isaac's scream. When I went to check on him, he was in the shower and there was a bloody black feather in the trash can. It might have been the first time I saw it, but it sadly wasn't the last. Over time, he grew immune to the pain. And now that I know what his dad did to him, I understand now why it didn't hurt Michael."

"Fuck," I whisper, my stomach sinking as I start to feel sick. "The thought of how many feathers Michael has pulled is messed up."

"But enough of the sad stuff. It's in the past. Luke and I, we're helping Isaac the best we know how. It's not easy, but thankfully he's allowing us to be there for him this time."

"How's he doing?" I ask as we head inside.

"He's trying. I can see the guilt eating at him. It's like he spent so long pushing everything down, trying to pretend it wasn't there, but now that it's surfaced, it's slowly draining him. He hates himself for hurting Luke and me. He hates himself for the way he treated you. He loves you, you know?"

That has me stopping. "What?"

"I know it's hard to believe, but he does. I think a part of him always has. He's giving Luke and me the time to grow with you, but I know he wishes he could do the same."

"Could have fooled me," I sigh. "I mean, I see him trying, I see the change in him. But he's hardly tried to talk to me alone, and anytime he does say something, it's him randomly saying sorry before walking away. The first time he really talked to me was the same day he told Heather what he did."

Noah helps me out of my coat. "He doesn't want to make any of this about him. He wants you to know that he craves something between the two of you, but he wants to make sure Luke and I get it before him. Because as much as Isaac craves it, he doesn't think he deserves it."

"He doesn't," I tell him as I take my boots off. "Yet."

"He will keep working at it until he does. And even if you don't give him a shot, he will still spend every day trying."

"I guess we will see how things go."

As I change out of my wet clothes and into something dry, so I'm warm when we go back outside, what Noah said plays on a loop in my mind. Isaac has been groveling in his own way. But he's doing it in ways that won't get him recognized for it. Like he wants to earn my forgiveness but won't take credit for anything. He's been leaving me little cupcakes at my door for the past week. My favorite, red velvet with cream cheese.

I overheard him tell Mary, the head housekeeper, not to do my laundry, so I waited around to see why, and found him washing my clothes. The confusion and dedication on his face as he tried to fold everything was cute because he clearly hasn't done his own laundry ever.

I'm the only one in the house that likes Red Delicious apples, but the fridge is always stocked with them.

It's the little things with him that I find are getting to me, in a good way, more than his words. If it was anyone else but him, I'd make him work harder than ever, grovel like crazy, but I don't have it in me.

I see the light in his eyes slowly dimming, and it's breaking my heart.

What Isaac needs is love, support, and people on his side. I'll be one of them, if he'd let me.

Noah and I spend the next hour playing in the snow. After we make a very wonky–but adorable–snowman, we grab the sleds from the shed and go to a hill nearby.

I laugh and smile the whole time. I don't think I've had this much fun in a really long time.

When we're tired and the sun is fully set, we head inside. After changing again, I head back to the living room to find Noah sitting on the couch in front of the fireplace with two mugs of hot chocolate on the coffee table.

"Thank you," I say, taking a seat next to him and grabbing a cup. I take a sip and moan. "This is so good."

"Thanks. It's my mom's recipe. All from scratch."

Putting the mug back on the table, I look over at Noah. He grins and opens his arms. With giddy excitement, I snuggle against him and sigh happily. The bond is a powerful thing. It has the power to control everything, if you let it. And in moments like this, I don't mind.

Tonight is a go with the flow kind of night, and I'm hoping it ends with me and Noah taking that next step and officially making him mine.

CHAPTER NINETEEN

ABBY

"Okay, so skiing and snowboarding ended up a lot like skating," I say as I climb off the snowmobile.

Last night, I ended up falling asleep in Noah's arms. When I woke up this morning, I was in his bed with him sleeping soundly next to me. Like a creeper, I watched him for a little while with a smile on my face. This time with him has been amazing. Getting to know him on his own, away from everyone else, is just what we needed for him to open up.

After he woke up, we got something to eat, then took the snowmobile to the ski resort. There I quickly learned that, while I like the snow and think it's pretty, outside of sledding, snow activities are *not* my thing.

Noah seemed to have enjoyed himself, but he didn't get to fully do what he wanted because he kept having to pull me out of the snow.

"It was fun, though." Noah smirks as he climbs off too.

Bending over, I grab some snow and make a snowball.

"Yeah, I'm sure you had a lot of fun, laughing at me every time I fell on my ass," I sass and toss the snowball at him

He's not expecting it, so he doesn't try to dodge it, and it hits him right in the face.

My hand flies to my mouth, trying to smother my laugh as the snow drips down his face.

"Oh, it's like that, is it?" he asks, wiping the melting snow off.

"Noah," I say in a warning tone as he bends over. "You don't want to do this." I slowly back up, heart racing with excitement.

"Oh, but I do." He chuckles and launches a snowball at me. I move, raising my arms with a screech, and it hits me in the side.

"It's on!" I shout, grabbing more snow.

We start a snowball fight, running around the front of the cabin, using what we can to block the other's snowballs. I manage to get over to a tree and duck behind it.

My face hurts with how big my smile is, belly cramping from laughing so hard.

"Where are you, Hellcat?" Noah calls out as I take a moment to catch my breath. I can hear the crunch of the snow under his boots as he makes his way closer to me. "Just come out and surrender. We both know I won."

"Never!" I shout with a laugh.

"Then I'll just have to come get you."

Everything is silent for a moment and I wait, wondering what he's going to do next.

"Gotcha." He steps around the tree. But he doesn't throw a snowball. He grabs me by the waist and spins me around.

We both fall into the snow, me on my back, him looming over me.

Both of us are breathing heavily, his lips so close to mine.

181

As he rocks himself against me, pressing his very hard cock against my core, I feel the snow around us melt.

"Noah," I whisper. "I think it's about time you take me inside and make me yours."

His eyes search mine before he kisses me. My eyes flutter shut, and I moan as his tongue slips in and over mine. We kiss slow and sweetly for a little while, but my body quickly becomes an inferno with the need for Noah.

As if he feels the same way, Noah breaks the kiss, wraps his arm around my back and pulls me up, standing with me in his arms.

I wrap my legs and arms around him while he carries me into the house. We don't say anything, the sexual tension thick in the air, as he sits me on the table. My heart races, anticipation filling me as Noah takes my boots off, then my jacket.

Once he takes his own off, he steps between my legs and cups my face. "Abby, I know you didn't choose this, having me or any of the others as your mates, but there's not a day that goes by since finding out you were mine that I haven't been overjoyed. I'm sorry for the part I played in what was done to you, I know I've said this before, but I need you to know. You are smart, funny, kind, and amazing. You make my day brighter, you make me smile wider and laugh harder. You have no idea how happy I am to get to call you mine, to be able to spend the rest of my life with you, if you let me have that honor."

"Noah..." my voice breaks as I say his name, tears falling down my cheeks that he kisses away. "I love you." I do, I feel it in my heart.

"Fuck," he groans before crashing his lips to mine.

Our kiss isn't like moments before. It's desperate, needy, and raw as we both work at ridding the other of their clothes.

We break the kiss long enough to take off our tops before finding each other's lips again.

Once we're both in only our underwear, Noah picks me up and carries me to the bedroom.

The moment he lays me down on the bed, something inside me takes over. The need for him is so strong. The bond goes crazy with each touch, and it has me aching for him to be inside me.

"You don't need condoms," I blurt, taking off my bra and panties as he reaches for the bedside table. "I'm good and on birth control."

"Oh, okay," he says, his attention back on me. His eyes widen as he takes in my naked body. "Holy shit," he whispers, licking his lips.

He stands there, cock straining against his boxers as I crawl over to him. Grabbing the waist band, I pull them down, letting his hard length spring free. I hear his breaths coming in quick pants as I grab a hold of his cock and lick the bead of pre-cum off the tip before licking his very impressive sized dick like a damn lollipop.

"Abby," he moans as I take him into my mouth as far as I can before pulling back and doing it again. "Fuck, baby, if you keep doing that, this is going to be over before I'm even inside you."

I let his cock fall free with a pop. "Good point." I grab his arm and pull him down on the bed, grunting at the force. I straddle him and bite my lip as I grind my wet pussy along his cock.

He's looking at me in awe, the hunger in his eyes matching how I feel. "How do you want me, Noah?" With the guys, I know he lets them take control. But this is his chance to be the one in charge, if he wants. Although, the idea of being the one in charge for once sounds like a hell of a good time for me.

Something we have in common is I'm normally the one to follow what my guys do.

"Any way you'll have me." He gasps as the tip of his cock pushes inside me before I pull back.

"Perfect," I purr, lifting my ass up enough to reach between us to grab his cock. His shaft is already drenched in my juices as I line his cock up with my entrance, so when I sink down all the way, he slides in with ease.

"Yes!" I cry as he fills me up, his cock stretching me so damn good.

"Abby," he grunts, his hands gripping my thighs. "Fuck, baby, you're so wet."

"I need you, Noah," I pant out as I start to rock my hips. Grabbing his hands, I pin them over his head and hold them there. I ride him, our eyes locked together as I bring us both to new heights.

I love watching him surrender to me, his pupils black with lust, his lips part as he pants, and when I start to fuck him harder, faster, his eyes roll back as a sexy as sin moan leaves his plump lips.

"That's it, Noah, take it. Lay there and fucking take it." I moan as my breasts bounce with every thrust of my hips. I love this position. Not only does it feel amazing, but I feel powerful. The way Noah is looking at me makes me feel sexy and loved.

"So fucking hot," he whimpers as an orgasm creeps up on me. I don't want to cum, not yet, so I sit up and lean back, the new position making me moan as I dig my nails into his muscled thighs.

"Touch me," I beg. "Play with my clit, Noah. I want to feel your hands on me." He does as he's told, pressing his thumb against my clit, working it in firm, slow circles. "Yes!" I shout. "Oh! Fuck yes, Noah," I whimper as the orgasm starts to build again. This time with his cock hitting me in my sweet spot and the work of his thumb, I let it wash over me.

I scream his name as the pleasure becomes too much, making me crumble in on myself. I slump forward over him, my pussy locking around his cock as I cum hard.

Noah wraps his arms around me, holding me tightly through my release as he fucks up into me. My body feels like it's on fire in all the best ways.

Thankfully, Noah takes over and flips us both. He starts to pound into me, a look of determination on his face.

"I love you, Abby," he grunts as I cling to him, another orgasm already building. Or maybe the first one hasn't even ended.

"Fuck, fuck, Noah!" I sob. I need to say it now before this is over. I want to feel him cum inside me as we make things official. "I, Abigail– Oh, fuck!" I sob as he hits my sweet spot. "Morningstar." I'm panting like crazy, my mind fuzzy as the bond hums to life. It feels like I'm being shocked with little bolts of electricity. "Accept you, Noah, as my mate."

Noah growls, his eyes wild, pupils so blown his eyes look black. "I, Noah," he grunts, slowing his thrusts to long, deep motions. "Take you, Abigail Morningstar, to be my mate."

And just like that, the bond explodes. It feels like fireworks going off as we both suck in a gasp, followed by Noah's roar and my scream as we both find our release.

His cock jerks inside me violently, filling me with rope after rope of hot cum. The sound of him coming undone for me is one of the hottest things I've ever heard.

I smile like I'm drunk, eyes closing as he peppers kisses all over my face, my chest, my breasts while murmuring how much he loves me, how happy he is.

I feel the same way, but I'm too wrung out to speak, like everything short circuits my brain.

Noah flips us again so that I'm on top, his cock still buried deep inside me. He holds me tight, like he never wants to let me go.

"I don't ever wanna leave," I murmur as he plays with my hair. Looking up, I grin as I see his new mate mark on his neck. It looks good on him.

"I know, me too." He chuckles, kissing my forehead. "But we have mates who would be very sad if we didn't go back."

"I know," I sigh dramatically, making him chuckle again. "Good thing we love them."

"Yes, a very good thing, but they love us too."

"Noah?"

"Yes, love?"

"We're going to be okay." I sigh. "Me, you, Luke, and Isaac we're going to be okay."

Noah makes a choked sound as he pulls me tighter. "Thank you," is all he whispers. It's the last thing said before sleep finds me, bringing me into a dream just as sweet as reality.

CHAPTER TWENTY

ABBY

"There she is!" Leo greets me as I walk through the front door of the house.

With a big smile on my face, I drop my bags and run over to him. He laughs, catching me as I jump into his arms while he spins us around. "I missed you." I manage to get in quickly before his lips are crashing against mine.

"Don't hog her." Zed pulls Leo off me and takes his place. I sigh happily into his kiss as I'm surrounded by their familiar scents and the buzz of our bond.

After they let me come up for air, I look to see where Noah went because he was right behind me when I came into the house. A soft smile finds my lips as I see him greeting Luke and Isaac with their own kisses.

"So, how was it?" Luke asks, striding over to me with a big grin on his face.

"Amazing." I lean back in Zed's arms as Luke steps into me. He gives me that cocky, sexy smirk before giving me a kiss of my own. It's something I'm not used to but love every time. It's an adjustment adding the guys on as my mates, but it's going better than I thought.

Luke breaks the kiss, bringing his lips to my ear. "I'll get Noah to tell me all the juicy details while I'm balls deep in him later."

I whimper, the image of the two of them filling my belly with heat.

"Don't get our girl all worked up. She just got home, I don't think she wants to be bombarded with cocks." Zed chuckles.

"I mean...." I tilt my head back with a grin.

"Cheeky Little Bird, you are," Zed growls, nipping at my nose and making me giggle.

"Abby, love, I'm going to go put our stuff away, okay?" Noah comes over and I step away from Zed to let Noah kiss me. "I love you," he whispers loud enough for just me to hear.

I bite my lip, grinning as butterflies fill my belly. I'm glad, so damn glad, that this is all working out in the end. Because each of these guys are perfect for me in their own way.

Leaning up on my tip toes, I bring my lips to Noah's ear. "I love you too," I whisper back before taking his ear lobe into my mouth, giving it a little suck and nibble, making him groan.

He steps away from me, heat in his eyes before turning back to the bags. I don't miss the bulge in his pants as he carries the stuff out of the room.

I find Isaac watching Noah and Luke leave with an amused look on his face.

"Little Bird," Zed murmurs, getting my attention. "How about you spend the night with those three."

"Are you sure?" I ask, turning to look at Leo and Zed.

"I think they need some Abby-loving." Leo grins. "You should have seen the two of them without you guys, and it was only for two days. Pouting like big babies."

"Really?" I laugh.

"Oh, yeah." Zed chuckles. "Isaac was all broody and Luke was all *'I miss them'* and *'when are they coming home?'* They are lost without the two of you."

I look over to see Isaac still standing there awkwardly. He looks at Zed for a moment, and when Zed gives him a nod, Isaac comes over.

"Ah, I was wondering if you wanted to watch a movie with me and the guys tonight? If not, it's cool, I get it. You just got—"

"I'd love to," I interrupt his adorable rambling.

"Oh." He blinks at me. "Okay, cool."

"Fuck, you're so lame," Zed groans, earning a glare from Isaac.

"Oh, shut up. I heard you just now. You were just as bad at the moping, the both of you." Isaac flips off Zed, and they both chuckle.

Fuck. This, this right here, is what I didn't know I needed. To see the two of them getting along. Tears sting the back of my eyes with how happy I am.

"Come on, Starbright, let's go upstairs and away from this crazy man's ramblings." Leo throws his arm over my shoulder, escorting me up the stairs toward my room.

"You were totally lost without me too, weren't you?" I smirk up at Leo.

"Oh, one hundred percent." He grins down at me. "You're our world, Starbright. Without you, what's the point?"

"Ugh." I poke him in the side. "You're being all cute and shit. Stooooop."

"Never!" he shouts when we get to the top of the stairs before hiking me over his shoulder.

"Leo!" I burst into laughter as he takes me up the second set of stairs.

"Enough out of you, woman!" He slaps my ass making me yelp. "I need me some Abby-loving before sending you away for the night to your other boyfriends."

"Such a drama queen." I giggle. He bursts into my room and tosses me onto the bed. "What are you doing?!" I laugh as he starts to pull my clothes off.

He pauses. "Are your ears not working?" He narrows his eyes. "I said, I need some Abby-loving. And I'd like that to be with you naked and my cock inside you."

"Oh," I breathe, liking the idea of that. I let him take my clothes off, and the moment my pussy is bare to him, he's diving between my legs.

A minute later, Zed walks into the room, his eyes growing dark with hunger as he takes us in. Grabbing the door, he slams it closed behind him and starts to take his clothes off too.

Well, shit... this is a welcome home I could get used to.

"I was wondering if you changed your mind." Isaac chuckles as I step off the bottom step of the stairs leading into the basement. Since finding out all of them are my mates, they've been spending more time down here together, rather than separately in their own rooms.

While I'm glad they're open with their love now and don't feel like they need to hide it, I'm a little jealous. Not because of their love, but because I want to spend time and be with them too.

So when Isaac asked me to hang out with them tonight, I jumped at the chance.

"Sorry." I have no shame as all three of them look at me over their shoulders from where they're sitting on the couch. "Got a little busy."

"Because my brother was balls deep inside you?" Isaac grins, raising a brow. He seems to be in a better mood today. It's like he's a little more like himself, minus the asshole part.

"Maybe." I grin playfully. "What can I say? He's got a big dick and knows how to use it."

"I bet he does." Luke grins. "One day we need to all have some group fun so I can see it up close and per–" Isaac slaps Luke upside the head. "Hey!"

"Stop talking about wanting to see my brother's dick," Isaac growls.

"Are you jealous, baby?" Luke teases him. "Don't worry, I love your cock."

Rounding the couch, I sit down in Noah's lap and bring my legs up to lie across Luke's lap. "I've seen your dick, Isaac, and let's just say, I can tell you're related." I smirk, loving the way his jaw slacks.

"Nice!" Luke chuckles, raising his hand for a high five, and I, of course, give him one, proud of our men's cocks.

"Ah..." Isaac clears this throat. "Well, then. That's something I didn't want to know about my brother."

I just shrug my shoulders and snuggle into Noah, grinning at Isaac. He watches as Noah wraps his arms around me, kissing the top of my head, then how Luke rubs his hands up and down my shins.

Giving me a little smirk of his own, Isaac grabs my feet and starts to rub them. My eyes fall shut, and I moan at how amazing it feels. Being with all of them like this feels natural. I love it. Who knew this would be my life?

"Alright, let's start this movie before this turns into a fuck fest." Luke chuckles. I can feel his cock harden under my legs.

"Fine," I sigh. "Not that I would mind, though."

"Soon, Spawny, soon," Luke promises. I look at Isaac and wink. The dark promise in his eyes has me turned on.

This time, I do end up watching most of the movie. But of course, I fall asleep before it's over. I wake again when I feel someone put me down in a bed.

"You think she will be mad if she wakes up next to all of us?" Isaac whispers. I hear the rustling of clothes and then the bed dips.

"No. Why would she? She's already fucked two of us and cemented the bond," Luke says, sounding close as he snuggles next to me.

"Okay, let me rephrase the question. Will she be pissed that I'm in the bed?" Isaac growls.

"Babe, get in bed. She's not going to be mad. She wants you too. I know she does. Just, give it time, remember?" Noah encourages, voice soft as he takes my other side.

"I know," Isaac sighs. I feel fingers brush my hair out of my face. "I hate how I treated her. I wanted her so fucking bad from the moment I saw her but was blinded by unwarranted hate."

"She understands now, Isaac. She's an amazing person. She's not going to hold it against you."

"She should; I was horrible to her. I hated it too. Every night, I'd hate myself for anything mean or rude I said or did to her that day. Yet, I still woke up and did it all over again." He moves his hand, and I miss the warmth of his touch. "I'm fucked in the head, and she deserves better than me. I'll only drag her down."

"I mean this with all my love, shut the fuck up!" Luke growls. "We love you for who you are. You were dealt a shitty hand, and it fucked with you for a while. It wasn't your fault. But you realized your mistakes and you're changing to be a better person. That's what matters. We see it, and I know she does too. So stop talking negatively about the man we love— our mate—before we kick your ass. Now get in this fucking bed and cuddle with us, damn it."

The room is silent, and I want to open my eyes to see how Isaac is taking this, but I don't. The bed dips, and my heart rate settles.

"I love you," Isaac whispers.

Noah and Luke say it back.

We all drift off to sleep, wrapped in each other's embrace. I'm overwhelmed with the feeling, so much love between the three of them, the bond is going wild, and I know they can feel it too. But no one says anything and just enjoys the moment.

We have no idea what tomorrow will bring, so right now I'll take all the time with the three of them I can get and hope I get more in the future.

CHAPTER TWENTY-ONE

ZED

"Why is he here?" Abby asks, pacing back and forth. We're getting ready to have a quiet evening in for New Years, wanting to take it easy for the night because this holiday has been crazy for all of us in some kind of way.

But then dear-old-deadbeat-sperm-donor thought it would be fun to crash our evening. Odd thing is, he's here alone. No Veronica, Raphael, or Gabriel.

I hate seeing my Little Bird stressed. I know she's only like this because she's worried about Michael starting shit with Isaac.

Looking over at my brother sitting on the edge of Abby's bed, Noah, and Luke at his side, I see him trying to hold himself together, but I know being around Michael makes him uneasy, rightfully so.

"This is technically his house," Isaac points out.

Abby stops pacing and shoots him a glare. "So? No one wants him here. Hell, his own wife doesn't even live here. He should just stay in Heaven or wherever the fuck he goes to when he's not here."

"Let's not let him ruin our night," Leo tries to soothe, pulling Abby into his embrace. She sighs, but gives in, wrapping her arms around him. "We can just go outside like we planned to, put some music on, and have a few drinks before going swimming. I'm sure he won't come outside."

"I don't want him here," Abby murmurs against his chest.

I haven't told them what I have on video. I didn't mean to keep it to myself, but with the craziness of Christmas and what Abby's mom told me, I didn't know how to go about it.

But this would be a good time to follow through with my plan. "I'll be right back, baby," I tell Abby, kissing her on the side of her head.

"Where are you going?" she asks, peeking her head up to look at me.

"Going to tell him to leave." I grin with a wink.

"Zed..." she says my name like she's not sure I should go.

"Don't worry, Little Bird. He won't try shit with me. He knows he can't bully me."

"I don't trust him. He might try something." I hate the concerned look in her eyes, but I love that she cares just as hard for us as we do for her. I lean over and kiss her softly on the lips, licking her taste off of mine when we pull apart.

"I'll be fine, baby. Stay here, it won't take me long."

"Zed, you don't have to. We can just ignore him," Isaac adds.

"No." I give him a hard look. "He's not ruining our night, and we are not going into the new year with this asshole lingering around like a bad fucking smell."

I turn and leave, not giving anyone else a chance to voice their opinion.

I hate this man and not because he broke my mom's heart or left me without a father; no, I fucking thanked him for leaving. It's because he brought a child into this world and instead of loving and protecting him, he abused him. He did fucked up shit to his own son, beat his wife. While the fucking world thinks he's some sort of saint. He taught the people on this island that the Devil was evil, but the only evil person I see is him.

No more. I won't let him hurt the people I love anymore.

Not bothering to knock, I swing his office door open, finding him on the phone. "I'll call you back," he rushes out to whoever he's talking to before looking over at me, a death glare in his eyes. He hangs up. "What do you want?" he spits.

"Who was that, Pops? Was that your little fuck muffin?"

"What are you talking about?" He narrows his eyes.

"Hold up." I raise a finger, reaching for my phone. "I'll show you, maybe it will jog your memory."

I find the video and turn the volume up as high as it will go before pressing play and turning it so that he can see it.

The sounds of raunchy sex fill the air, and Michael is up out of his seat in a flash. "Where the hell did you get that?"

"Oh, I had front row seats to this show." I chuckle. He reaches for my phone, but I pull it away. "Doesn't matter if you take my phone, I have it uploaded to so many places you won't be able to find them all. They're just sitting there, waiting for me to show the world just how much of a sad fucking excuse for an Archangel you really are. I wonder what the Pure Bloods would say? Or maybe even God?"

"You stupid little boy," he snarls, stepping closer to me. "You don't wanna fuck with me, trust me!"

"I'm not afraid of you." I laugh. "Here's how this is going to go. You're going to leave this house tonight and never come back again. No one wants you here. Take whatever is important and leave. If you don't, I'll send this video to every single person on this island. I'm sure it will get back to God eventually."

"I should have made your mother get an abortion." He gives me a disgusted look.

"Ahh, doesn't that go against what you preach?" I raise a brow.

"Fuck you," he spits.

"So, we have a deal? Oh, and you're going to divorce Veronica."

"The hell I will!" He balls his hands into fists, and I know he really wants to hit me right now, but he's not as stupid as he looks, he won't risk it. What people think of him means too much. Gotta keep the reputation pure. "Fine, you want me to leave your pathetic excuse of a brother alone? Done. He's nothing but a joke. Both of you are. But what makes you think I'm going to leave my wife?"

"Because you're nothing but a narcissistic asshole who gets off on abusing people to make yourself feel like some kind of god." I snort, shaking my head. He doesn't like that comment, his face turning an ugly shade of red. "You're going to do it. You're going to leave, never come back and never go near Isaac or Veronica again. Because I will release that video, and you know it."

His jaw ticks, and I know he's holding back on wanting to do to me what he's done to Isaac. "This isn't over. I'll leave, but you will regret messing with me."

"Yeah, yeah. Come on, old man, pack your shit and get the fuck out." I wave my hand.

He bitches the whole time, calling me all the lovely names

in the book as he grabs what he can out of his desk and around the room.

"I hate you," he states, pausing before he leaves. "I wish you were never born. But the biggest joke was having your mom as my mate."

"That's okay." I grin. "You're not her only mate."

His face drops. "What the hell are you talking about?"

"Funny you mention Hell. Turns out, the man you hate the most in the world, more than your son's mate, is also her mate."

Yup, there goes that vein in his forehead, it popped. And like a toddler throwing a tantrum, he yells his way down the hall. I follow after, a shit eating grin on my face the whole time.

Isaac and the others step out of Abby's room, and Michael stops. "You're dead to me," Michael sneers.

"Same goes for you," Isaac replies, but I see the pain in his eyes. Makes me want to fucking push this asshole down the stairs. Sadly, he won't break his neck if I did, but it would be funny to watch.

Michael scoffs, shaking his head. "Such a waste."

"Get fucked, you sack of shit!" Abby yells from behind the guys.

"Stupid whore!" Michael calls back. "Your mother was right to leave you with your monster of a father."

Fuck it. I lift my foot and with all my force shove it into Michael's back. He jolts, his hands flying out to catch himself, but he doesn't have enough time and goes head first down the stairs, his stuff tumbling down after him.

"Fuck, that was gold," Frankie cackles.

I grin over at her. "Worth it." We high five before turning back to the others. The door slams shut a second later.

"How did you get him to leave?" Isaac asks.

Pulling out my phone, I show him and everyone else the video.

"Eww. No, gross, stop!" Abby shouts, covering her eyes. "Warn a girl next time."

"Sorry, Little Bird." I chuckle.

"How long have you had that?" Abby asks, peeking through her fingers.

"Christmas," I grimace.

"Zed!" she shouts.

"I know, baby, I'm sorry. I was going to show you all sooner; I wasn't meaning to keep it a secret, but with everything going on, it really did slip my mind."

"Fine." She glares at me. "So, what? You used this video to blackmail him?"

"Yup." I smirk.

"Isaac, don't hate me, but your brother is really turning me on right now." Luke chuckles. "That's so genius, it's making my cock hard."

"Here, watch this," Noah says, showing him the video.

"And now it's soft as a cookie. Thanks." Luke looks ready to puke.

"You're welcome." Noah grins with a chuckle.

"So... he's really gone? He won't come back?" Isaac asks.

"Nope. Not if he wants to keep his perfect reputation." I wink. "Oof." Isaac practically tackles me in a hug. My eyes widen as I'm taken by surprise.

"Thank you." Isaac sighs, his voice thick with emotions.

"Yeah..." I wrap my arms around him, meeting Abby's watery stare and happy smile. "You're my brother."

Abby mouths *I love you,* and I grin.

This Isaac isn't the cocky fucker I met before. I know that part of him is still there under all the hurt and pain. After he heals, he'll find himself again.

199

I'm glad we have this second chance at being brothers. At being there for one another. I hate that the reason why we weren't was because of the man who should have been there for the both of us; but in the end, he didn't care about anyone but himself.

It's no loss to me, but I know Isaac had some good moments with him, and even though Michael is a monster I know he's going to miss those.

We will give him his own good memories to replace the bad ones. Memories that are made by people who are not toxic or harmful, but who love him and have his back.

ISAAC

I know Zed said he was gone. I watched him leave with my own eyes. But I can't help but think that it's all too good to be true.

"Isaac?" Zed's voice pulls me out of my thoughts. I look over at my brother. I still can't believe he did what he did. *For me.* I hated him for a very long time. More than I thought I hated Abby. He was the son of my father's mate. I used to think that my dad would regret leaving Megan and go back to her and his first son, and leave me behind.

But now I know, Zed is not the enemy; the man who helped make us is. I like Zed, he's a good man, a good mate, and after seeing who he really is, there's just no way I can hate him.

"Yeah?" I ask, my attention only on him for a few seconds before finding Abby again.

"Go to her. Be her midnight kiss."

"What?" My head snaps over to him. "Why?"

"Because she's your mate. You're crazy about her, and you look like a love sick puppy watching her over there. Or a creeper, both would work." He grins with amusement.

"I am not," I mutter, but prove his point by finding Abby again. She's sideways in Luke's arms as they cuddle on a lawn chair. Her legs on Leo's lap, who's sitting in a chair next to them.

Noah is on Luke's other side, playing with his blond locks as Abby talks to Frankie, who's sitting with Libby and her mate.

Abby looks good enough to eat in that bikini. I don't want to think with my dick, but it's really hard when you have someone as fucking stunning as her as your mate while being unable to touch her.

"Isaac, I know you don't think you deserve her, but you do. And I know you've been working your ass off doing things for her without her knowing."

"You do?" I narrow my eyes. "How?"

Zed raises a brow. "Really? Do you know how obsessed I am with that girl? I know when she eats, sleeps, and pisses. So, I'd know if there was someone sneaking around, watching her."

"I'm not watching her," I huff. Okay, well, that's a lie. I do watch her any chance I get, but I'm not like his crazy-ass and just watch her sleep. Okay, maybe the other night when she slept in our bed, but that's different.

"Why are you leaving cupcakes at her door when you could be giving them to her yourself? Or doing her laundry? And Frankie told me about the few times she stumbled upon you telling the Heathers to leave Abby alone before they fucked with her. Well, not your Heather, Frankie already warned her to fuck off."

"Okay, fine. Yes, I've been doing all of that. I don't know how to be a good person, Zed. With the guys, we grew up together, we formed this natural flow of a friendship at a young age. I don't have friends outside of them. I don't know how to... *people*. And I don't know how to properly grovel. Abby isn't the type of person you can buy forgiveness for, she wants actions of chance, but I don't know how to do that."

"I think you're doing a good job as it is. She told me about how you stopped her in the hallway that one time. Be more like that."

"What? That was a moment of weakness, I was sure I had lost points when it came to her."

"Nah." He chuckles. "I just know her pussy was wet for you."

"You're weird, you know that?"

"Yeah." He shrugs, taking a drag of his smoke. "But being normal is boring. Now, stop looking like a little bitch and go talk to our girl. Get a little tongue action when the clock strikes midnight." He grins before turning around and heading inside the house.

Abby leaves the guys and heads over to the hot tub. I see them getting up to join her, but when they look at me, I shake my head, and they sit back down. Luke gives me a shit eating grin, followed by him raising his fingers up into a V and flicking his tongue between it. I glare at him, flipping him off.

But Noah gives me a soft encouraging smile. *I love them.*

"Hey," I say as I slip into the hot tub, trying to ignore the way my heart is pounding in my chest. God, I feel like some kind of virgin when I'm around her.

"Hey." She grins. "So, have you finally grown a pair?"

"What?" I furrow my brows.

"Isaac, let's stop playing games." She slides over to me, and I'm fucking shocked when she straddles my lap. I look up at her stunned. Is she drunk? I know she had a few, but I don't think she is. "You're my mate."

"Yes." I nod slowly.

"You want me."

I blink. "More than you will ever know."

She gives me a smirk. "And I want you."

"Hold up, what?" I know she agreed to starting over, but I've been keeping my distance for the most part, so she can have time with Luke and Noah. Since when does she want me?

She rolls her eyes. "I know this might be hard to believe. What you did was fucked up, it hurt me, it really fucking hurt me. But that's the past. There were underlying things that contributed to your asshole ways. But I'm not going to hold it against you because I've seen the change in you. I see how much you love Luke and Noah. I see the amazing person you truly are when you're with them."

"And you," I add, swallowing hard.

"And me what?"

"You make me want to be a better person."

She smiles at me, brushing some of my wet hair out of my face. Fuck, having her touch me, sitting on me like this, it's like I was handed the damn moon. "I remember what you said to me at school. I need you too. It's just taken me a little longer to see it. We said we would start over, but you've been holding back. No more, okay?"

"Fuck, Abby." I close my eyes, taking a deep breath. "You say no holding back, but I don't think you understand what that means for me."

"Then tell me."

Opening my eyes, I stare into her bright blue ones. "I want to touch you, like all the damn time."

"Okay." She smirks, and my brows raise.

"I have a lot more in common with my brother than you might think." Not wanting to flat out say I'm ready to stalk her, to be glued to her side, killing anyone who looks at her funny, and freak her out.

She leans in, brushing her lips against my ear. "I don't see any issues with you having anything in common with Zed. I love how he is with me." She sucks my ear lobe into her mouth, and I almost cum in this damn hot tub. "I like the growly, I like the dominant. I like to be put in my place in the bedroom."

"Fuck," I hiss as I tighten my hold on her hips.

"But nothing happens until our date." She pulls back.

"What do you mean? What date?"

Her brows rise. "Oh, don't think you're getting off easy. Your boys wined and dined me. Now it's your turn. Make it good, and just maybe I'll make it worth your while. Oh, and Happy New Year." She kisses me, her soft mouth pressing against mine. I groan and part my lips, letting her tongue slip in and over mine. But the kiss is over way too fucking soon for my liking when she pulls back. "That one's a freebie. No more until our date night." She winks before climbing off me, leaving me with the biggest case of blue balls known to man—and angel—kind.

Date. I should have known. It's not that I didn't want to take her out, it's that I didn't know if she would want me to.

And what a fucking way to go into the new year.

Alright then, I guess I'm planning a night she won't forget.

CHAPTER TWENTY-TWO

ABBY

"Do you think your dad still needs me to be here?" Frankie asks me as we meet up between classes.

"What do you mean?" I look up at her. She's so damn sexy. My fingers itch to reach up and touch her bright hair. But I can't, that would be weird, right?

"Well, Michael is gone, and I don't think he's coming back anytime soon. So I don't really have anything to report back to him. Did the guys even find out what Michael's been doing?"

"No," I sigh. "Luke and Noah are going to try to find some time to talk to their dads and see if they will tell them anything since the four of them are on good terms."

"Turns out, I'm not a fan of school." Frankie chuckles.

"Wait, if you're no longer needed here, then he's going to send you back, right?" My question comes out in a bit of a panic. The idea of her leaving, not being able to see her, makes my stomach drop.

"I mean, maybe?" She sounds like she hasn't thought that far ahead.

"So what, you're just going to come here, get Zed's hopes all up, make friends with me, and then just leave?!" I don't mean to raise my voice, but I'm starting to spiral with no idea as to why.

"Hey, Abby, it's okay."

"No, it's not! You can't just make people care about you and then leave!" Tears sting my eyes as I turn away from her and take off down the hallway.

I'm not one to let emotions get the better of me, but when it comes to Frankie, I don't know how to think, how to feel.

I'm not stupid, I know I have feelings for her. At first, I thought it might just be attraction, but the more time I spend with her, the less I feel like we're friends and the harder I fall.

What would the guys think? Would they think I'm selfish for wanting someone else when I already have the five of them?

I leave the building and go to the one place on campus I feel like I can breathe. My feet lead me to the pond in the garden.

But when I go to the bench, I find it's not empty.

"Hey." I stop in front of the bench. Isaac looks up at me.

"Hey." He smiles. "What are you doing here?" His brows furrow when he sees my face. He jumps to his feet, saying, "You've been crying."

"I have?" I whisper, my hands reaching up to feel my wet cheeks. "Oh."

"What's wrong?" he growls, crowding me as he cups my face. "Who do I have to kill?"

That makes me laugh. "No one." I sniff as he wipes my eyes. "I'm just being overly emotional."

"Why do you say that?"

Letting my head fall to Isaac's chest, I wrap my arms around his middle, needing a hug.

He seems stunned for a moment, but then he wraps his arms around me, holding me tight. I like this Isaac, and I'd like to see this side of him more often.

"Because I should be focused on Luke, Noah, and... and you. But here I am, falling for yet another person." I let out a humorless laugh, tears springing to my eyes again.

"Is it Frankie?" He rubs his hand up and down my back, kissing the top of my head.

"How do you know?" I murmur into his chest.

He lets out a little chuckle. "Abby, Angel, it's kind of hard not to notice with the way the two of you look at one another when the other isn't paying attention."

"Doesn't that upset you?" I lean back to look at him, wiping my eyes with the back of my hand.

"No." He raises a brow, a small smirk quirks on his lips. "Why should it?"

"Because I have five mates, I shouldn't be feeling something for someone else."

He shakes his head. "Doesn't work like that, babe. Sometimes you can't help who you like."

"But she's not my mate. It's different."

"It really isn't." He runs his thumb over my lower lip, making me shiver.

"She's Zed's best friend. What if he gets mad?"

"He won't." Isaac laughs. "That man loves you more than anything in this world. All he wants is to see you happy. If he's willing to let us explore things, then Angel, Frankie will have his support. And Leo's too."

"What about you and the others? I don't want any of you to

think you're not enough, because all of you are, but I can't ignore the way Frankie makes me feel."

"You support our love, and we will do the same for you, and whoever you choose to be with. We just want some of that love, you know." He kisses me on the nose, and fuck, he's right; he is a lot like his brother, but his own person too. Both sure do know how to make me swoon and get me all hot and bothered too.

"Thank you." I hate that I'm getting so choked up right now, but between my freak out with Frankie and Isaac's change in... well, everything, it's a lot to take in.

"For what?"

"For not hating me anymore. For wanting to change and be a better man for me." I let out a little sob, my emotions opening like a dam. "I wanted you when I shouldn't have. It hurt so fucking much. I thought I'd have to live with the pain for rejecting you for the rest of my life. I regretted it, then hated myself for feeling that way."

"Shhh." Isaac grabs the back of my head, pulling me against his chest and holding me tight. "Hating you was the hardest thing I've ever done, but Abby, loving you is the easiest."

I don't say anything, just break down in his arms. I feel his words ringing true as he holds me. I stay there, letting everything out.

"It's okay to not be okay," he murmurs against the top of my head.

"That goes for you too," my voice cracks as I look up at him with bleary eyes.

"Even when I'm not okay, I know I will be because I have you, Luke, and Noah."

"You do," I promise him. Something inside me is healing. I

don't want to hold onto the pain of the past. I want to move on. I have no control in who my mates are, but I can choose how to deal with it. People change and grow from the mistakes in their past. I see that in Isaac.

"So, about Frankie?" he smirks. I groan. "She doesn't like me, but I can't blame her. I don't like me very much right now, either. But I think she's good for you."

"Really?"

"You need someone to help you escape all this testosterone, and I think she was meant to be the person to keep you from going crazy with the lot of us."

I laugh, wiping my nose. "I'm gross."

"A little." He grins.

I slap him on the chest with a laugh. "I think I should get back. I missed most of class, but it's lunch soon so I'm going to find Frankie and apologize."

"Talk to her. See where she stands with everything. I can't speak for her, but anyone with eyes can see she wants you. And if she doesn't, then she sucks and would be missing out on something amazing."

"Walk me back?"

"Yeah." He laces his fingers through mine and a giddy feeling takes over me. He's willing to be seen with me, in public, holding hands. My eyes flick up to the feather on his neck, and I smile, a warm feeling washing over me.

Maybe everything will be okay.

"Ah, Angel, I think someone wants to talk to you," Isaac says, stopping us as we get back to the main school building. I look over in the direction that Isaac is to see Frankie standing by the tree. She's watching us, a dark look on her face, but I think it's pointed at Isaac. "See, I told you. Hates me."

"I'll see you later, okay?"

He leans down, his black hair falling over his eyes as he kisses me on the nose. "See you later, Angel. Be a good girl." *Fuck. Why does that get me hot?* I bite my lip, cursing that damn smirk he gives me as he walks away, knowing how much he affects me.

"Hey."

"Dear god, Frankie!" I hiss, jumping as I almost piss myself. I look over to see her standing next to me.

"Sorry." She chuckles.

"Hey." I look up at her, nibbling on my lower lip. "Sorry about earlier. It was wrong of me to freak out on you like that. I was... I was just afraid, I guess. That you would leave."

"You know, if you would have stayed just a liiiittle bit longer," she starts, holding up her pointer finger and thumb with only a sliver of space between them. "I would have told you, that even if I wasn't here at the school on the assignment, I would have fought to stay."

"Really?" I ask hopefully.

"Yes, because I don't wanna leave." She bites her lower lip. "I have some very good reasons to stay."

Relax, Abby, this girl's senses are killer, and she can probably smell how turned on you are right now. And only so much of it can be blamed on Isaac.

"Good, because I don't want you to leave," I sass, putting my hands on my hips.

She grins. "Good, because I don't want to."

We both chuckle. "Then good." I sigh, feeling tired, but I can't go home. So I'll settle for eating. "Wanna go grab food?"

"Yeah, I could eat."

We head inside and walk toward the food court. The whole way there we each catch the other stealing glances. By the time we get where we're going, we each have a big smile on our face.

I'm not ready to tell Frankie how I feel. I think Isaac still needs me to put him first. Until we have that moment we desperately need, I don't want to add another person's feelings into the mix, to have another person I have to take into consideration. Not while I'm still working on another.

But I will. I need to. I just hope when I tell her, I don't get my heart broken again. Because that shit really fucking hurts.

CHAPTER TWENTY-THREE

ISAAC

"Stay up!" I snarl as I try for the tenth time to get these fucking fairy lights to stay up. I feel like an idiot right now, but I know this is something Abby would love. And because of that, I'm getting over myself and doing whatever I can to make her happy.

I'm used to being with the guys. And as much as they enjoy going out and doing things together, they're not into big romantic gestures... I think... *Fuck, are they?* God, I'm a shitty boyfriend and mate. I should ask them if this would be something they would want too.

But this isn't about them right now, it's about Abby. And this is one of her favorite places to come to. I may have stalked her a few times when she would end up here for hours.

She hasn't been here much lately with trying to tend to all her mates. I overheard her talking to Leo about it the other day. After struggling for days on what to do for her, how to top Luke and Noah's dates, I realized it wasn't about that. It was about doing something that would make her happy, no matter how big or small, and that it meant something to me also.

So, here I am in the dark, in the middle of this creepy-ass cemetery setting up fairy lights.

"Take that!" I huff out my victory as I finally get them to stay in place. Switching on the lights, I'm surprised how pretty they make the gazebo look. Looking at my phone, I curse when I see the time. I told Abby to meet me at seven, and it's six fifty-five.

Grabbing the blanket I brought with me, I lay it out in the middle, then grab the pillows and set them around it. After placing the picnic basket on the blanket, I grab the candles. Lighting them, I set them up around the gazebo on its ledge.

"This is romantic enough, right?" I mutter to myself. "She's going to hate it." I groan, running a hand through my hair, pulling at the roots as I second guess myself.

"No, she's not." A soft voice has me spinning around. Abby stands on the gazebo steps, eyes wide as she takes everything in.

My heart sinks into my stomach as I wait for her to say something else. Her eyes glisten in the lights, and I pray it's happy tears.

"Isaac," her voice cracks, eyes meeting mine. "I love it."

Relief floods through me. My hands twitch at my side with the need to touch her. I'm about to go over to her, when she starts to walk over to me. She's in front of me within a few strides. "Thank you," is all she says when she leans up and grabs the back of my head, crashing her lips to mine.

Something inside me snaps. Snarling, I grab her by her thighs and hoist her up into my arms. I slam her back against the pillar, grinding my thickening cock against her pussy.

For a brief moment, I think I went too far, but Abby moans

into my mouth as she rocks against me, grabbing handfuls of my hair and pulling hard.

Fucking hell, this girl drives me insane.

All ideas of this date go out the window, and the only thing I have on my mind is getting her naked and my cock inside her.

I feel like I'm underwater, my lungs about to burst as they scream for air; and Abby, she's the fucking air. She's the only thing right now that can save me.

Cradling the back of her head, we kiss harder, our lips moving faster in a bruising kiss. Her little gasps for air between kisses don't stop her from taking more from me.

"More," she murmurs against my lips as she sucks in air, her lips finding mine again.

A low feral sound rumbles in my chest as I put my weight against her, holding her up, so I can free my hands. Finding the hem of her dress, I pull it up her body. She raises her arms, breaking the kiss long enough for me to pull it off before her lips are back on mine.

"Fucking hell, Abby," I let out a panting snarl. "I need you. Please."

She nods frantically, licking her lips with her eyes wide and wild.

Sexy isn't what I'd call her right now. No, she's fucking stunning. Her hair is a mess, her lipstick smudged... she's fucking perfect.

"Let me help," she says, ripping off her own panties and tossing them to the side.

"That was fucking hot," I growl, needing to taste her lips again. I tongue fuck her mouth as I struggle a little to get my fucking pants off.

Finally, I'm able to get them undone and let them fall to my ankles. I couldn't care less that my ass is on display for any poor soul who could be around right now. No one could tear me away from my girl in this moment.

Gripping Abby's hips, I adjust her so that the tip of my cock pushes against her entrance. I break the kiss, both of us panting heavily, bodies covered in a light sheen of sweat. "Know this, Abby. The moment I'm inside you, you're mine. I won't hold back anymore, I won't throw any more pity parties. You are *my* mate. I will spend every fucking day letting you and the whole damn world know that I'm yours. You, just like Luke and Noah, own me, Abby. My mind, body, and every inch of my broken, tainted soul. It's not much, but it's yours. I'm giving you one last chance to walk away."

She lifts her chin, the fire in her eyes that I fucking love shining bright. "Never." The word is strong and firm. It's also my undoing.

On a savage growl, I thrust forward, making her take every inch of my cock. Her eyes widen, her nails clawing at my back as she screams. "That's it, Angel," I grunt as I start to pound into her. She clings to me, little whimpers and whines escaping her as her cunt strangles my cock, only making me harder. "You're mine. All fucking mine."

"Isaac!" she sobs. Nothing about this is sweet and romantic. Who was I fooling? There's only so much of me I can change, but sex with any of my mates? Yeah, fat fucking chance I can keep myself in check.

The bond is going crazy. It feels like I've been electrocuted, my whole body coming alive.

"Look at you, baby," I grunt, cupping her chin. "Your greedy little cunt is dripping for me, isn't it?"

"Yes," she moans, her eyes falling closed as she holds on for the ride.

"No, open your eyes, Angel. I want to see you when you

shatter in my arms. But don't worry, I'll be here to put you back together."

"Oh fuck!" Her eyes snap open. I'm sure she's drawing blood, the sting of her nails on my shoulders feeling so fucking good.

"So fucking gorgeous. My mate. Mine," I growl as I nearly come apart as she grips me so fucking hard. I can feel her juices dripping down my thighs and god, it's making me feral.

I feel my orgasm creeping up on me, but I don't want this to be over. I could fucking live inside her pussy.

"I-I, Abigail," she gasps out, her eyes lock on mine in an intense stare. My brows furrow, confused with what is happening. "Morningstar. Oh, fuck!" Her eyes close as she arches her back, her nails digging into my shoulders. I can tell she's close as her body trembles against mine. "Rescind... my rejection... to you, Isaac."

Her eyes snap open as she sucks in a breath, her pussy clamping around me as an orgasm rips through her.

She... did she just?

A wave of power hits me, and I'm a goner. "Abby!" I roar, slamming into her one last time before my cock starts to jerk inside her. I cum hard, so fucking hard that I almost drop her. "Fuck, fuck!" My fist beats against the pillar as my jaw clenches so tight that I fear my teeth might break.

"Holy shit," Abby pants out as I tuck my face into her neck. We're both breathing like crazy as we take a moment to recover. That's what I'm telling myself; instead, I'm really hiding the tears in my eyes over the fact that she took it back. I'm no longer rejected, and the relief of that pain alone is enough to make a grown man sob like a fucking baby.

"You didn't have to," I murmur against her neck before kissing it.

"I wanted to," she whispers, her hand finding my hair. She

starts to play with it as I feel her pulse against my lips. "You're not the same man I rejected, Isaac. This one, I have no reason not to want."

"Angel," I growl before biting down on her neck, making her moan.

"I'm not done," her voice cracks, making me pause.

"I, Abigail Morningstar, accept you, Isaac, as my mate."

My eyes close, and I can no longer stop the tears from falling. My heart hurts from beating so hard, but it's also so damn full right now. I take a few deep breaths, getting a hold of myself.

Pulling us away from the pillar, I bring her over to the blanket. Moving the food out of the way, I lay her down.

"I, Isaac, accept you, Abigail Morningstar, as my mate." I groan when I feel a new wave of magic creep into my bones as the bond that already made me feel so much, now consumes me.

"You wanted me to be myself, didn't you, Angel?" I ask her, grinning as I brush the hair from her face.

"Yes." She nods.

"Good, then get on all fours like a good fucking girl."

Her eyes widen, but damn the way she pulls herself off my cock and scrambles to her hands and knees for me, presenting her perfect ass in the air as my cock gets ready for round two.

My hand comes down hard on her ass making her let out a lusty moan. "Dirty little mate." I chuckle, grabbing a handful of her hair and yanking her head back. "My naughty Angel." Gripping her hips, I hold her still as I thrust back into her.

Her eyes roll back as I lean forward, devouring her in a dirty, sloppy kiss before shoving her down, pressing her face into the blanket.

I start to fuck into her with slow deep thrusts. Her pussy

warm and wet for me, I watch my cock pump in and out of her, covered in our mixed release.

A part of me inside her, my cum coating her walls. Mine, fucking mine.

Releasing her hair, I let my hand slowly trail down her back, her body arching with my touch.

"So pretty," I whisper. And then I'm gone again, control out the fucking window. My hands dig into her hips, holding her as I fuck her within an inch of both our lives.

The night is filled with my grunts, growls, and groans mixed with her sobs of pleasure, pleas for more, and whines of it being too much.

"No. You can take it. One more, Angel. Be a good girl and give me one fucking more." My nostrils flare as I feel myself ready to cum again.

"I'm so close. Fuck, Isaac, yes!"

"Play with your clit, Abby. I wanna hear you scream my name." My pelvis snaps against her ass, and I'm mesmerized by the way it bounces.

"Oh, fuuuck," she moans as she starts to play with herself.

Tossing my head back, I close my eyes and revel in this moment. I've never felt this with her. The bond hums happily, love flooding it in waves.

"Isaac!" she sobs. "I'm gonna cum. Oh, fuck. Isaac."

"That's it, let go, Angel," I growl with another slap of her ass, barely hanging on.

"Oh, oh, oh, oh fuck!" she screams. It's not my name, but it's good enough. "I love you. Oh fuck, I love you."

"Fuck!" I snarl, slamming into her and holding her flush to my body as I cum again, almost as hard as before because hearing those words, it does shit to me. I thought I'd never hear her say them.

Once I give her every drop of cum I have in me, I pull out,

watching it flow from her pussy. Using two fingers, I scoop it up the best I can, shoving it back inside her. She whimpers, her core overly sensitive as I pump my fingers in and out of her slowly.

"Isaac," she whimpers. I smirk, removing my fingers and bringing them, covered in my cum, to her lips.

"Be a good girl and clean me up."

Cheeky little thing she is, she smiles lazily up at me and opens her mouth. I slide my fingers in, and she cleans them so well, it's almost erotic.

Then she shocks the fuck out of me as she gets onto shaky arms and turns around. My cock is still hard, covered in our release, and she looks up at me, biting her lower lip before sticking her tongue out and licking my length from root to tip.

She teases me as she takes me fully into her mouth, her tongue swirling around, lapping up our cum. "Fucking hell, Abby," I growl, nostrils flaring as I resist the urge to hold her head down and fuck her mouth. But I can't go for another round. Though I'd never admit this, I wish Leo was here. Fucker was good at keeping my dick hard, at least this time I want it.

She releases my cock with a pop. "So, what's in the basket?" she asks, tilting her head to the side.

I burst into a chuckle. "Fuck, I love you."

She rises to her knees and this is the first time I'm seeing her fully naked body tonight. My eyes go to her tits, her nipples hard and pointed right at me.

"Eyes up here, big boy," she teases in a seductive tone.

I ignore her and lean over, taking one of her nipples into my mouth. She moans as I suck before biting down, making her gasp. I do the same to the other, then pull back with a smug grin. "Lay down, Angel."

She lays down on the blanket, looking like the angel she is as her messy hair falls around her head in a halo.

Butt-ass naked, I get up, my half-hard cock bobbing as I go over to my bag and grab the extra blanket and head back to Abby.

I sit down and pull the blanket over us, then reach over and grab the basket. Leaning back against the pillows, I pull her into my arms.

Everything feels right in the world for the first time... ever, as I feed her the chocolate covered strawberries I packed.

We talk about nothing special, but it means everything to me. Before I know it, we're both drifting off to sleep.

And even though it's outside in the open, I have one of the best sleeps I've ever had.

CHAPTER TWENTY-FOUR

ABBY

"Luke, stop!"

"Just one more," someone chuckles. "Look at them, they're so damn cute."

My eyes blink open. Everything is bright, making me shield my eyes as they adjust. "What's going on?" I groan. Blinking a few times, I realize I'm not in my bed.

"Hey there, sleepy head." Luke gives me a wicked grin as he stands at the edge of the blanket.

"Shit," I hiss, pulling the blanket up to cover my boobs. Isaac mumbles something before pulling me closer into him. "We fell asleep. Zed and Leo must be losing their minds."

"Nah, don't worry. We came looking for you last night and found the two of you fucking like rabbits. Had a feeling you would end up here all night. But seeing how school starts in like a half hour, and you still weren't back, we came looking for you again."

"School!" My eyes widen as I jump to my feet, the

blanket falling to the ground. I'm about to slap my hands over my body to cover up but then remember these are my mates, and they have seen me naked. So, I grab the clothes that Noah is holding out to me, an adorable blush painting his cheeks. "Thanks." I quickly grab my bra and put it on before tossing my school shirt and skirt on. "I need to shower." I cringe, realizing that I have cum dried on my inner thighs.

"I enjoy how you smell." Luke steps closer and tucks his face into my neck, taking a deep inhale and moans.

Arousal spikes through me, but I shake it off and push past him. "I'll be right back." I run over to the groundskeeper's building where I know there's a bathroom. Having a whore's bath isn't my proudest moment, but I don't have time to go home and shower.

Once I'm done, I toss my hair up into a messy bun and head back to the gazebo, finding the guys packing everything up. Isaac looks over at me and grins, giving me a knowing look.

I smile back, my belly heating with the memory of last night. We're official. And I'm so happy I could cry. The pain is gone, not one trace of it left behind. It's like breathing in the crispest, freshest air.

"Morning, Angel," Isaac murmurs as he pulls me into his arms. He kisses me slow and deep, and I melt into his hold.

"As much as I'd like to sit here and watch as the two of you give us a repeat of last night, we need to get going." Luke slaps Isaac's ass, earning himself a low growl. Luke just smirks before stealing his own kiss.

"Come on, Hellcat." Noah chuckles, pulling me into his arms before wrapping one around me and guiding me toward their car. "Did you have a good night?"

"It was amazing," I sigh wistfully.

What Isaac did was sweet and perfect. While the events of

the night were not in order at all, I wouldn't have changed anything.

After he fed me, we just laid there and talked, music playing quietly in the background. It's exactly what we needed. I'm so damn glad to see Isaac more like himself. I hope it sticks.

During the drive to school, Isaac kept looking at me in the rearview mirror and Luke kept making eye-fucking comments.

"Well, I guess I'll see you at lunch," I say to Isaac after giving Luke and Noah a kiss. I turn to leave but Isaac grabs me by my arm and pulls me into his body.

"Where do you think you're going?" he growls before crushing his lips to mine. He kisses me until I'm melting into the floor before pulling back, leaving me a panting mess. "Have a good day, Angel. Be a good girl." He nips my bottom lip before spinning me around and slapping me on the ass.

I'm shocked and dazed as I walk toward Leo and Frankie who are waiting for me inside. Leo has a knowing grin while Frankie looks over at the guys with a stink eye.

"Have a good night?" Leo asks with a chuckle.

"So good," I giggle.

The day has been full of whispers involving me and the guys. It used to bother me, but not anymore. They can judge me all they want, but at the end of the day, I have amazing mates who blow my fucking mind.

I had someone stop me and Frankie between classes to ask me if it was true, if Isaac was also my mate. I said yes, and by the end of the day the whole school knew.

"This school is far more toxic than they want to admit,"

Frankie comments, flipping off a group of people who are staring at us as we walk to my car.

"Yeah, but there's no use letting it bother you. They won't change no matter what you say to them." I roll my eyes as the people gasp.

"Brainwashed, I tell you," Leo states.

"Pretty much," I sigh, slowing my steps when I hear shouting.

By my car are Luke, Isaac, Noah, and all three of the Heathers. My brows furrow as I wonder what is going on. As I get closer, I catch what Isaac is saying.

"Don't fucking test me, Heather," Isaac snarls. "You must be fucking delusional if you think I'm going to just let you get away with this."

"I have no idea what you're talking about," Heather, the nasty bitch who fucked Isaac's dad denies, jutting out her chin.

"Don't play stupid," Noah scoffs.

"Not much playing going on," Luke snickers, and Heather shoots him a death glare.

Isaac pulls out his phone and turns the screen towards her. A second later, sex noises fill the air. Heather's eyes widen in horror as her face pales. "Yeah, I know you fucked my dad. You're so pathetic. You are so desperate to have money and power that when you couldn't have me, you went to my dad? A married man too."

"T-that's a lie. Someone made that. It's not me," she stammers, trying to defend herself.

"Cut the crap." Frankie steps forward. "The person who took this saw it like a live-action, bad porno." Frankie looks to Isaac. "What's going on?"

Luke answers, saying, "We came out here to meet Abby and found these three fucking with her car."

"You're fucking kidding me," Frankie sneers. "I fucking told you if you fucked with her again, I'd do something about it."

"I didn't do anything!" Heather protests, looking like she's seconds away from pissing her pants. Good, this girl needs some fear, maybe she will learn a lesson.

"No. No, you didn't, because I compelled you not to fuck with Abby."

"You did?" I ask. Is it fucked up that it makes me happy she would protect me like that?

Frankie shoots me a look that says she will explain later before looking at the other two Heathers who are standing off to the side like they're ready to bolt any second. "No, you found a way around it by getting these two fools to do it for you."

"Hey!" Luke's old Heather whines.

"What did they do to my car?" I ask Isaac, who looks at me with murder in his eyes. Not toward me, but toward Heather, and fuck, it's a really bad time to be turned on right now.

"She cut your brakes."

I burst out laughing. "You're kidding me, right? What did you think would happen? I'd lose control over my car and crash?"

"Well... yeah," Noah's old Heather admits.

"Shut up, Heather!" the other two both shout at the same time.

"You do know I can't die, right?" I blink at her, then look to the other two. "Any cuts or bruises I'd get would be gone just as fast as I got them."

"See... no harm, no foul," Heather states. "Now delete that clearly edited video, and we'll call it even. We won't mess with Abby anymore."

"Oh, I know you won't." Isaac chuckles "Because no, I won't be deleting this video. And no, it's not edited, and you damn well know it. But what I am going to do is threaten you."

Isaac steps closer to Heather, trapping her against the car. "If you fuck with Abby again, I will end you. If you so much as look her fucking way, I will send this video to everyone, including your parents. I will ruin you. Do you understand me?" His voice is low, lethal, and like I said before, it's a really bad time to be turned on.

"Y-yes." She nods her head quickly. At least this is one smart move, realizing she's not going to be getting out of this.

"Just to make things clear," Isaac looks at the three of us. "None of us ever wanted you. We never planned on marrying you." One of the Heathers goes to open her mouth but Isaac holds up his hand, silencing her. "You never loved us, you just loved the money and power that would have come with marrying us. Do us all a favor, get some self-respect and find someone you actually love, because trust me, money and power doesn't buy happiness. At the end of the day, money won't take away the loneliness. Love is the best way to go. Now get the fuck out of here," he barks, sending the three of them scurrying away.

"I don't like you," Frankie says to Isaac, making us all look at her. "But you earned some brownie points for that one."

Isaac steps up to Frankie, and my heart drops. I really don't want them to fight, but I know they have issues with one another. More so Frankie toward Isaac.

"I know you don't like me. Hell, I don't even like me. But I need you to know this—I'm not going anywhere. That woman, right there," he points to me. "She's mine. She's my mate, and I will fight for her until my last breath. And there's nothing you, or anyone else, can do to stop me."

I watch as a slow grin takes over Frankie's lips. "You are so much like your brother, it's crazy. Alright, Angel Boy, you won me over."

"What?" Isaac looks taken aback.

"Nice to see your balls dropped and you turned into a real man. About damn time." Frankie pats him on the shoulder and turns to me. "Come on, Leo. Since you drove Abby's car to school and it's no longer drivable at the moment, we may as well go get Zed from work and give Abby some alone time with her newly formed mates."

"Alright." Leo chuckles. "Love you, Starbright." Leo kisses me. "Be a good girl."

"She better not be when she's with us." Luke jokes, making me bite my lower lip.

"What was that?" Isaac asks, stunned as we watch Leo and Frankie, two of my best friends, walk away.

"I don't know." I laugh. "So, wanna give me a lift home? I'm going to need to get those brakes fixed."

"Get in, Spawny," Luke says, opening the door to his car, which is next to mine.

I slide in, expecting him to come in after me, only it's Isaac who takes a seat next to me. "No," he says, taking the seatbelt from my hand and tossing it away before grabbing my hips and pulling me into his lap.

"Isaac." I laugh as he wraps his arms around me, holding me tight.

"What?" he murmurs as he tucks his face into my neck. "You said it yourself, we can't die from a car crash. I'll be your seat belt."

He kisses my neck, and my body starts to heat. "You're crazy," I chastise, but snuggle into him deeper.

It's like I can't get enough of his touch, his smell, just... him. And now I'm craving the other two just as much now that our bonds are all connected. Like Isaac was the missing link.

"If loving you makes me crazy, then, babe, all of us belong in a psych ward."

And just like that, my heart explodes.

"I still don't think this is fair," Luke mutters as he takes off his last piece of clothing. All three of them are sitting around the poker table they have in the basement, butt-ass naked.

Only we're not playing poker because I don't know how to play. So I suggested a game I almost never lose at called Seven Up.

It's also a game they've never played, but when I explained how, they were confident that it sounded easy.

Every round someone lost, they had to remove a piece of clothing. Yet here I am, only missing my socks.

"Looks fair to me." I lick my lips, my eyes glued to his cock that is getting harder the longer I stare.

Luke sits down, blocking my view. I pout and look up to find him smirking, giving me a knowing look. I roll my eyes and hand out fresh cards to everyone.

Tonight has been fun. When we got home, Noah cooked steaks on the grill for us. We did a little swimming where I enjoyed watching Noah and Isaac make out while Luke played with me. And by played, I mean finger-fucked me until I came on his hand and got the attention of the two others who were shooting hungry stares our way.

Then we came down here to watch a movie, only none of us wanted to watch the same thing, so we played some video games.

Isaac got pissed off and started to argue with Luke, so I suggested something a little less competitive.

We continue the game, and because I won the last round, I

get to go first. The guys watch as I flip my cards, and then groan as I win. "Winner, winner, chicken dinner."

"That's it," Isaac says, standing up and kicking his chair behind him.

I'm taken by surprise as the other three do the same. I swallow hard as I take in how hard they are.

"What are you doing?" I ask as my three mates look at me like they're hungry, and I'm the thing they want to devour. A thrill spikes through my body as I slowly get up and back away.

"We don't like to lose, Angel," Isaac growls, rounding the table. I keep walking backward, not paying attention to where I'm going, and my back hits the wall. I was too focused on Isaac that I didn't notice Noah and Luke coming at me from my sides.

All three of them box me in against the wall.

"We want what's owed to us," Luke demands, a dark cocky smirk curving on his sinful lips as he leans over me, bracing himself against the wall with one hand.

"And w-what's that?" I ask on a shaky breath.

Luke takes a piece of my hair and twirls it around his finger before giving it a little tug. "Your body."

My breaths come in quick shallow spurts as my body breaks out in a sweat. Heat pools in my lower belly because I know what's about to happen, and fuck, if I'm not thrilled.

"Strip," Isaac gravely instructs, and I shiver in pleasure.

With shaky hands I pull my shirt off over my head, their ravenous eyes watching every move I make. Tossing it to the ground, I take my shorts off next.

"Ah, ah, ah," Luke tuts. "Underwear too."

All three of them turn around and walk to the couch. My eyes fall to their toned asses, and a little groan slips past my lips. Noah and Luke take a seat while Isaac moves the table out of the way before joining them.

I try to calm my breathing as I slowly make my way towards them, reaching behind my back to unclasp my bra.

Letting it drop to the ground, my breasts fall free. All three of them let out low growls, making my nipples pebble.

I feel powerful under their stare, the way they look at me like I'm perfect.

"Stop," Isaac commands, and my steps falter. "Turn around."

"Now take your panties off." I grin, knowing they can't see me. I can play their game. This is going to be fun.

Hooking my thumbs into the waistband, I pull them down over my ass, bending over to step out of them. My ass and pussy are on full display, and I'm rewarded with a string of curses.

"I'm fucking that ass tonight," I hear Luke mutter to the guys, and a thrill runs through me.

"Turn around, Angel," Isaac commands. When I do, my breath hitches because I find all three of them stroking their cocks. These three sexy, powerful men have no idea how gorgeous they look right now. *And they're all mine.*

"On your knees." The look in Isaac's eyes is dark, feral.

I drop to my knees, finding myself wanting to obey every one of their commands.

Luke licks his lips, his chest rising and falling quickly. Noah's cheeks are flushed as he works his hand a little faster.

"No cumming," Isaac tells them. "Save it all for our dirty girl." Fuck. Yes, please!

He looks at me, taking his hand off his cock and placing his arms on the back of the couch behind the guys. He raises his chin. "Crawl to us."

Holy shit. Is he for real? He wants me to crawl to him.

I don't move, and I see a flicker of uncertainty in Isaac's eyes, like maybe he's doubting himself, thinking that he's pushing me too far. He's being himself, but I see the fear of my disapproval shining back at me, and that simply won't do.

Not wanting him to be ashamed of who he is or what he likes, I do what I never thought I'd do for anyone. Me, the princess of Hell, starts to slowly crawl on my fucking hands and knees for my step brother.

Even though I'm down here like this, the way they're looking at me isn't like someone who's beneath them. No, they're looking at me like I'm a fucking Queen.

And Isaac looks like a dark, regal King. They all do. But Isaac... his soul is dark, tainted. But that doesn't make him any less of the man who proved himself to me. *My mate.*

"Such a good girl." Isaac coos as I stop before him. He leans over, cupping my cheek in his hand. My eyes flutter closed, and I lean into his touch, his praise pleasing me. "You look fucking breathtaking on your knees for us, Angel. Are you mine? Ours?"

"Yes." The word slips past my lips on an exhale as my eyes open to look at his striking blue ones.

"Do you want to be our good, dirty little mate for us tonight? Because, baby, we want your body to be ours, to use as we please. We want to touch you, fuck you, and stuff every one of your holes with our cocks, then fill them with our cum. Would you like that?"

"Yes, please," I whimper, my pussy dripping for them now.

"Climb into my lap, Angel. Come sit on my cock," he growls, grabbing a handful of my hair and pulling toward him.

I go eagerly and straddle his lap. "Now, take my cock." I wrap my hand around his stiff length, my hand twitching to stroke him, but not daring to do anything I'm not told to. "Line it up with that tight cunt of yours." I do and bite my lower lip as I wait for his next command. "Now take your fucking throne where you belong."

Fucking hell. I whimper as I sink myself down on his length. Isaac is big, really fucking big. I don't know if I could survive both of them at the same time.

"Fuck," Isaac growls through clenched teeth, his jaw ticking, nostrils flaring. "It's taking everything in me not to flip you over onto this couch and pound into you like a feral fucking beast." I want to tell him to do it, beg him to, but I also know that's not going to happen. Luke and Noah are going to play too.

I don't move as Luke gets up. My eyes are locked with Isaac, neither of us wanting to look away first. Or maybe we just can't, too mesmerized by the other.

It's not until I feel Luke's hand trail down my back that I snap out of this trance. "Lean forward, baby."

I do, molding my body to Isaac's chest as I tuck my face into his neck. His arms come around me, moving us both to a new position, making it easier for Luke.

Isaac moves his hands to my ass cheeks, parting them and giving Luke a view of my tight hole. My heart beats faster. I feel exposed but desired.

"Mine," Luke growls and I gasp when I feel his warm, wet tongue swipe over it. My blood is pounding in my ears as I wait for Luke to do something. Then I feel the blunt tip of his cock against my hole.

"Breathe, Angel, relax and let him in," Isaac whispers, breaking character to make sure I'm okay. And I love him more for it. I nod and let out a deep breath.

Luke pushes forward. Anal isn't new to me, but it's not something I've done often with Leo or Zed. "So fucking tight," Luke grunts. "Fucking perfect."

I focus on my breathing as he inches his way into me fully,

the burn quickly turning to pleasure. I'm used to prep, but there was none. Maybe they're so used to doing this with each other that it didn't cross their minds. But it's alright, I don't mind the little bit of pain, it feels good. I'm grateful he used lube though.

All three of them go still as if they know they fucked up. "Fuck," Isaac hisses.

"Are you okay, Abby?" Luke asks, fear coating his voice.

I feel full, so deliciously full as I adjust to having both of them inside me. "I'm fine," I sigh, kissing Isaac's neck. "I'm good."

"Prep her next time, dickhead," Isaac growls.

"I'm sorry. Fuck. I'm sorry. This is new to me. Shit, I'm sorry."

I move my head to look back at Luke, giving him a dopey smile. "I'm okay, babe. But you know what would be even better?"

"What?" he asks me, eyes wide.

"If you both fucked me until I'm boneless." I sit back a little bit, bracing myself against Isaac's chest and look at Noah, who's kneeling next to us, cock level with my face, watching with concern. "And Noah made me choke on his cock."

"Fucking hell," Luke groans.

"You heard our mate." Isaac chuckles darkly. "Let's give our dirty girl what she wants."

Noah looks down at me with pure love in his eyes. I part my lips, letting my tongue peek out to lick the bead of pre cum from his tip. He groans, thrusting forward, pushing the tip against my lips. I open my mouth, taking him all the way.

"Doesn't she look stunning with our man's cock down her throat?" Isaac asks as I start to bob my head slowly, my tongue memorizing every inch of Noah's fat cock.

"So fucking good," Luke groans as he pulls all the way out

and thrusts back in.

It's like both of them snap at the same time. Isaac grabs my hips, holding me in place as he starts to fuck up into me, while Luke uses one hand to grip the top of my shoulder and the other to shove my head down on Noah's cock. I gag as he hits the back of my throat.

"That's it," Luke pants as he fucks into me. "Take his cock. Fucking choke on it."

My eyes roll back as the three of them use me for their pleasure.

Noah starts to take control, replacing Luke's hand with his own. And in true Noah fashion, he's softer than the other two.

"You're doing so good," Noah pants out, his fingers rubbing the back of my head as he fucks my throat. Saliva is trickling down my chin, over his cock, making a mess that no one cares about.

"I can feel your cock against mine," Isaac grunts, thrusting up.

"Feels good." Luke slaps my ass. "You gotta fuck this ass sometime, babe. She's so fucking tight."

My body is burning, my veins on fire as pleasure fills me to the brim. Reaching between Isaac and myself, I find my clit and whimper around Noah as I play with my swollen bud.

"Oh shit," Noah pants out. "I'm not going to last much longer." His grip on my hair tightens as his hips move faster. I'm struggling to breathe through my nose, so overwhelmed by all the new sensations.

"Angel, you're going to take Noah's cum, aren't you? You're going to be a good girl and take every last drop. I don't want any of it wasted."

I nod, moaning as I move my fingers faster.

"But I don't want you to swallow."

"Fuck, fuck, I'm gonna cum!" Noah shouts, letting out a

groan as the first spurt of salty cum hits my tongue. His cock jerks in my mouth, filling me so much I can feel it dripping from the side. I'm doing my best to listen and resist the urge to swallow, but it's hard.

Noah pulls back, letting his cock fall from my lips. "I love you," he whimpers, kissing my forehead before falling back on the couch, exhausted and spent.

I can't say it back, but I feel it.

Isaac grips my chin, forcing me to look at him. My pussy grips his cock like a vice as he adds pressure to my jaw, forcing me to open my mouth as he opens his. He angles my head down and Noah's cum spills past my lips and onto his tongue. He lets go of my jaw as he closes his mouth and swallows, licking his lips

I'm done for. My orgasm slams into me like a fucking truck as I cum so hard. A scream breaks from my throat so loud my voice cracks as my body locks up.

The guys fuck me harder through my release, unable to hold back anymore. "That's it, baby, gush all over my fucking cock," Isaac growls, his arm holding me in place as he pounds up into me.

"I'm cumming. Fuck, this ass is too damn good," Luke shouts before slamming into me one last time. "Fuck!" he snarls as he cums, spilling himself deep in my ass.

"Looks like it's down to just the two of us, Angel." Isaac chuckles as Luke pulls out of me. He parts my cheeks and groans, watching his cum spill from my hole. I whimper as he takes two fingers and pushes it back inside.

"Your hole looks so fucking good with my cum dripping out of it, baby." Luke kisses my back before taking the couch on Isaac's other side.

Finding whatever strength I have, I sit up. "Ride me, Angel."

Letting my head fall back, I rock my hips and ride his cock. This angle feels so good, hitting me perfectly. I take my time, and I know the guys don't mind, enjoying the show.

But Isaac can only hold off for so long before he takes control again.

Grasping my hips, he starts to rock me faster, leaning forward to take my nipple into his mouth. He sucks on it, the sensation flooding me with pleasure.

"I'm about to cum, Angel. Tell me what you want."

"Touch me," I pant out, feeling another orgasm coming. "Make me cum, then fill me with yours."

He growls as he brings his thumb to my clit and starts to rub. I cry out, almost falling forward. My clit is sensitive, a bundle of exploding nerves.

"Take it, Abby," he grunts. "Take it all."

Gripping my ass tightly with his free hand, he rocks me on his cock faster, harder, as his thumb works me over.

"Isaac!" I cry. "Oh, fuck. It's too much."

"You're doing so fucking good, Angel. You can take a little more."

My wild, frantic eyes meet his as I resist the urge to pull away from the overwhelming feeling and give in. I let go, allowing myself to cum again. This time, it's different. I sob out my release as Isaac growls out his. I squirt all over his cock, soaking his belly and my thighs.

"Holy shit," Isaac groans. "Did my good girl just squirt for me?"

"Yes," I whimper, slumping forward. I'm done for. Angel or not, I can't move. Sex is one thing that's both human and the most inhuman thing at the same time.

"You did so good," Luke murmurs as he kisses the back of my neck. "Noah, clean her up."

I sigh, relaxing into Isaac, waiting for Noah to go grab a wet cloth to clean me up.

But he doesn't. My eyes fly open as I feel a tongue at my asshole. I'm stunned, shocked, and also really turned on again as Noah eats my ass, cleaning me from Luke's cum. Holy shit, these guys are going to kill me.

"Noah's our little cum slut, aren't you, baby?" Luke chuckles. "He loves it."

When Noah's done, Isaac moves and lays me down on the couch. "You did so good, baby." He kisses me as he lifts my legs up and pulls out.

I'm confused as to why he's holding me in this position as I feel his cum dripping out of me. But it doesn't make it to the couch, nope, Noah is between my legs. He growls as he starts to lick my cunt clean of Isaac's cum before devouring my pussy like a starved man.

I cum for the third time on a broken sob, body soaring to new heights, and instead of coming down, I black out.

I wake a few times throughout the night. Once when they worked together to clean me in the shower and then another as we all snuggled in bed.

"She's everything," Isaac mumbles, kissing my forehead. "I'm sorry I'm the reason why this wasn't how things were sooner."

"It's alright. What matters is she's ours now. And we are not doing anything to fuck it up," Noah says.

"She completes us, you know?" Luke adds.

"Yeah. I know." Isaac holds me tighter, like if he lets go I'll be gone.

I don't want to leave them. I don't think I could If I wanted to. They're mine now, and I'm theirs. My mates are where they're supposed to be.

Now, with everything how it should be with them, what the fuck am I going to do about Frankie?

CHAPTER TWENTY-FIVE

FRANKIE

Abby has been really quiet today. She won't look me in the eye, and she's only been giving me one-word answers. *I hate it.* My stomach is in knots thinking that she's mad at me, or maybe now that she's in a good place with all her mates, she doesn't see a use for me, doesn't have time for me.

I know I'm overreacting, and it's not like Abby to be that kind of person, but I'm freaking out.

"Abby." We're at a park near Zed's work, swinging on the swings as we wait for him to get off his shift. There's no kids here right now and the place has been overall empty since we got here. The only sounds are the swing chains squeaking, and my heartbeat pounding in my ears.

"Yeah?" she asks absent-mindedly, not bothering to look at me. It kills me, and now I'm in full blown panic mode. It's like when she freaked out on me and ran away when she thought that if I wasn't here to keep an eye on things for her dad, I'd go

238

back to Hell. But that was never the plan. Lucifer gave me the go ahead to be with Abby, to stay here if she chooses me. Of course, she doesn't know that.

"You're quiet today, and I don't like it. What's wrong?"

"Nothing's wrong," she sighs, lifting her gaze to look out in the distance.

"Are you mad at me? Did I do something to upset you?" We were fine yesterday. Hung out after school, laughed, smiled, and swam until I went home for the night. It's like everything changed overnight.

Her eyes snap to mine. "Mad at you? No, why would I be?"

"Because you won't even look at me." I hate how vulnerable I sound. I've killed hundreds of grown demons with my bare hands yet, this woman—this sexy, smart amazing woman has the power to bring me to my knees, to second guess everything in fear of not having her. Did I just convince myself that she liked me? Was I mistaken in the way she looked at me, the lust, desire and need in her eyes?

I sure as hell smelt it, that can't be mistaken, but was it just a physical attraction?

Her eyes start to water, and I curse myself for saying something. "I'm sorry."

My stomach drops. "Why? What do you have to be sorry for?"

"I don't want to lose you. You're my best friend. I know I have the guys, but with you, it's different. I love what we have."

My heart is beating so fast. Good thing; if it stops, I won't die, but it might feel like it. "Why would you lose me?"

She stops the swing, putting her feet down to the ground. Her hands grip the chains tightly as she closes her eyes and takes a deep breath. "Because if I tell you how I feel about you, and you don't feel the same way, I could risk losing you." Tears slide down her cheeks as a breath gets caught in my thought. "And losing you would put me in a world of pain I thought I'd gotten rid of."

I stand, moving to stand before her. My fingers itch to touch her, but not yet, not until she tells me how she feels. *Come on, Princess, just say the words, and I'll give you the world.* "And how do you feel about me?" I ask, emotion thick in my voice. It's like I have everything I ever wanted within my grasp and all I have to do is reach out and take it.

Her eyes are still closed as she takes in a shuddering breath. In the smallest of whispers that my enhanced hearing allows me to hear, she says, "I'm in love with you."

Who knew that one sentence could bring me so much joy. It's like being handed everything good in the world, the universe, wrapped into one. "Princess," my voice is low and husky as my body hums with the bond, begging me to touch her. She opens her eyes, blinking her bright blue stunning eyes up at me. "I love you too."

Her eyes widen, but I don't give her much time to think as I lean down. At the same time I grip her chin, I place my lips on hers.

She lets out a gasping moan, one hand coming up to grip the back of my hair while the other one grabs my wrist that's holding her chin. The spark explodes inside us, the bond flowing from me to her. Everything clicks into place. She's my mate, and now she knows it. Only thing is, did I just fuck everything up? I should have asked her, but I was just so caught up in the moment; those weeks of being so careful not to touch her, no matter how badly I ached to, just gone.

She kisses me back, standing, so I can wrap my arms around her, pulling her flush to my body. Our lips part, tongues clashing, and it's fucking magnificent.

Abby clings to me, kissing me desperately. The smell of her

blood makes me fucking feral, my fangs aching to drop, to sink into her perfect creamy skin and drink from my mate. Animal blood keeps me going, but the blood of your mate is supposed to be like nothing else.

Holding her tightly to me, I use my speed, bringing her to the tree next to the swings and pushing her up against it.

One of her hands pulls at my hair while the other one grips at my shirt. Her whimpers and moans are music to my ears, but the smell of her soaked pussy has me going wild.

We keep kissing like we're each other's air to live. I grab her ass, slipping my leg between hers. She grinds against my leg, her needy cunt chasing the friction. And I do the same. My pussy pulses, my clit aching as I start to rub against her leg.

My mind is hazy; the only thing I can think about is her blood and making us both cum.

We're frantic as we use each other for our pleasure. Breaking the kiss, I find her neck and start to suck and kiss at her pulse.

"Frankie." Abby lets out a desperate whimper as she continues to rock against me. "Oh, fuck, yes."

I thrust harder, ecstasy filling my veins, the pressure just what I need. I can feel my orgasm race to the surface as Abby urgently chases hers. My fangs pop free, nicking her neck. She hisses as her tangy blood hits my tongue. I feel myself going full vampire as I sink my teeth into her pulse. Abby clings to me as she screams, her release hitting her hard and fast. Mine does too. I let out a savage growl, my eyes rolling back as I suck in mouthfuls of her intoxicating blood, euphoria filling me in waves.

When Abby climbs in my arms, panting as she tries to catch her breath, I pull back, swallowing the last bit and lick my lips.

"I'm so fucking sorry," my voice comes out hoarse as I put

my forehead to hers, dizziness like I've never felt before hits me, but I feel so fucking good right now.

"Don't be," she huffs out a laugh. "That was, fuck, that was amazing. You bit me."

"I know, I'm sorry."

"I liked it. Really liked it. Fuck, I came so hard."

"So did I." I chuckle, pulling back to look at her, to make sure she's okay.

Her eyes are half lidded, cheeks flushed with a bright pink blush. "Frankie?"

"Yes, Princess?" I murmur, smiling so hard. I'm extremely fucking happy.

"We're mates, aren't we?"

"Yes, baby." I steal a soft kiss. "We are. How do you feel about that?"

"Relieved," she sighs. "I don't feel guilty about my feelings anymore. I was hoping this would be how things ended up but didn't want to fill myself with false hope."

"You're not mad? Not overwhelmed?"

"No." She shakes her head, still smiling. "This feels different. I got to know you first, fell for you in my own time. It wasn't out of nowhere with someone I just met, or someone I wasn't in a good place with. It was right."

"Good." I smile harder. "That's what I wanted."

"What?" Her brows furrow.

"I wanted you to get to know me first, to decide if I was someone you wanted to be with. I gave you the time to get into a good place with the guys because I didn't want to spring this on you and add to the pressure you were already under."

"You knew I was your mate?" she asks, a little bit of hurt flashing in her eyes that makes my heart ache "How long?"

I grimace. "A few years."

"What!" she shouts, making me flinch.

"I'm sorry. At first, it was my job. Vampire guards make their job their whole world. And the fact that you're the king of Hell's daughter, I didn't know how that would work. And you had Leo. You looked so happy. You were meant to take over Hell. I was just some worker."

"You're not just some worker, Frankie. You're an amazing person, my best friend... My mate," she whispers the last words, tears in her eyes. "Fuck, I can't believe you're my mate."

"It's the greatest honor I could have ever been given. I wanted you for so long. But you had no idea who I was, and I wasn't allowed to let you know. But I watched over you, made sure you were safe."

"You did?"

I nod. "And then you came up here, and I thought I lost you for good. It hurt, but I just wanted what was best for you. The reason why I knew you were my mate before touching you was because vampires can smell it in their mate's blood. Not being with you would have hurt, but not as much as if I already had a taste of your blood, or if we sparked."

"So, you want me?" she asks, so much hope shining in her eyes.

"More than anything in the world. I love you, Abby."

"I love you too." She throws herself at me, and I hold on to her tightly, everything in the world feeling right, until I open my big fat mouth and ruin everything.

"We wanted to tell you when I came to earth, but you were already dealing with Luke, Isaac, and Noah."

She pulls back, looking up at me. "We?" *Fuck. Shit. Fucking hell.* "Who's *we*?"

I bite my lower lip, her blood still on my tongue. "Zed. He could tell pretty much the moment we met."

"Zed!" Her eyes widen, anger filling them, and I know I really fucked up.

"I asked him not to tell you. I asked him to give us time." I try to reason with her, but... oh shit, her demon is showing. She's pissed. Really pissed.

She pushes past me, her wings bursting from her back. One beautifully black and the other blindingly white. "Abby!" I shout as she takes off into the sky toward Zed's work.

I take off running, dread filling my stomach. *Way to go, Frankie.* Things went from perfect to a shit show with just one word.

Thankfully, with my speed, I make it to the garage at the same time Abby does. Zed looks up from the car he's working on. He smiles brightly; it's filled with so much love it hurts to see as it falls the closer Abby gets. "Little Bird, what's wrong?" His brows furrow as he looks between a frantic me and furious Abby.

"How could you!" Abby shouts. "You told me you weren't going to keep anything else from me. I told you I can handle stuff, that you didn't need to protect me. You lied!"

"No, baby. No, I didn't." He steps toward her, and she steps back, hurt flashing across his face.

"You knew Frankie was my mate. You knew since she came to earth."

His face pales, eyes flicking up to mine then back to her. "We didn't want to overwhelm you. You had so much going on. After everything the guys put you through, only to find out they were your mates. It was a lot. I hated seeing you in pain, it hurt me to see you hurt. Little Bird, I didn't do it to be mean, I just wanted you to have time to breathe before finding out about another mate."

"I get that, Zed. I do, but you can't keep doing this. It's my choice, my feelings, my decision. You can't keep making them for me! I have the right to know these things."

"I know, baby, I know. I'm sorry. I'll stop, I promise. I'll tell you everything from now on." I've never seen my best friend look so distraught as he pleads with his mate. It's hard to watch and fucking hurts.

"I need some space." Abby shakes her head. "A few days to just process everything."

"Little Bird..." The way his voice cracks around her name has my heart cracking right along with it. I never wanted this, I didn't mean to cause any issues. I fucked up, I should have told her. She's right, this is her life, her right to choose. Fuck!

"Just a few days." Abby backs away. "I love you, Zed. I just wish you could see that I don't always need to be protected."

She turns around, launching herself into the air.

"Fuck, no!" Zed is about to take off after her, but I stop him.

"I'll go," I tell him, his watery eyes turning to me.

"I can't lose her, Frankie. She's my everything. I'd rather be dead than lose her."

"You won't. I got her. I promise. Everything will be okay. She just needs time."

"Take care of her."

"Always."

We hug so hard that my bones would be crushed if I wasn't a supernatural. He lets go, giving me one last hopeless look before I take off after our mate. Zed's scream follows behind.

I won't let this ruin us.

CHAPTER TWENTY-SIX

ZED

My mind is a whirlwind of emotions. I'm furious with myself for being so fucking stupid and keeping another thing from Abby. I didn't want to, but my best friend pretty much begged me not to tell her. Her reasoning made sense at the time, but at the end of the day I fucked things up, yet again, because I can't get it out of my head that I need to protect her. I should have said no. I should have told her.

Any thoughts of hurt or pain towards Abby in any way turns me into a fucking caveman. Normally, I don't give a shit, as long as my baby is safe. Only now, she's pissed off at me.

The look of betrayal on her face when she walked towards me at the garage was something I never wanted to see. I caused her to be hurt, I caused her pain.

I fucking hate myself. I want to go to her, to beg her to forgive me, to give her the whole fucking world if it means she never looks at me like that again. But I can't, I'd only make things worse. Frankie has her; she will make her see that I only did it because I love her. I'd never hurt her, at least, not willingly. *Have I loved her too hard that I suffocated her?* I gave her space with Luke, Isaac, and Noah, even though I wanted to wring their necks for the first while. But they love her, I see that. So I stepped back.

It wasn't enough. I should have tried harder to convince Frankie to at least tell Abby that they were mates, to not touch her just yet, that way they could have time.

As I walk to my house, I feel empty. Everything hurts, my heart taking the brunt of it. I've never felt so hopeless, so defeated in my life. I can't lose her.

If anything happened to my mom, or my sister, it would hurt; it would nearly kill me, but I'd get myself together eventually because I'd have Abby to stay strong for.

But if I lose Abby, that would break me and not even my family could get me through that. Like I told Frankie, I'd rather be dead, than be without Abby. Simple as that.

The heel of my hand rubs at my shattered heart as I walk down the path leading to my door.

A heavy thud makes me spin around, hoping that Abby flew back to tell me she forgives me.

Only when I turn around, it's not Abby. "What do you want?" I snarl, not in the mood to deal with this crap today. "I thought I told you if you ever came back, I'd show everyone on this fucking Island what you're really like," I snarl, taking a step towards Michael.

He gives me a cruel laugh, shaking his head. He doesn't look good. His hair is a mess, and his eyes look manic. They're the eyes of a man who has nothing left to lose.

"You're a fool! You think I'd just sit back and let some fucking bastard of a son control me? You're going to give me every copy of that recording."

"Or what?" a booming voice comes from behind me. Right, I forgot my mom texted me, telling me that she and Lucifer were here for a visit to check in on Libby.

"Lucifer," Michael spits. "I shouldn't be surprised to see you here, I guess this is where all the useless wastes of space gravitate to. First, that bitch of a mate of mine, then this mistake we made." He tosses his hand toward me. "And now you. How fitting."

His words about me mean nothing. They don't hurt. But I won't stand by and let him talk about my mother like that.

LEO

"Do you think he's mad at me?" Abby asks, biting on the nail of her thumb as we drive down Zed's street.

"No, Starbright. He's not mad. He's probably worried sick about you."

"I didn't mean to blow up like that, I was just so mad and caught up in the moment."

"I know," Frankie says, wrapping her arm around Abby's shoulder.

When Abby came home, she was in tears. Frankie wasn't far behind. Luke, Noah, and Isaac joined us as I held Abby while she cried and Frankie told us what happened.

She yelled at Frankie too for keeping this from her, and Frankie sat there and took it, knowing she deserved some of Abby's anger.

I knew I had to tell her I knew too. Even if it wasn't as long as they did. After Frankie and I both talked to her about why we didn't say anything, she realized why we did it. And as much as she didn't like being kept in the dark, she understood and wasn't mad anymore.

Then she started to cry again because of how upset she got with Zed. So, here we are, driving to Zed's so Abby can apologize.

"What the fuck?" Luke mutters as we pull up to Zed's house. We park across the street and get out.

"What is he doing here?" Abby growls as we walk across the street.

"Don't you fucking talk about my mom like that!" Zed roars as he steps toward Michael. Megan runs down the stairs and pulls her son back.

"Zed, love, he's not worth it. He's just some sad man who hates to lose. You're better than him."

Michael lets out a booming laugh. "Better than me? You're such a dumb cunt."

"I'm going to fucking kill you," Lucifer says in a low, demonic tone, his eyes going black.

"Stay out of it, Abby." I grab her arm, pulling her back as she takes a step in their direction.

"But..." she looks up at us with anger swarming in her eyes.

"Your dad will handle him," Isaac assures, stepping up next to us. We stand back and watch.

Megan steps back, trying to get Zed to go with her, but he's yelling at Michael alongside Lucifer.

Lucifer bursts into flames, taking a step toward Michael. Fear flashes in his eyes as he takes a step back. Michael's wings pop out and, like the fucking coward he is, he takes off into the air to run away. Only Lucifer isn't letting him go without a fight. His wings emerge, dark as the darkest night, as the flames grow along the feathers before he's fully engulfed and takes off after Michael.

"No, no!" Abby starts to shout.

"He's going to be fine," Isaac says. "Your dad is the devil, he's got this."

"No!" Abby shouts, spinning around with frantic eyes. "You don't get it. The only people who can kill an Archangel is another Archangel or God himself. Yes, my dad is the devil, a fallen angel, but he still is technically an Archangel! If Michael dies, God will bring him back. But if my dad dies? There's no one to bring him back. I'll lose him. I can't lose him."

"If you go up there, Michael could kill you!" Frankie shouts.

There's a big boom in the sky. My eyes snap up, fear blanketing me as the two of them go at it, clashing together as the skies rage above them. Rain falls from the sky in angry fat drops.

The two of them get struck by lightning, sending them crashing to the ground. But that doesn't stop them. They get to their feet. Punches are exchanged, foul words following.

Megan and Zed's shouting gains my attention. They're not yelling at the two holy beings at war, they're shouting at each other.

"Zed!" Megan shouts as Zed storms over to the fighting men.

Everything feels like it slows down as we all stand there, frozen in place unable to do anything or to stop what is about to happen.

Michael pulls his fist back, ready to take another go at Lucifer, only Zed pushes Lucifer out of the way.

Dread fills my body as Zed's eyes widen, Michael's fist embedding itself into Zed's chest. The whole world stops around us, the only one who moves is Michael as he pulls his fist back, taking Zed's heart with him.

"No," Abby whispers.

Michael stumbles back, looking at the bloody heart in his hand with horror in his eyes. He lets go of it, letting it drop to the ground with a thump before taking off into the sky.

Pure disbelief fills me, my eyes snapping over to Zed, eyes still wide, mouth gaped open as he drops to his knees. Abby lets out an agonizing scream as Zed falls back onto the ground.

Dead. Zed is dead.

ABBY

No, no, no. This isn't real. This is some kind of sick and twisted fucked up nightmare. It has to be. This can't be reality, I refuse to believe it.

I watch in horror as Zed drops to the ground, his lips parted, eyes trapped in a moment of terror.

"Zed!" I scream so loud my voice breaks, lungs aching. "No, no, no!" I run over to him, my heart shattering inside my chest. I drop to the ground, practically on top of him and take his cold, wet face into my hands. "Wake up." I brush his black hair out of his face and tap his cheek. "Please, baby, wake up. Come on, it's time to wake up now." My throat is raw, clogged by panic. "I'm sorry, I'm so sorry. Please. I'm not mad at you. I promise. Zed, baby, I'm not mad anymore. Wake up and we can go home. Come home with me, so I can cuddle in your arms. We can forget about the fight. It doesn't matter anymore. Please." My cry comes out cracked and broken, tears streaming down my face. I lean forward and kiss his cold lips. "Come on, baby, wake up." I keep kissing him, praying for one of those moments from the movies where the prince kisses the princess and she wakes up. I need that to happen. It has to!

Thunder crashes above us as the rain pelts down over our body. "Someone get him an umbrella! He's wet and cold! His lips are turning blue. We need to get him warm!" I shout, tears stream down. Someone touches my shoulder.

"Abby, baby."

I shrink away from whoever's touch it is and look up to Megan who's sobbing in my dad's arms.

"I told him not to," she cries. "I told him to stay back, but he wouldn't listen. He knew Michael was going to try to kill you, and he knew that you wouldn't come back from it. He didn't want Abby to lose her father. God, why!" She crumbles, but my dad holds her up, keeping her from hitting the ground.

My eyes find Zed's again. They're not closed, but he's not awake.

I look over my shoulder. Zed's heart lies there in the mud. My heart, my everything.

"Oh, no!" Megan screams, my head snapping back to Zed.

His body starts to disintegrate, disappearing before my eyes. "No, no, no!" I scream. "No, baby, don't go. You can't leave me. You promised you would never leave me. Come back. Please. You promised." I claw at his ashes, trying to grab it with my hands, only the water is too fast, washing them away. Within seconds there's nothing left. Zed's body is gone.

And just like a switch, I'm not Abby anymore.

Slowly, I get to my feet, my powers rippling along my arms, running down to my fingertips. Closing my eyes, I let the Queen of Hell take her rightful place within me.

When I open my eyes I know they're black. My skull tingles

as I feel my horns grow, my tail breaking free as my wings burst from my back. Fire ignites, covering me head to toe.

Looking up into the sky, I find Michael still there, watching his wings fluttering against the raging winds.

I take off, launching myself into the sky, ignoring the shouts of my mates below me. Rain pelts my face as I race toward Michael, my wings beating faster than they ever have before.

"I didn't mean to!" he screams over the thundering winds. "It wasn't supposed to be him!"

I don't want to hear his voice, to listen to his pathetic excuses. A hellfire ball forms in my hands, and I start to launch one after the other. He dodges the first few, but I manage to hit him with the last one. He lets out a scream of pain.

"I don't want to kill you, little girl, but I will if you don't fuck off!" he roars as he takes off higher than the sky.

I just laugh, tossing my head back, laughing until my sides hurt. Then in the blink of an eye, the smile is gone, the laughter stops, and I'm shooting though the fucking sky like a bullet.

My body crashes into Michael. He tries to pull me off, but I lock my legs around his neck from behind. His fingers claw at my thighs, fists pounding against my muscles, but I don't care. I grab ahold of his head, getting a good grip and pull.

My body starts to vibrate as powers I didn't even know I had fill me. It's almost too much to handle. My head feels like it's about to burst, my veins on fire.

I scream as I use every ounce of my strength. And then I feel it. Michael screams in agony as I rip his motherfucking head from his body.

I watch as his body falls below me, nothing but his head still grasped tightly in my hands. His body hits the ground, exploding into dust on impact. My eyes flick to his decapitated head as it starts to disintegrate in my hands.

I'm not sure how I did it, I didn't even think it was possible, but I killed Michael the archangel.

Only because he killed Zed.

Zed is dead. My mate, my heart, my soul, is dead.

Everything hits me all at once, punching me in the chest.

Letting out a wail–a soul crushing, blood curdling scream, my body gives out–my wings stop beating, and I let my body plummet toward the ground.

As I fall, every memory of Zed flashes before my eyes. My body shuts down, and I feel nothing. I am nothing. I tell myself there's no way I could survive another bond rejection. There's no way I can live through a mate dying.

But Zed is *dead*. It's as simple as that.

To be continued in Tainted Souls- Angelic Academy Book Four

Also by Alisha

Book One: Little Bird

Book Two: Venomous Queen

Book Three: Dark Soldiers (Coming Soon)

Boys Of Kingston Academy:

Tantalizing Kings

Boys Of Rose Briar Hill:

Just A Summer Fling (Prequel)

Broken Prince (TBD)

A Forbidden Game (MFM Step brother hockey)

A Game Of Choice

STANDALONES

We Are Worthy- A sweet and steamy omegaverse.

We Are Destiny A steamy poly omegaverse

Wild Child- A steamy poly omegaverse (cowrite)

If You Go Into The woods- Steamy MF Shifter Novella

A Mid Nights Bloody Dream (TBD)

Knot Going Anywhere (TBD)

Fated To Save Her FF Vampire (TBD)

CO-WRITES

Solidarity Academy

Knock 'Em Down: Book One

Take 'Em Out: Book Two

Rise 'Em Up: Book Three

Coral Springs University

Hooves & Heartstrings- An MF Monster Romance

Lost Between The Pages

Mad For The Sea Witch

Wild Thorn Ranch

Marshall

Wyatt & Weston

ANTHOLOGIES

Beach Shots & Monster Knots: A Monster Romance Anthology

For the Love of Villains: Anthology (Coming soon)

Autumn Spells: A Charity Anthology (Coming Soon)

Knotty Holiday Nights: An Omegaverse Holiday Anthology (Coming Soon)

SHARED WORLDS

Naomi (Dressed to Kill)

ACKNOWLEDGMENTS

As always, I'm beyond grateful for Jessica, Jennifer, Cassie, Mylene and Martha. You ladies are family more than anything! Thank you for all the time and energy you put into all my books.

Many thanks to my Beta and ARC teams for your time and efforts to help each of my books be the best they can be!

ABOUT ALISHA

Writer, Alisha Williams lives in Alberta, Canada, with her husband and her two daughters. She has three crazy kitties who she loves. When she isn't writing or creating her own graphic content, she loves to read books by her favorite authors.

Writing has been a lifelong dream of hers, and this book was made despite the people who prayed for it to fail, but because Alisha is not afraid to go for what she wants, she has proven that dreams do come true.

Wanna see what all her characters look like, hear all the latest gossip about her new books or even get a chance to become a part of one of her teams? Join her readers group on Facebook here - Naughty Queens. Or find her author's page here - Alisha Williams Author

Of course, she also has an Instagram account to show all her cool graphics, videos, and more book related goodies - alishawilliamsauthor

Sign up for Alisha's Newsletter

Got TikTok? Follow alishawilliamsauthor

Printed in Great Britain
by Amazon